The Infamous Arrandales

Scandal is their destiny!

Meet the Arrandale family—dissolute,
disreputable and defiant! This infamous
family have scandal in their blood, and
wherever they go their reputation
will *always* precede them!

Don't miss any of the fabulous books
in Sarah Mallory's dazzling new quartet!

The Chaperon's Seduction
Temptation of a Governess
Return of the Runaway
The Outcast's Redemption

All available now!

Author Note

This is the fourth in The Infamous Arrandales mini-series, and Wolfgang's story is the one that started everything off for me. The Arrandales are a wild family, but Wolfgang Arrandale has always been the worst of them all—a rake and a rogue who fled to France after murdering his wife. His story is like a cloud on the horizon of the other stories, faint but always there, and finally in this book I have the chance to bring Wolf home.

In *The Outcast's Redemption* Wolf returns to England to clear his name, and in the process falls in love with a good woman. A *very* good woman—because Grace is the daughter of a clergyman. She has lived a blameless life, a world away from Wolf's own experiences. Grace has suffered heartache, but her belief in justice and goodness have never yet let her down. However, saving Wolfgang Arrandale proves to be her greatest challenge.

I do hope you enjoy Grace and Wolf's adventure. In the process of discovering the truth of what happened at Arrandale Hall ten years ago they discover each other, and if they can overcome all the obstacles in their way they might even find their happy ending.

Enjoy!

THE OUTCAST'S REDEMPTION

Sarah Mallory

First published in Great Britain 2016
By Mills & Boon, an imprint of HarperCollins*Publishers*
1 London Bridge Street, London, SE1 9GF

Large Print edition 2016

© 2016 Sarah Mallory

ISBN: 978-0-263-26323-7

Our policy is to use papers that are natural, renewable and recyclable
products and made from wood grown in sustainable forests.
The logging and manufacturing processes conform to the legal
environmental regulations of the country of origin.

Printed and bound in Great Britain
by CPI Antony Rowe, Chippenham, Wiltshire

Sarah Mallory was born in the West Country and now lives on the beautiful Yorkshire Moors. She has been writing for more than three decades—mainly historical romances set in the Georgian and Regency period. She has won several awards for her writing, most recently the Romantic Novelists' Association RoNA Rose Award in 2012, for *The Dangerous Lord Darrington*, and 2013, for *Beneath the Major's Scars*.

Visit the Author Profile page
at millsandboon.co.uk for more titles.

For TGH.
Thank you.

Chapter One

March 1804

The village of Arrandale was bathed in frosty moonlight. Nothing stirred and most windows were shuttered or in darkness. Except the house standing within the shadow of the church. It was a stone building, square and sturdy, and lamps shone brightly in the two ground-floor windows that flanked the door. It was the home of Mr Titus Duncombe, the local parson, and the lights promised a welcome for any soul in need.

Just as they had always done, thought the man walking up the steps to the front door. Just as they had done ten years ago, when he had ridden through the village with the devil on his heels. Then he had not stopped. Now he was older, wiser and in need of help.

He grasped the knocker and rapped, not hard, but

in the silence of the night the sound reverberated hollowly through the hall. A stooping, grey-haired manservant opened the door.

'I would like to see the parson.'

The servant peered out, but the stranger kept his head dipped so the wide brim of his hat shadowed his face.

'Who shall I say is here?'

'Tell him it is a weary traveller. A poor vagabond who needs his assistance.'

The servant hesitated.

'Nay, 'tis late,' he said at last. 'Come back in the morning.'

He made to shut the door but the stranger placed a dirty boot on the step.

'Your master will know me,' he stated. 'Pray, take me to him.'

The old man gave in and shuffled off to speak to the parson, leaving the stranger to wait in the hall. From the study came a calm, well-remembered voice and as he entered, an elderly gentleman rose from a desk cluttered with books and papers. Once he had passed the manservant and only the parson could see his face, the stranger straightened and removed his hat.

'I bid you good evening, Mr Duncombe.'

The parson's eyes widened, but his tone did not change.

'Welcome, my son. Truscott, bring wine for our guest.' Only when the servant had closed the door upon them did the old man allow himself to smile. 'Bless my soul. Mr Wolfgang Arrandale! You are returned to us at last.'

Wolfgang breathed a sigh of relief. He bowed.

'Your servant, sir. I am pleased you remember me—that I have not changed out of all recognition.'

The parson waved a hand. 'You are a little older, and if I may say so, a little more careworn, but I should know you anywhere. Sit down, my boy, sit down.' He shepherded his guest to a chair. 'I shall not ask you any questions until we have our wine, then we may talk uninterrupted.'

'Thank you. I should warn you, sir, there is still a price on my head. When your man opened the door I was afraid he would recognise me.'

'Truscott's eyesight is grown very poor, but he prefers to answer the door after dark, rather than leave it to his wife. But even if he had remembered you, Truscott is very discreet. It is something my servants have learned over the years.' He stopped as the object of their conversation returned with a tray. 'Ah, here we are. Thank you, Truscott. But what is this, no cake? Not even a little bread?'

'Mrs Truscott's gone to bed, master.'

Mr Duncombe looked surprised. 'At nine o'clock?'

'She had one of her turns, sir.'

'Pray do not worry on my account,' put in Wolfgang quickly. 'A glass of wine is all I require.' When they were alone again he added drily, 'Your man does not want to encourage dubious fellows such as I to be calling upon you.'

'If they knew who you are—'

'They would have me locked up.'

'No, no, my boy, you wrong them. Not everyone in Arrandale believes you killed your wife.'

'Are you quite sure of that, sir?' asked Wolfgang, unable to keep a note of bitterness from his voice. 'I was found kneeling over her body and I ran away rather than explain myself.'

'I am sure you thought it was for the best, at the time,' murmured the parson, topping up their glasses.

'My father thought it best. He was never in any doubt of my guilt. If only I had called here. I am sure you would have counselled me to stay and defend myself. I was damned the moment I fled the country.'

'We cannot change the past, my son. But tell me where you have been, what you have done for the past ten years.'

Wolfgang stretched his long legs towards the fire.

'I have been in France, sir, but as for what I did there—let us just say whatever was necessary to survive.'

'And may one ask why you have returned?'

For a long moment Wolf stared into the flames. 'I have come back to prove my innocence, if I can.'

Was it possible, after so long, to solve the mystery of his wife's death? When the parson said nothing he continued, giving voice to the thoughts that had been going round in his head ever since he decided to leave France.

'I know it will not be easy. My wife's parents, the Sawstons, would see me hanged as soon as look at me. I know they have put up the reward for my capture. Florence's death might have been a tragic accident, but the fact that the Sawston diamonds went missing at the same time makes it far more suspicious. I cannot help feeling that someone must know the truth.'

The parson sighed. 'It is so long ago. The magistrate is dead, as are your parents, and Arrandale Hall has been empty for years, with only a caretaker there now.' He shifted uncomfortably. 'I understand the lawyers wanted to close it up completely, but your brother insisted that Robert Jones should remain. He and his wife keep the house up together as best they can.'

'Jones who was footman in my day?' asked Wolf.

Mr Duncombe nodded. 'Yes, that is he. I am afraid your lawyers will not release money for maintaining the property. Your brother does what he can to keep the building watertight, at least.'

'Richard? But his income will not cover that.'

'I fear it has been a struggle, although I understand he has now married a woman of…er…comfortable means.'

'Ah, yes. I believe he is now step-papa to an heiress,' said Wolf. 'Quite a come-about for an Arrandale! Ah, you are surprised I know this. I met Lady Cassandra in France last year and she gave me news of the family. She also told me I have a daughter. You will remember, sir, that Florence was with child and very near her time when she died. I thought the babe had died with her but apparently not.' He gazed into the fire, remembering his shock when Cassie had told him he was a father. 'The child is the reason I must clear my name. I do not want her to grow up with my guilt hanging over her.'

'An admirable sentiment, but how do you begin?'

'By talking to anyone who might know something about that night, ten years ago.'

The old man shook his head.

'That will not be easy. The staff are gone, moved away and some of the older ones have died. However, Brent, the old butler, still lives in the village.'

He stopped as a soft, musical voice was heard from the doorway.

'Papa, am I so very late? Old Mrs Owlet has broken her leg and I did not like to leave her until her son came—oh, I beg your pardon, I did not know you had a visitor.'

Wolf had risen from his chair and turned to face the newcomer, a tall young woman in a pale-blue pelisse and a matching bonnet, the strings of which she was untying as she spoke to reveal an abundance of silky fair hair, neatly pulled into a knot at the back of her head.

'Ah, Grace, my love. This is Mr…er…Mr Peregrine. My daughter, sir.'

'Miss Duncombe.' Wolf found himself being scrutinised by a pair of dark eyes.

'But how did you come here, sir?' she asked. 'I saw no carriage on the street.'

'I walked from Hindlesham.'

She looked wary and he could not blame her. He had been travelling for over a week, his clothes were rumpled and he had not shaved since yesterday. There was no doubt he presented a very dubious appearance.

The parson coughed. 'Mr Peregrine will be staying in Arrandale for a few days, my love.'

'Really?' she murmured, unbuttoning her pelisse. 'I understand the Horse Shoe Inn is very comfortable.'

'Ah, you misunderstand.' Mr Duncombe cleared his throat again. 'I thought we might find Mr Peregrine a bed here for a few nights.'

Grace sighed inwardly. Why did Papa think it necessary to play the Good Samaritan to every stranger who appeared? She regarded the two men as they stood side by side before the fire, the guest towering over his host. She turned her attention to the stranger. The dust of the road clung to his boots, his clothes were positively shabby and as for his linen—the housewife in her was shocked to see anything so grey. Grace was not used to looking up at anyone, indeed she had often heard herself described as a beanpole, but this man topped her by several inches. His dark curling hair was as rumpled as the rest of him and at least a day's growth of black stubble covered his cheeks. She met his eyes and although the candlelight was not sufficient to discern their colour they held a most distracting glint. She looked away, flustered.

'I do not think…' she began, but Papa was not listening.

'And we have been very remiss in our refreshments, my love. Mrs Truscott is unwell, but I am sure you will be able to find our guest a little supper?'

'Why, of course,' she answered immediately, glad of the opportunity to get this man away from her father, who was far too kind-hearted for his own good. 'Perhaps Mr Peregrine would like to accompany me to the kitchen?'

'The kitchen?' her father exclaimed, surprised. 'My dear—'

'It will be much easier for me to feed Mr Peregrine there, sir, since he will be on hand to tell me just what he would like.' She managed a smile. 'I came in that way and noted a good fire in the range, so it is very comfortable. And you may finish your sermon in peace, Papa.'

Her father made another faint protest, but the stranger said, 'Pray do not be anxious for me, sir. If you have work to finish, then I must disturb you no longer.' He picked up his battered portmanteau and turned to Grace. 'Lead on, Miss Duncombe. I am at your service.'

It was most gallantly said, but Grace was not fooled. She merely inclined her head and moved towards the door.

'Oh, Grace, send Truscott to me, when you see him, if you please. I need to apprise him of the situation.'

She looked back in surprise. 'There is no need, Papa, I can do that.'

'It is no trouble, my love. I want to see him on other matters, too, so you had best send him up. As soon as you can.'

'Very well, sir.' Her eyes flickered towards the stranger. 'Come along.'

She crossed the hall and descended the stairs to the basement with the man following meekly behind. No, she amended that. There was nothing meek about *Mr Peregrine*. Hah, she almost laughed out loud. That was no more the man's name than it was hers. Clearly Papa had made it up on the spur of the moment to give him some semblance of respectability. It was the sort of thing her father would do. Papa was a scholar and Grace's own education was sufficient for her to know that the name meant traveller in Latin. No doubt Papa thought that a good joke.

She went quickly to the kitchen, despatched Truscott upstairs to see his master and turned to face the man.

'Very well, you may sit at the table and I will see what we have in the larder.'

'A mere trifle will do,' he murmured, easing his long legs over the bench. 'A little bread and butter, perhaps.'

She pursed her lips. Even sitting down he dominated the kitchen.

'I do not think *a mere trifle* will do for you at all,' she retorted, reaching for an apron. 'You look the sort of man who eats heartily.'

'You have it right there, mistress, but with your cook indisposed I would be happy to have a little bread and cheese, if you know where to find it. Perhaps your man Truscott will help us, when he returns.'

Grace had been thinking that she would serve

him just that, but his words flicked her on the raw. She drew herself up and fixed him with an icy look.

'I am quite capable of producing a meal for you. It is a bad housewife who has to depend upon her servants for every little thing!'

Wolfgang rested his arms on the table as he watched Grace Duncombe bustling in and out of the kitchen. She must be what, twenty-three, twenty-four? He couldn't remember seeing her, when he had lived at Arrandale, but ten years ago he had taken very little notice of what went on in the village. He had been four-and-twenty, reluctantly preparing to settle down with his wife. He thought of Florence, lying cold and broken on the stone floor, and her daughter—their daughter. The baby he had always believed had died with her. He rubbed his temples. He would consider that tomorrow. For now he was bone-tired from travelling and ravenously hungry. From the delicious smells coming from the frying pan his hostess was rising admirably to the challenge of feeding him.

When Truscott returned, Wolf knew he had been informed of their guest's identity. The man was bemused and not a little embarrassed to find Arrandale of Arrandale sitting in the kitchen. Miss

Duncombe was absent at that moment and the man-servant stood irresolute, shifting uncomfortably from one foot to the other.

'Sir, I—'

Wolfgang stopped him. 'Hush, your mistress is returning.'

She came in from the yard.

'Truscott, pray fetch a bottle of wine for our visitor.'

'Nay, not just for me,' said Wolf quickly. 'Bring a glass for your mistress, too.'

He thought for a moment she would object, but she merely frowned and went back to her cooking. The kitchen was warm and comfortable and Wolfgang felt himself relaxing as he watched her work. She was well named, he thought, there was a gracefulness to her movements, and an assurance unusual in one so young.

When Truscott went out again, Wolf said, 'Are you only preparing a meal for me?'

'Father and I dined earlier,' she replied, dropping pieces of lamb into the pan. 'Papa will take nothing more than a biscuit or two until the morning.' She finished cooking the meat and arranged it neatly on the plate. 'There,' she said with a hint of defiance. 'Your dinner.'

Wolf regarded the meal she had set before him. Besides the collops of mutton there was a dish of fried potato as well as cold potted hare and a parsnip pie.

'A meal fit for a lord,' he declared. 'Will you not join me?'

'No, thank you. I told you I have already dined.'

'Then at least stay and drink a glass of wine with me.' When she shook her head he murmured, *'"Better a dinner of herbs where love is, than a stalled ox and hatred therewith."'*

She glared at him, but at least she stayed. She slid on to the end of the bench opposite. 'What an odd thing to say. I do not hate you, Mr Peregrine.'

He poured wine into the glasses and pushed one across the table towards her. She cradled it in her hands before sipping the contents.

'Then what *do* you think of me?' he asked.

'To begin with,' she said slowly, looking down at her wineglass, 'I do not think you are deserving of Papa's best claret.'

'The best, is it?' Wolf murmured. 'Perhaps your man made a mistake.'

'Truscott does not make mistakes.'

No, thought Wolf, but it would be his undoing if

the man showed him too much respect. For all that he could not help teasing her.

'Then clearly he sees the worth of the man beneath these sorry clothes.'

She put her glass down with a snap. 'Who *are* you?'

'What you see, a humble pilgrim.'

'Yes, I know that is what you would like me to think, Mr Peregrine, but I will tell you to your face that I find nothing humble about you!'

'Humility comes hard for a gentleman fallen on hard times.'

She was silent and Wolf gave his attention to the food. It was really very good, but it troubled him that she had been obliged to cook it.

'You have only the two servants?' he asked her. She bridled at his question and he went on quickly. 'You have a large, fine church here and this area is a prosperous one, I believe.'

'It was used to be,' she told him. 'There has been no one living at the Hall for several years now and that has had an effect. Without a family in residence our shopkeepers cannot sell their goods to them, the farmers do not supply them with milk and meat.'

'But the estate is very large, it must provide a good living for many local families.'

'With an absentee landlord the farms do not thrive and there is no money to maintain the houses. Many families worked at the Hall, when it closed they lost their positions. Some moved away and took up new posts, others found what work they could locally.' She looked across the table at him. 'There is much poverty here now. My father does what he can to relieve it, but his own funds are limited. We have very little of value in this house.'

Wolf understood her, but the fact she thought he might be a thief did not matter at that moment, what concerned him was that the people—his people— were suffering. Duncombe had told him the lawyers were being parsimonious with his money, but clearly they did not realise the effect of that. Richard should have started proceedings to declare him dead. Instead he preferred to put his own money into Arrandale.

He closed his eyes for a moment, as the weight of responsibility pressed down on him. He had thought himself unfairly punished, exiled in France for a crime he had not committed, but he saw now that he was not the only one to suffer.

'How long do you intend to stay in Arrandale?' Grace asked him.

'A few days, no more.' He glanced up at the clock.

'It is growing late and I should indeed be grateful for a bed, Miss Duncombe, if you can spare one.'

'My father does not turn away anyone in need.'

'Thank you.' He pushed aside his empty plate. 'Then with your permission I will retire now.'

'Of course.' She rose as the elderly manservant shuffled back into the room. 'Ah, Truscott, Mr Peregrine is to be our guest for a few days. Perhaps you would show him to his room. Above the stable.'

She took a large iron key from a peg beside the door.

'The…the groom's quarters, mistress?' The servant goggled at her.

'Why, yes.' She turned her bright, no-nonsense smile on Wolf. 'We have no stable hands now, so the garret is free. I have already made up the bed for you. Truscott will show you the pump in the yard and where to find the privy. I am sure you will be very comfortable.'

And I will be safely out of the house overnight, thought Wolf, appreciatively.

'I am sure I shall, Miss Duncombe, thank you.'

Truscott was still goggling, his mouth opening and closing like a fish gasping for air. Wolf clapped him on the shoulder.

'Come, my friend, let us find a lamp and you can show me to my quarters.'

The servant led him across the yard to the stable block, but when they reached the outer stairs that led to the garret, Truscott could contain himself no longer.

'Mr Arrandale, sir,' he said, almost wringing his hands in despair. 'Miss Duncombe's as kind as can be, but she don't *know*, see. I pray you'll forgive her for treating you like this.'

'There is nothing to forgive,' said Wolf, taking the key from the old man's hands. 'Your mistress is very wise to be cautious. I should not like to think of her letting any stranger sleep in the house. Now, go back indoors and look after her. And remember, tomorrow you must treat me as a poor stranger, no serving me any more of your best wines!'

Wolf climbed the stairs to the groom's quarters and made a quick inspection. Everything was clean and orderly. One room contained a bed, an old chest of drawers and a washstand, the other a table and a couple of chairs. Wolf guessed the furniture had been consigned there when it was no longer of any use in the house. However, it was serviceable and the bed was made up with sheets, blankets and pillows upon a horsehair mattress. He lost no time in shedding his clothes and slipping between the sheets. He could not help a sigh of satisfaction as he felt the soft linen against his skin. After a journey of twenty hours aboard the French fishing boat that had put him ashore near Eastbourne, he had travelled on foot and by common stage to reach Arrandale. The most comfortable bed on his journey had been a straw mattress, so by comparison this was sheer heaven.

He stretched out and put his hands behind his head. He could not fault Miss Grace Duncombe as a housekeeper. A smile tugged at his mouth as he recalled her shock when the parson said he was to stay with them. She had come into the room like a breath of fresh air. Doubtless because she brought the chill of the spring evening in with her. She said she had been visiting a Mrs Owlet. He frowned, dragging back old memories. The Owlets had worked at the great house for generations. It was a timely reminder that he would have to take care in the village, there were many such families who might well recognise his lanky frame. Grace Duncombe had no idea of his true identity, but she clearly thought him a rogue, set upon taking advantage of her kindly father, which was why she was housing him in this garret. That did not matter. He was here to find out the truth, but he must go carefully, one false move could cost him his life.

It was Grace's habit to rise early, but this morning she was aware of an added urgency. There was a stranger in the garret. She was quite accustomed to taking in needy vagrants at the vicarage, giving them a good meal and a bed for the night, but Mr Peregrine disturbed her peace. She was afraid her father would invite the man to breakfast with him.

As soon as it was light Grace slipped out of bed and dressed herself, determined to make sure that if their guest appeared he would not progress further than the kitchen. When she descended to the basement she could hear the murmur of voices from the scullery and looked in to find Mrs Truscott standing over the maid as she worked at the stone sink in the corner. They stopped talking when Grace appeared in the doorway.

'Ah, good morning, Miss Grace.' Mrs Truscott looked a little flustered as she came forward, wiping her hands on her apron. 'I was just getting Betty to wash out Mr—that is—the gentleman's shirt. So dirty it was, as if he had been travelling in it for a week. We didn't heat up the copper, not just for one shirt, Miss, oh, no, a couple of kettles was all that was needed and look—hold it up, Betty—you can see it has come up clean as anything. All it needs now is a good blow out of doors and it will be as good as new.'

'Did Mr Peregrine ask you to do this?' asked Grace, astounded at the nerve of the man.

'Oh, no, Miss Grace, but I could see it needed washing, so I told Truscott to fetch it off the gentleman at first light, saying I would find him a shirt from the charity box to tide him over if need be, but he said he had another to wear today, so all we have to do now is get this one dry.'

Betty had been nodding in agreement, but she stopped, putting up her nose to sniff the air like a hound.

'Begging your pardon, Mrs Truscott, but ain't that the bacon I can smell?'

'Oh, Lordy yes.' The housekeeper snatched the wet shirt from the maid's hands and dropped it into the basket. 'Quick, girl, it will be burned to a crisp and then what will the master say? Oh, and there's the bread in the oven, too!'

Grace stepped aside and the maid rushed past her.

'Give me the shirt, Mrs Truscott, I will peg it out while you attend to Father's breakfast.'

'Oh, Miss Grace, if you are sure?'

'I am perfectly capable of doing it, so off you go now.' Smiling, she watched the housekeeper hurry back to the kitchen then, putting a handful of pegs in the basket on top of the shirt, she made her way outside. The sun was shining now and a steady breeze was blowing. Grace took a deep breath. She loved spring days like this, when there was warmth in the sun and a promise of summer to come. It was a joy to be out of doors.

A clothes line was fixed up in the kitchen gardens, which were directly behind the stable block. As she crossed the yard Grace heard the noise of the pump being worked and assumed it was Truscott fetching more water for the house, but when she turned the corner she stopped, her mouth opening in surprise to see their guest, stripped to the waist and washing himself.

Her first reaction was to run away, but it was too late for that, he had spotted her. She should not look at him, but could not drag her eyes away from the sight of his half-naked body. The buckskins covering his thighs could not have been tighter, but although he was so tall there was nothing spindly about his long legs. They were perfectly proportioned. He had the physique of an athlete, the flat stomach and lean hips placing no strain on those snugly fitting breeches, but above the narrow waist the body widened into a broad chest and muscled shoulders, still wet and glinting in the morning sun. He bent to pick up his towel, his movements lithe, the muscles rippling beneath the skin. As he straightened she noted the black beard on his cheeks and watched as he flicked the thick dark hair away from his face. Droplets of water flew off the tendrils, catching the light. Like a halo, she thought wildly. A halo for a dark angel.

'Good morning, Miss Duncombe.'

Her throat had dried. She knew if she tried to speak it would be nothing more than a croak so instead she inclined her head, frowning in an effort not to blush. She forced her legs to move and walked on, feeling very much like one passing a strange dog and not knowing if it was going to attack. The line was only yards away from the pump and, keeping her back to him, she concentrated on pegging out his shirt. Her fingers felt stiff, awkward and her spine tingled at the thought of the man behind her. She had noticed faint scars on his body, signs that he had not lived a peaceful life.

* * *

It was very quiet, perhaps he had gone, after all he had finished washing himself and it must be cold, standing in this chill wind, naked...

'Thank you for going to so much trouble for me.'

She jumped at the sound of his deep voice. She turned to find he was very close, towering over her. He was towelling his wet hair and with his arms raised he looked bigger and broader than ever. The skin beneath his ribcage was drawn in, accentuating his deep chest with its shadow of dark hair. What would it be like to touch him, to run her hands over his skin and feel those crisp, dark hairs curling over her fingers?

Shocked, Grace stepped back and hastily picked up the washing basket, holding it before her like a shield while she tried to gather her scattered wits. She must answer him.

'It was nothing. We c-cannot have you going about the village like a beggar.' She began to move backwards, as if she was afraid to turn her back on him. 'Once you are dressed Mrs Truscott will serve you breakfast in the kitchen.'

He kept his eyes on her, his look dark, unfathomable. She felt like a wild animal, in thrall to a predator.

'Then I had best make myself presentable.'

She swallowed.

Pull yourself together, Grace!

'Yes. Please do. And do not take too long about it. My servants have a great deal to do today.'

From somewhere she found the strength to turn and walk away. She wanted to run, she could feel his eyes boring into her and a shiver ran the length of her spine. She had never met anyone who made her feel so ill at ease. Or so deliciously alive.

When Grace went down to the kitchen later she found their guest sitting at the table, enjoying a hearty breakfast. Mrs Truscott was also there, but Grace's relief at finding that she was not alone with the man was tempered by the housekeeper's behaviour. She was standing at one end of the table, watching the stranger with a look of motherly satisfaction while he addressed his plate of bacon and eggs. It was understandable, thought Grace, fair-mindedly, for the stranger had clearly made an effort to clean himself up. His hair was still damp but the dark curls were now brushed and gleaming and his lean cheeks were free of stubble, making him look much younger.

And much more attractive.

He looked up at that moment and she blushed.

'Good morning again, Miss Duncombe.'

He rose, but Grace quickly gestured to him to sit back down. He was so tall she did not want him towering over her. Again.

'Pray, go on with your breakfast,' she told him, not meeting his eyes. 'I came to fetch tea. My father and I always enjoy a cup at this time, before he goes to his study to work.'

'I beg your pardon, Miss Grace. I've been that busy I forgot all about it. I will make it now, just as soon as I have cut some more bread for Master... er...Mr...um...'

'Peregrine,' said Wolf, as the housekeeper stumbled over how to address him. He gave her a reassuring smile, which would have included Grace, if she had been attending, but she was already busy at the range, preparing tea. He had noted the telltale flush on her cheeks when she saw him and thought how well the extra colour suited her. She was a long Meg, no doubt about it, but not thin. He watched her now as she bustled about gathering cups, milk and sugar. Her movements were actually very pleasing to the eye.

Wolf told himself this was no time to be considering a flirtation. But he could not resist one more small tease.

He said, 'I would very much like some tea, ma'am, if you can spare it.'

She was pouring tea into the two fine porcelain cups as he spoke and he saw her hand shake a little.

'You may have what is left in the pot.' Still she would not look at him. 'Mrs Truscott shall pour more water on the leaves for you, but if you will excuse me I must take these upstairs. Papa will be waiting.'

And with that she whisked herself out of the kitchen. The housekeeper let out a whistling breath.

'Well now, I've never known the mistress so curt before. I'll make fresh tea for you, master, don't you fret.'

'No, no, you heard Miss Duncombe. The remains of this pot will do well enough for me. And do you sit down and join me.'

'Nay, Master Wolf, that wouldn't be fitting, me being a servant and all.'

He pushed his plate away. 'I have sat at table with much worse company than honest servants, Mrs Truscott, believe me. And I pray you will stop treating me like some great gentleman.'

'But you are master of Arrandale, sir. How else am I to treat you?'

'Like the scrubby schoolboy that used to creep into the parson's garden and steal the best plums from the tree! Lord, how you used to scold me in those days. What a rogue I was.'

'Aye, a rogue, sir, but never a villain,' replied the old woman, her eyes unnaturally bright. 'That I will never believe.'

But could he ever prove it? thought Wolf. He saw the housekeeper surreptitiously wiping her eyes and he continued cheerfully, 'Now let us have that tea while it is still drinkable.'

'It will serve several times yet,' she told him, fetching more cups. 'I shall use the leaves again for Truscott and me, and then dry them and give them to the poor.'

'Times are hard here?'

'Times are hard everywhere, Master Wolf, what with the war and everything, but there's no doubt that since your parents died, life has become much more difficult in Arrandale. The steward was carried off in the same epidemic and that made matters even worse, for there was no one to run the estate. These London lawyers don't understand, you see. They expect their rents every Quarter Day and make no allowances for bad harvests, or sickness. What charity there is in the village comes from Mr Duncombe and his daughter.' She hesitated. 'There is some hereabouts that blames you for the troubles, Master Wolfgang.'

'And with good cause. If I had not been so wild no one would have believed me capable of murdering my wife, I would not have fled the country and my parents would not have died.'

'You don't know that, sir.'

'No, but it is what many believe, is it not?'

'Aye, sir, it is. Which is why you must take care. There's some in the village as would give up their own mothers for a shilling.'

'I am aware of that, but I must talk to Brent, our old butler. Where will I find him?'

'He lives with his niece and her husband in the house beneath the elm trees, at the far end of the village. His sight is very poor now and he rarely goes out.'

'I need to see him alone, if possible.'

'Then this morning would be a good time, the others will be off to market.'

'Then I will go now.'

He rose and began to pack up the dishes, but Mrs Truscott stopped him.

'You be on your way, Master Wolf, but be careful. There's plenty hereabouts with long memories, and though you ain't dressed like your old self there's no disguising that tall frame of yours.'

'I have been disguising this frame of mine for years, Mrs T., but don't worry, I'll take the lanes and skirt the village.'

'Shall I tell Mr Duncombe you will join him for dinner?' she asked. 'He'd like that, I'm sure.'

Wolf paused at the door. 'I would, too,' he admitted. 'But what of his daughter?'

The housekeeper gave him an enigmatic look.

'Miss Grace will come round when she knows you better, sir, you'll see. You could always charm the birds from the trees and that's a fact!'

Chapter Two

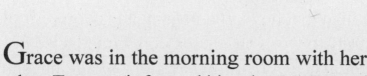

Grace was in the morning room with her father when Truscott informed him that Mr Peregrine had gone out, but would join him for dinner. Mr Duncombe received the news with equanimity, but not so Grace.

'Mr Peregrine is very sure of his welcome,' she remarked, when they were alone again.

'And why not?' replied her father mildly. 'We have offered him hospitality, as we would any of God's creatures.'

'But we know nothing about the man.'

'He has a good heart.'

Grace shook her head. 'You are too kind, Papa, too trusting. I have put him over the stables.'

'Yes, so I understand.' Her father chuckled. 'I am sure he has slept in worse places.'

'But you will have him sit down to dinner with us.'

'Yes, dear, and I would remind you of what the Bible says: *"Be not forgetful to entertain strangers."* Hebrews, my love, Chapter Thirteen.'

She smiled. 'Somehow I do not think Mr Peregrine is an angel in disguise, Papa.'

'Perhaps not, but I can assure you he is a gentleman and, I think, a man worthy of our help.'

More than that he would not say and soon retired to his study to work on his sermon. Grace tried not to think that he was running away from her, but she was left with the uneasy suspicion that Papa knew more about this stranger than he would tell her. She glanced out of the window. It was a fine day, if she hurried through her household duties there might be time for a ride before dinner.

Wolf found the little house under the elms without much difficulty. He had taken the back lanes around the village, his hat pulled low on his brow, and he adopted a slouching, shambling gait so that anyone seeing him would not think him a gentleman, let alone Arrandale of Arrandale. The house appeared to be deserted, but Wolf kept his distance for a while, watching and waiting. It was no hardship, for the sun was high and it was a warm spring day. At length the door opened and an old man limped out. Wolf recognised him immediately. The butler looked no older than he had done when Wolf had last seen him ten years ago. The old man sat down on a bench against the wall of the house and turned his face up to the sun. Wolf approached him.

'Good day to you, Brent.'

'Who is that?' The butler peered up short-sightedly.

'Do you not know me?' Wolf dropped down until his face was level with the old man's. He smiled. 'Do not say you have forgotten me.'

'I know the voice, but…' The faded eyes stared into Wolf's face. 'Is it really you, Mr Wolfgang, after all these years?'

Wolf grasped the frail, outstretched hands. There was no doubt of the old man's delight. He said gently, 'Yes, Brent, I am come back.'

'Lord bless you, sir, I never thought to see the day! Not that I can see very much, for my eyes ain't what they was.' He frowned suddenly. 'But 'tis not safe to be out here. Pray, step inside, sir.'

'Let me help you up.' Wolf took his arm and accompanied him into the house.

'Forgive me if I sit in your presence, Master Wolfgang, but I've got a leg ulcer that pains me if I stand for too long.'

'I think you have earned the right to sit down,' replied Wolf, helping him to a chair and pulling up one for himself. 'You served my family faithfully for many years.'

'Aye, I did, sir, and very sorry I was when the old master and mistress died and the house was shut up for the last time. Very sorry indeed.' He brightened. 'Are you come back to stay, master?'

'Not quite yet. First I have to prove my innocence. That is the reason I am here, Brent, I want you to tell me what you remember, the night my wife died.'

'I remember it as clear as day, sir, but I told it all to the magistrate and he said there was nothing in it to help you.'

'I would like you to tell me, if you will. Starting with the argument I had with my wife before dinner.' Wolf's mouth twisted. 'I am sure you heard that.'

The old man sighed. 'Aye, the whole household heard it, but if you will excuse my saying so, sir, we was accustomed to you and your lady's disagreements, so fiery as you both were. You went out and Mrs Wolfgang ordered a tray to be sent up to her room. That left only the master and mistress and Sir Charles to sit down to dinner.'

'Ah yes, Urmston, my wife's cousin.' Wolf sat

back. Sir Charles Urmston had always been received warmly at Arrandale. Personally, he had never liked the man. Wolf and Florence had never needed much excuse to hurl insults at one another and on this occasion she had accused him of hating Charles because he was the man Wolf's parents would have liked for a son, rather than the wild reprobate Wolf had become. The idea still tortured him.

'I went out for a ride to cool my temper,' he said now. 'What happened while I was gone?'

'We served dinner and Meesden, Mrs Wolfgang's dresser, took up a tray for her mistress. Mrs Wolfgang did not come downstairs again. About eleven the mistress prepared tea in the drawing room, just as she always did, to be served with cakes and bread as a light supper. Then, shortly after midnight, I was coming upstairs to the hall when I heard a shriek, well, a scream, more like.' The old man stopped, twisting his hands together. 'If only there'd been a footman at the door, he'd have seen what happened, but it was late and they was all in the servants' hall.'

'Never mind that,' said Wolf. 'Just tell me what you saw.'

'Mrs Wolfgang's body at the bottom of the grand

staircase, her head all bloody and broken and you kneeling over her. I remember it so well. White as a sheet, you was. The master and mistress came running out from the drawing room and you said, in a queer sort of voice, "She's dead. She's dead."

'Such a to-do as there was then. Mrs Arrandale fell into hysterics and we was all in a bustle. The doctor was sent for and the master sent word that your horse was to be brought round, as quick as possible.'

'How incriminating must that have looked,' Wolf declared. 'If only I had waited, stayed and explained myself.'

'Ah but your father was anxious for you. Even if Sir Charles hadn't been pressing him I think he would have insisted—'

'Charles? You mean Urmston urged him to send me away?'

'Aye, sir. As soon as Sir Charles came in from the garden he told your father to send you off out of harm's way until they could find out what really happened. But they never did find out, sir. Instead…'

'Instead they found the Sawston diamonds were missing and I was doubly damned.' Wolf finished for him. 'Who discovered the necklace was gone?'

'Meesden, sir. She had been fetched down to her mistress, when it was found Mrs Wolfgang was still alive. The poor lady was carried to the morning room and Meesden stayed with her 'til Dr Oswald arrived. Fortunately he was dining at the vicarage and was soon fetched. Meesden went up to Mrs Wolfgang's bedchamber for something and came down screaming that the lady's jewel case was open and the necklace was gone.'

'And everyone thought I had taken it,' muttered Wolf.

'I never believed that, sir. Even though the evidence…' The butler's words trailed away.

'Aye,' growled Wolf. 'My wife always kept the key hidden behind a loose brick in the fireplace.' He was suddenly aware of his neckcloth, tight around his throat like a noose. 'To my knowledge only three people knew of that hiding place. Florence, her dresser and myself.' His mouth twisted. 'I have no doubt Meesden told everyone that fact.' The distress in the old man's face confirmed it. Wolf reached out and touched his arm. 'Think, Brent. Are you sure there was no one else in the house that night?'

'Well, 'tis only a feeling…'

'Tell me.'

Brent paused, his wrinkled brow even more furrowed as he struggled to remember.

'I told the magistrate at the time, sir, but he made nothing of it. You see, once I had taken the tea tray into the drawing room for the mistress I prepared the bedroom candles. I was bringing them up to the staircase hall when I heard a noise upstairs. Voices.' The old man sat up straight. 'I thought it was Mrs Wolfgang talking to someone.'

Wolf's lip curled. 'Some would say it was me. That I returned and pushed Florence from the balcony.'

Brent shook his head. 'When I saw you kneeling beside Mrs Wolfgang's body I could tell you'd just come in. It was bitter cold that day and we had the first heavy frost of the winter. There was still a touch of it on the skirts of your coat, as there would be if you'd been out o' doors for a length of time. I told the magistrate, but he paid no heed to me. He thought I was just trying to protect you.'

'And no one else in the house saw or heard anything?'

Brent shook his head slowly.

'No, sir. Your father and the magistrate gathered everyone in the servants' hall and asked them that very question, but 'twere bitter cold that night, so those servants who had not gone to bed was doing their best to stay by the fire in the servants' hall.'

'But the voices you heard upstairs, could it have been my wife's dresser? Surely Meesden might have been with her mistress.'

'No, sir. When Meesden brought her mistress's tray downstairs after dinner she said she was going to bed and she passed on Mrs Wolfgang's instructions that on no account was she to be disturbed again until the morning. Quite adamant about it, she was, and then she went to her room. The maid who sleeps next door heard Meesden pottering about there, until she was sent for, when it was known her mistress was still alive.'

Wolf frowned, wondering if there was some little detail he was missing. He said, 'I must visit the house. Jones is living there, I believe.'

'Aye, Master Wolfgang, he is, and he would be willing to talk to you, I am sure, but take care who else in the village you approach, sir. There's many who lost their livelihoods when Arrandale Hall was shut up and they would not look too kindly upon you.'

'That is understandable, but if I do not try I shall not make any progress at all.' Wolf rose. 'I must go.

Thank you, Brent.' He put a hand on the old man's shoulder. 'No, don't get up. I will see myself out.'

'You'll come again, sir. You'll let me know how you get on?'

'I shall, you may be sure of it.'

Wolf walked back through the lanes, going over all the old man had told him. He would not risk going through the village in daylight but he would make his way to Arrandale Hall later, and perhaps, once it was dark, he might call upon one or two of the families that he knew had worked at the house, the ones he felt sure would not denounce him. The pity of it was there were precious few of those. He had spent very little of his adult life at Arrandale. Some of the old retainers would remember him as a boy, but most of the newer staff would have little loyalty to him, especially if they believed he was the reason Arrandale was closed up.

The thud of hoofs caught his attention and he looked round to see Grace Duncombe riding towards him on a rangy strawberry roan. She sat tall and straight in the saddle, made taller by the very mannish beaver hat she wore, its wispy veil flying behind her like a pennant. Wolf straightened up and waited for her. She checked slightly, as if uncertain whether to acknowledge him, then brought her horse to a stand.

He touched his hat. 'That is a fine mare. Is she yours?'

'Yes.' Her response was cool, but not unfriendly. 'Bonnie is my indulgence. I have a small annuity from my mother that I use for her upkeep.'

He reached out and scratched the mare's head.

'You need not excuse yourself to me, Miss Duncombe.'

She flushed and her chin went up. 'I do not. But people wonder that I should keep my own horse when we have had to make savings everywhere else.'

'I imagine she is useful for visiting your father's parishioners.'

Her reserve fled and she laughed. 'With a basket of food hanging on my arm? I cannot claim that as my reason for keeping her.' She smoothed the mare's neck with one dainty gloved hand. 'I have had Bonnie since she was a foal and cannot bear to part with her.'

'I understand that. I had such a horse once. A black stallion. The very devil to control.'

'Oh? What happened to him?'

'He died. I am on my way back to your father's house now. Shall we walk?'

Grace used the gentle pressure of her heel to set Bonnie moving.

Perhaps he is a highwayman and his horse was shot from under him. That might also account for the scars on his body.

She quickly curbed her wayward imagination. She had seen a shadow cross the lean face and guessed he had been very fond of his black horse, so it was no wonder he did not wish to talk about it. She must follow her father's example and be charitable.

'You would find it quicker to cut through the village,' she said, waving her crop towards a narrow path that wound its way towards the distant houses.

'Not much quicker.'

'Ah. You are familiar with Arrandale?'

'I can see the church from here, Miss Duncombe, and it is clear this way will bring us to it almost as quickly as cutting back to the village.'

'And you would rather avoid the villagers,' she said shrewdly.

He shrugged. 'You know how these little places gossip about strangers.'

Grace pursed her lips. He frustrated every attempt to learn more about him.

She said now, 'That should not worry you, if you have nothing to hide.'

'I am merely a weary traveller, taking advantage of your father's hospitality to rest for a few days.'

'I fear *taking advantage* is just what you are doing,' she retorted, nettled.

'I mean no harm, Miss Duncombe, trust me.'

'Impossible, since I know nothing about you.'

'You could ask your father.'

'I have done so, but he will tell me nothing.' She paused. 'I understand you are dining with us this evening.'

'Yes. Do you object?'

She stopped her horse.

'I would worry less if I knew something about you.'

He looked up and she had her first clear view of his eyes. They were blue, shot through with violet, and the intensity of his gaze was almost a physical force. Her insides fluttered like a host of butterflies.

'One day I will tell you everything about me,' he promised. 'For the present I would urge you to trust your father's judgement.'

'He seems to have fallen completely under your spell,' she snapped, seriously discomposed by the sensations he roused in her. 'You might be an out-and-out villain for all we know.'

Grace inadvertently jerked the reins and Bonnie sidled. Immediately he caught the bridle, murmuring softly to the mare before looking up again.

'Your father knows I am no villain, Miss Duncombe.'

He placed his hand on her knee as if in reassurance, but it had quite the opposite effect on Grace. Her linen skirt and several layers of petticoats separated them, but the gesture was shockingly intimate. Waves of heat flooded her, pooling low in her body. Her alarm must have shown in her countenance, because his hands dropped and he stepped away.

'Perhaps you should ride on, if you are afraid of me.'

Afraid? Grace's head was full of chaotic thoughts and feelings. He unsettled her, roused emotions she had thought long dead, but, no, she was not *afraid* of him. Quite the opposite.

'I should,' she said, gathering her reins and her disordered senses at the same time. 'I *shall*!'

And with that she set Bonnie cantering away.

* * *

Wolf watched her go, the skirts of her russet riding habit billowing and accentuating the tiny waist beneath her tight-fitting riding jacket. He had to admit it was a fine image. He had thought when he first saw her that her hair was the colour of pale honey, but out of doors, with the sun glinting on her soft curls, it reminded him more of ripe corn. And those eyes. They were a rich, deep blue. Dark as sapphires.

With a hiss of exasperation he took off his hat and raked his fingers through his hair. Bah, what was this, was he turning into some foppish poet? And, confound it, what had come over him to talk to her like that? He had said he was a lowly traveller, he should have touched his cap and kept a respectful silence.

It might be wiser to eat in the kitchen this evening, but Wolf knew Mr Duncombe would be able to tell him more about his family. Ten years was a long time and Wolf wished now that he had kept in touch, but it had been his decision to cut himself off. He had thought he would never return to England, but that was changed now. He had a daughter, a responsibility. Settling his hat more firmly on his head, he set off once more for the vicarage. As the good parson said, the past was gone. He must look to the future.

Grace was determined to wear her most sober gown for dinner that night, but when Betty came up to help her dress, she rejected every one pulled out for her as too tight, too low at the neck, or too *dull*. In the end she settled for a round gown of deep-blue silk gauze with turban sleeves. Its severity was relieved with a trim of white silk at the neck and ankles and a run of seed pearl buttons down the front. She found a white shawl with blue embroidery to keep off the chill and, throwing this around her shoulders, she made her way downstairs to the drawing room.

'Oh.'

Grace stopped in the doorway when she saw their guest was alone. She had deliberately left her entrance as late as possible to avoid just such a situation.

'Do come in, Miss Duncombe. Your father has gone to his study to find a book for me. He will be back immediately, I am sure,' he said, as she came slowly into the room. 'I hope you will forgive me dining with you in my riding dress, but I am…travelling light. And I had not noticed, until I changed for dinner, that this shirt is missing a button.' Again that dark, intense look that did such strange things to her insides. 'I hope you will forgive me. It hardly shows beneath the cravat, and at least, thanks to your housekeeper's services, it is clean.'

Her training as a vicar's daughter came to her aid.

'If you will give it to Truscott when you retire this evening I will see that it is repaired. I will have your other shirt laundered, too.'

'Thank you, ma'am, but Mrs T. is already dealing with that.'

Mrs T.! She bridled at his familiarity with her servants, but decided it was best to ignore it. She turned thankfully to her father as he came back into the room.

'Here you are, my son.'

He held out a book and Grace's brows rose in surprise. *'The Mysteries of Udolpho?'*

'Mr Peregrine wanted something to amuse him if he cannot sleep,' explained her father. 'And he is unfamiliar with Mrs Radcliffe's novel.'

'I do not see how you could have failed to hear of it. It was a huge success a few years ago,' remarked Grace.

'I was out of the country, a few years ago.'

Heavens, thought Grace. *It gets worse and worse. Are we harbouring a spy in our midst?*

'Ah,' cried Papa. 'Here is Truscott come to tell us dinner is ready. Perhaps, Mr Peregrine, you would escort my daughter?'

Grace hesitated as their guest proffered his arm, staring at the worn shabbiness of the sleeve.

Oh, do not be so uncharitable, Grace. You have never before judged a man by his coat.

And in her heart she knew she was not doing so now, but there was something about this man that disturbed her peace.

'Do not worry,' he murmured as she reluctantly rested her fingers on his arm. 'I shall not be here long enough to read more than the first volume of *Udolpho*.'

'I am relieved to hear it,' she retorted, flustered by his apparent ability to read her mind.

His soft laugh made her spine tingle, as if he had brushed her skin with his fingers. When they reached the dining room and he held her chair for her the tiny hairs at the back of her neck rose. He would not dare to touch her. Would he?

No. He was walking away to take his seat on her father's right hand.

Wolf wanted to ask questions. Coming back here had roused his interest in Arrandale. His eyes drifted towards Grace, sitting at the far end of the table. It would be safest to wait until he and the parson were alone, but after ten years of resolutely shutting out everything to do with his family, suddenly he was desperate for news.

'So Arrandale Hall is shut up,' he said.

'But it is not empty,' said Grace. 'A servant and his wife are in residence.'

Wolf's mouth tightened at her swift intervention and the inference that he wanted to rob the place. He kept his eyes on the parson.

'Do you hear anything of the family, sir?'

'Alas, no, my son. I hear very little of the Arrandales now.'

'There was something in the newspapers only last week,' put in Grace. 'About the Dowager Marchioness of Hune's granddaughter, Lady Cassandra. She was married in Bath. To a foreign gentleman, I believe.'

Wolf laughed. 'Was she indeed? Good for her.'

Grace was looking at him with a question in her eyes, but it was her father who spoke.

'Ah, yes, you are right, my love, but that can hardly interest our guest.'

'No, no, of course I am interested.' Wolf hoped he sounded politely indifferent, as befitted a stranger. 'I take it there are no Arrandales living in the area now?'

'No. The house was closed up in ninety-five. There was a particularly bad outbreak of scarlet fever that spring and old Mr Arrandale and his wife died within weeks of one another.'

'Is *that* what they say killed them?' Wolf could hardly keep the bitterness from his voice.

'It was indeed what killed them, my son.' The parson turned his gentle gaze upon him. 'Nothing else.'

'There had been some trouble earlier that winter, had there not, Papa? At the end of ninety-four,' remarked Grace. 'I was at school then, but I remember there were reports in the newspapers. The older son killed his wife for her jewels and fled to France. It was a great scandal.'

The old man shook his head. 'Scandal has always followed the Arrandales, my love. Not all of it deserved.'

'You say that because your living is in their gift,' muttered Wolf.

'No, I say it because I believe it.'

'But, Papa,' said Grace, 'you believe the best of everyone.'

Wolf did not look up, but felt sure her eyes were on him. Mr Duncombe merely chuckled.

'I look for the best in everyone,' he said mildly, 'and I am rarely disappointed. Do pass me the fricassee of rabbit again, my dear, it really is quite excellent.'

Wolf wanted to ask about the child, his daughter. Had the parson seen her, was she tall, like him, or small-boned like her mother? Was she dark, did she have his eyes? The questions went round and round in his head, but he knew he must let the matter drop. When Mr Duncombe began to talk of more general matters he followed suit, but his long exile had left him woefully ignorant.

'You appear singularly ill informed of how matters stand in England,' observed Grace, clearly suspicious.

'I have been living in the north country, they have little interest in what goes on nearer London. That is why I have come south, to take up my life again.'

She pounced on that.

'Oh, are you a local man, then, Mr Peregrine? I do not recall any family with that name hereabouts.'

'No, the Peregrines are not local,' he replied truthfully.

The parson shifted uncomfortably.

'My dear, it grows late and I am sure Mr Peregrine would like to join me in a glass of brandy. I do not often indulge the habit, sir, but since you are here…'

Grace rose immediately. 'Of course, Papa.'

'If you wish to retire, Grace, I am sure our guest will not mind if we do not send for the tea tray.'

Wolf knew he should agree with his host. They could bid Miss Duncombe goodnight now and he would be free of her questions and suspicions, but some inner demon made him demur.

'If it is no trouble, a cup of tea before I retire would be a luxury I have not enjoyed for a very long time.'

Grace looked at him, eyes narrowed.

'You seem to be inordinately fond of the drink, Mr Peregrine.'

'I believe I am, Miss Duncombe.' He met her gaze innocently enough and at length she inclined her head, every inch the gracious hostess.

'Of course Mr Peregrine must have tea if he wishes it, Papa. I will await you in the drawing room.'

With that she swept out of the room.

As soon as the door was closed Mr Duncombe said, 'Was that wise, sir? My daughter is no fool.'

'I am aware of that, but I was not funning when I said I have missed life's little luxuries.' The old man's brows rose and Wolf's mouth twisted into a wry smile. 'Not tea-drinking, I admit, unless it was in the company of a pretty woman.' Wolf saw the other man draw back and he hurried on. 'Pray, sir, do not think I have any thoughts of *that* nature towards your daughter, I would not repay your hospitality so cruelly. No, I have no interest in anything save clearing my name.' He looked around to check again that they were alone. 'On that subject, sir, what do you know of my own daughter?'

'Alas, my son, I cannot help you. She lives with Lord and Lady Davenport, I believe. Doctor Oswald was dining here the night your wife died and a servant came to fetch him. When we met again Oswald said it was a miracle the baby survived. Your wife never regained consciousness.' In the candlelight Mr Duncombe's naturally cheerful face was very grave. 'He told me, in confidence, that if it had not been for the missing diamonds the magistrate would have recorded your wife's death as a tragic accident. Alas, both the doctor and the magistrate are now dead.'

'So you have a new Justice of the Peace?'

'Yes, Sir Loftus Braddenfield of Hindlesham

Manor,' the parson informed him. 'And that is another reason you might wish to avoid being in Grace's company, my son. She is betrothed to him.'

Chapter Three

Grace blew out her candle and curled up beneath the bedcovers. She really could not make out Mr Peregrine. She turned restlessly. In general Papa was a very good judge of character, but he seemed to have fallen quite under this stranger's spell.

She had to admit that dinner had been very enjoyable, the man was well educated and there had been some lively discussions of philosophy, religion and the arts, but he lacked knowledge of what was happening in the country. Surely the north was not that backward. Fears of Bonaparte invading England were never far away, but she thought if the man was a spy he would be better informed. Had he been locked up somewhere, perhaps? She was more thankful than ever that he was in the groom's accommodation and that she had reminded Truscott to check the outer doors were secure before he went to bed.

Perhaps he had been in the Marshalsea. Many men of good birth were incarcerated there for debt, or fraud. With a huff of exasperation she sat up and thumped her pillow.

Such conjecture is quite useless. You will only end up turning the man into a monster, when he is probably nothing more than penniless vagrant, for all his talk of having business in Arrandale.

But would he be in any hurry to leave, if they continued to treat him like an honoured guest? She settled down in her bed again. The man had clearly enjoyed his dinner and he had been eager to take tea with her after. A knot of fluttering excitement twisted her stomach as she remembered his glinting look across the dining table. It was almost as if he was flirting with her.

Yet he barely spoke two words to her in the drawing room. Once the tea tray appeared he lost no time in emptying his cup and saying goodnight. She tried to be charitable and think that he was fatigued. Sleep crept up on Grace. No doubt matters would look much less mysterious in the daylight.

* * *

'Good morning, Mrs Truscott.' Grace looked about the kitchen. 'Is our visitor still abed?'

'Nay, Miss Grace, he went out an hour ago.'

'Goodness, what can he be up to?'

Mrs Truscott smiled. 'Well, you know what your father always says, miss. Only those who rise early will ever do any good.'

Grace laughed.

'It is quite clear you approve of Mr Peregrine! But never mind that. I have come down to fetch tea for Papa. We are taking breakfast together and then I am going to visit Mrs Owlet. Perhaps you would pack a basket for me to take to her.'

'I will, Miss Grace, but it goes against the grain to be helping those that won't help themselves.'

'Mrs Truscott! The poor woman has broken her leg.'

'That's as may be, but if she hadn't been drinking strong beer she wouldn't have tumbled off the road and down the bank, now would she? And that feckless son of hers is no better. I doubt he's done an honest day's work in his life, not since the hall closed and he lost his job there.' The older woman scowled. 'It's said there's always rabbit in the pot at the Owlets' place, courtesy of Arrandale woods.'

'I am sure young Tom isn't the only one to go poaching in the woods and there is more than enough game to go round, since the woods are so neglected.'

'That's not the point, Miss Grace. It's breaking the law.'

'Well, if the law says a man cannot feed his family when there is such an abundance of rabbits on hand, then it is a bad law.'

'Tsk, and you betrothed to a magistrate, too!' Mrs Truscott waved a large spoon in her direction. 'Don't you go letting your man hear you saying such things, Miss Grace.'

'Sir Loftus knows my sentiments on these things and I know he has some sympathy with the poorer villagers, although it would never do for him to say so, of course, and I suppose I should not have said as much to you.'

'Don't you worry about me, Miss Grace, there's many a secret I've kept over the years. Now, let's say no more about it, for the kettle's boiling and the master will be waiting for his tea.'

Later, when she had seen her father comfortably ensconced in his study, Grace set off with her basket. Mrs Owlet lived at the furthest extremity of the village, at the end of a small lane backing on to Arrandale Park. Grace stayed for some time, trying to make conversation, although she found the widow's embittered manner and caustic tongue very trying. The sun was at its height when Grace eventually emerged from the ill-kept cottage and she stood for a moment, breathing in the fresh air. Having spent the past hour sympathising with Mrs Owlet, Grace was not inclined to walk back through the village and listen to anyone else's woes. Instead she carried on up the lane into the park. There was a good path through the woods that bounded the park itself, and from there she could walk past the hall and on to the vicarage. It was a well-worn path that cut off the long curve of the High Street.

It was a fine spring morning and the woods were full of birdsong. Grace's sunny nature revived and she began to feel more charitable towards Mrs Owlet. She had fallen on hard times when Arrandale House had been closed up. Now she lived a frugal existence with her son in what was little more than a hovel. It was no wonder that she was bitter, but Grace could not help thinking that less indulgence in strong beer and more effort with a broom would have improved her condition. Seeing her now, with her grubby linen and dirty clothes, it was difficult to think that she had once been laundress in a great house.

Grace recalled Mrs Truscott's dark mutterings about young Tom Owlet poaching in these very woods and she looked around her. Not that anyone could mistake her tall form in its blue pelisse for a rabbit, but she strode on briskly and soon reached what had once been the deer park. Arrandale Hall was ahead of her, but her path veered away from the formal gardens and joined an impressive avenue of elms that lined the main approach to the house and would bring her out very close to the vicarage.

She had walked this way many times and always thought it regrettable that such a fine old house should stand empty. It was looking very grand today in the sunshine, but there was something different about the building that made her stop. She frowned at the little chapel beside the main house: the wide oak door was open.

Grace hurried across to the chapel. It was most likely Mr Jones had gone in there for some reason, but it could be children from the village, up to mischief, and the sooner they were sent on their way the better. She stepped inside and stood for a moment, while her eyes grew accustomed to the gloom. Someone was standing by the opposite wall, but it was definitely not a child.

'Mr Peregrine! What on earth are you doing here?'

Wolf turned. Grace Duncombe stood in the entrance, a black outline against the sunshine.

'The door was open and I was curious to see inside.' He saw the frowning suspicion in her eyes. 'I have not been stealing the church silver, Miss Duncombe, if that is your concern.'

'There is nothing of that sort left in here now,' she replied. 'But what business can you have at the Hall?'

'Curiosity,' he repeated. 'After what your father said last night I was interested to see the house, but you may be easy. The caretaker knows better than to let strangers into the house.'

Aye, thought Wolf, Jones would turn a stranger away, but the man had been happy enough to let Wolf wander through the familiar rooms. If Grace had arrived ten minutes earlier she would have found him in the entrance hall of the house itself. That would have been more difficult to explain away.

'It was remiss of Mr Jones to leave the chapel

open,' she said now. 'I must remind him of his duties.'

'Must you?'

'Why, yes. While the family are absent we must respect their property.'

'Very commendable, Miss Duncombe, but since we are here, would you object if I took a moment to look around? You may stay, if you like, and make sure I do no damage.'

'I shall certainly do so.'

Silently he turned to study an ornately carved edifice with its stone effigies. A curious stranger would ask whose tomb this was, so he did.

'That is the tomb of Roland Arrandale and his wife,' said Grace, stepping up beside him. 'He was the first Earl of Davenport. The second and third earls are buried here, but the Hall was not grand enough for James, the fourth earl. He built himself a new principal seat and bequeathed Arrandale Hall to his younger son, John. His descendants are buried in the vault below us and you can see the carved memorials on the walls.'

'Including these,' murmured Wolf, looking up at two gleaming marble tablets.

'They are recent additions. For the late Mr and Mrs Arrandale, and Florence, the poor wife of Mr

Wolfgang Arrandale. I believe the younger son arranged for these to be installed at his own expense when the trustees refused to pay.'

Wolf kept his face impassive. What were those cheese-paring lawyers about to deny money for such things? And Richard—confound it, his little brother should not be bearing the cost. This was his fault. All of it.

'It was fortunate there were no children,' he said, keeping his voice indifferent.

'Oh, but there was,' she corrected him, as he had hoped she would. 'There was a little girl. She was adopted by an Arrandale cousin, I believe.'

'I am surprised her maternal grandparents did not bring up the child.' He glanced at Grace, hoping she might answer the question he dare not ask. She did not disappoint him.

'The Sawstons moved away from the area after their daughter's death. They wanted nothing more to do with the Arrandale family, nor their granddaughter.' Disapproval flickered over her serene countenance. 'It was cruel of them to abandon the baby at such a time. The poor child had done nothing to warrant it, except to be born.'

And that was his fault, too. A shudder ran through

Wolf and he turned away, saying curtly, 'There is little of interest here.'

'Unless you appreciate craftsmanship,' she told him. 'The font cover is by Grinling Gibbons.'

'Is it now?' Wolf went to the back of the church where the stone font stood behind the last box pew. He ran a careful hand over the elaborately carved wooden cover. 'What a pity I did not know that earlier, I might have carried it off to sell in the nearest town.' His mouth twisted. 'Is that not what you think of me, Miss Duncombe, that I am a thief?'

'I do not know what you are.'

'Your father trusts me.'

'Father trusts everyone.'

'True. He is a saint and I will not deny that I am a sinner. But I am not here to steal from the chapel.' Her darkling look was sceptical. He shrugged. 'I have seen enough here now. Shall we go?'

She indicated that he should precede her out of the church, then she carefully locked the door. She stood on the path, as if waiting for him to walk away.

He said, 'If you are going to the vicarage, I will escort you.'

'Thank you, but before I leave I am going to take the key back to Mr Jones.'

'Very well, I will wait for you.'

She looked dissatisfied with his answer, but she turned on her heel and hurried away to the house. Wolf followed more slowly. He could only hope that Jones would not give him away.

A few minutes later she returned and he was relieved by her exasperation when she saw him. Clearly she had no idea of his real identity.

'Yes, I am still here,' he said cheerfully. 'I shall escort you back to the vicarage. It is not at all seemly for a young lady to walk these grounds alone.'

'I have done so many times without mishap.'

'So you are an unrepentant trespasser.'

'Not at all, there is a right of way through the park.'

'And you walk here for pleasure?' he asked her.

'Not today. I have been visiting an old lady. It is much quicker to walk home this way than through the village.'

'It would be quicker still to ride. And having seen you in the saddle I know you ride very well, Miss Duncombe.'

'One cannot live within twenty miles of Newmarket *without* riding.' He detected the first signs of a thaw in her response. 'However, riding today would not have been so convenient. You see, I came through the village and carried out several errands. I passed on Mrs Truscott's recipe for a restorative broth to one family, called in upon a mother with a newborn baby to see how they go on and took a pot of comfrey ointment to old Mr Brent, for his leg. That would have been much more difficult if I had been riding Bonnie. I would have been forever looking for a mounting block to climb back into the saddle.'

'I quite see that. But do you never ride here, in the park?'

'I would not presume to do so without the owner's permission.'

'Are you always so law-abiding?'

'I am the parson's daughter and betrothed to Sir Loftus Braddenfield. I am obliged to set an example.'

'Of course.'

She looked up. 'I think you are laughing at me.'

'Now why should I do that?' He saw her hesitate and added, 'Come, madam, do not spare my feelings, tell me!'

'I think…' she drew a breath '…*I think* that you have very little respect for the law!'

His lip curled. 'You are wrong, ma'am. I have a very healthy respect for it.'

Grace did not miss the sudden bitterness in his voice. A convict, then. She should be afraid, he might be dangerous.

Not to me.

A strange thought and one she was reluctant to pursue. Instead she looked about her as they made their way through the avenue of majestic elms that led to the main gates and the High Street.

'It is such a pity that the park is now turned over to cattle,' she remarked. 'It was a deer park, you know. I used to love watching them roaming here.'

'You remember the house as it was? You remember the family?'

'Of course, I grew up here. At least, until I was eleven years old. Then I was sent off to school. As for knowing the family, my father may be a saint, as you call him, but he was careful to keep me away from the Arrandales. The old gentleman's reputation as a rake was very bad, but I believe his two sons surpassed him. Thankfully for Papa's peace of mind, by the time I came back the Hall was shut up.'

'And just when did you return?'

'When I was seventeen. Seven years ago.'

His brows went up. 'And you are still unmarried?'

She felt the colour stealing into her cheeks.

'I came home to look after my father, not to find a husband.'

'The local gentlemen are slowcoaches indeed if they made no move to court you.'

He is flirting with you. There is no need to say anything. You owe him no explanation.

But for some inexplicable reason she felt she must speak.

'I *was* engaged to be married. To Papa's curate, but he died.'

'I am very sorry.'

For the first time in years she felt the tears welling up for what might have been. She said quickly, 'It was a long time ago.'

'And now you have a new fiancé,' he said.

'Yes. I am very happy.'

There was a touch of defiance in her words, but Wolf also heard the note of reproof. He had been over-familiar. She was the parson's daughter and not one to engage in flirtatious chatter, but he had been curious to know why she was still unmarried. She was very tall, of course—why, her head was level with his chin!—and she had no dowry. Either of those things might deter a suitor. But they should not, he thought angrily. She was handsome and well educated and would make any man an excellent wife. Any respectable man, that is.

When they reached the park gates he saw they were chained, but there was a stile built to one side. Wolf sprang over it and, having helped Grace across, he pulled her fingers on to his arm. Silently she disengaged herself. Understandable, but he could not deny the tiny pinprick of disappointment.

Grace was relieved to be back on the High Street and with the vicarage just ahead of them. This man was far too forward and the tug of attraction made her feel a little breathless whenever she was in his company.

You are very foolish, she told herself sternly. *His only advantage is his height. He is the only man in Arrandale taller than you and that is hardly a recommendation!*

'You are frowning, Miss Duncombe. Is anything amiss?'

'No, not at all.' Hastily she summoned a smile. 'Here we are back at the vicarage. It will be quicker if we walk up the drive rather than going around to the front door and summoning Truscott to let us in.'

Grace pressed her lips together to prevent any further inane babbling.

* * *

She is uneasy, thought Wolf. *But how much worse would she feel if she knew I was a wanted man?*

A large hunter was standing in the stable yard and Mr Duncombe was beside it, talking to the rider, but seeing them approach he smiled.

'So there you are, Grace, and in good time.'

The rider jumped down. 'My dear, I am glad I did not miss you altogether.'

Wolf watched as the man caught Grace's hand and raised it to his lips. He looked to be on the shady side of forty, stocky and thick-set, with a ruddy complexion and more than a touch of grey in his hair. His brown coat was cut well, but not in the height of fashion, and he greeted Grace with an easy familiarity. Even before they were introduced Wolf had guessed his identity.

'Sir Loftus Braddenfield is our local Justice of the Peace.'

It did not need the warning note in the parson's mild words to put Wolf on his guard. Some spirit of devilry urged him to tug his forelock, but he suppressed it; Sir Loftus Braddenfield did not look like a fool. The man was coolly assessing him as Wolf made a polite greeting.

'So you are on your way to London, eh? Where are you from, sir?'

'I have been travelling in the north for some time,' Wolf replied calmly.

'And you thought you'd break your journey in Arrandale. Friend of Mr Duncombe's, are you?'

'I knew the family,' explained Mr Duncombe. 'A long time ago.'

Sir Loftus was still holding Grace's hand and it occurred to Wolf that he did not like seeing his fiancée escorted by a stranger. Wolf excused himself and as he walked away he heard Sir Loftus addressing Grace.

'I wish I could stay longer, my dear, but I have business in Hindlesham. I merely called to invite you and your father to dinner this evening. But if you have visitors…'

Grace's reply floated across the yard to Wolf as he ran lightly up the garret stairs.

'Mr Peregrine is not a visitor, Loftus. More one of Papa's charitable cases.'

He winced. That cool description should allay any jealous suspicions Braddenfield might have. Clearly the lady had a very low opinion of 'Mr Peregrine'. He went inside, but as he crossed the room he could not resist glancing out of the window, which overlooked the yard. The little party was still there, but the parson and Braddenfield appeared to have finished their discussion, for the magistrate was taking his leave of Grace, raising her hand to his lips. Wolf scowled. She was smiling at Braddenfield more warmly than she had ever smiled at him.

Kicking off his boots, he threw himself down on the bed. It did not matter what Miss Grace Duncombe thought of him. There were more pressing matters requiring his attention. Putting his hands behind his head, he thought of all he had heard from old Brent and from Jones, the caretaker at Arrandale Hall. He closed his eyes and conjured his own memories of the tragedy. He remembered the servants coming up to the hall while he knelt beside Florence's almost-lifeless form. Jones had added one small detail that Wolf had forgotten. It had been Charles Urmston who pulled Wolf to his feet, saying as he did so, 'You have done it this time, Arrandale. Your temper has got the better of you.'

Everyone would think Florence had met him on the landing, ready to continue their argument, and he had pushed her away so that she had fallen to her death. There were witnesses enough to their frequent quarrels. And the theft of the necklace was also laid squarely at his door.

He sat up abruptly. Whoever stole the diamonds knew the truth about Florence's death, he was sure of it. Wolf glanced out of the window again. The stable yard was empty now. Mr Duncombe and his daughter were invited to dine with Sir Loftus, so he was free to patronise the local inn this evening.

'Well, well, that was a pleasant dinner.'

Grace wished she could agree with her father, but if she were truthful, she had found the evening spent with Sir Loftus and his elderly mother a trifle dull. Mrs Braddenfield was a kindly soul, but her interests were narrow and her son, although well educated, lacked humour. Grace supposed that was partly to do with his being Justice of the Peace, a position he took very seriously. They did not even have the company of Claire Oswald, Mrs Braddenfield's young companion, to lighten the mix, for she was away visiting relatives.

The conversation over dinner ranged from local matters to the weather and the ongoing war with France, but it had all been very serious. Grace compared the evening to the previous one spent in the company of their mysterious guest. They had discussed a whole range of topics and her own contributions had been received without the condescension she often detected in her fiancé's manner. Berating herself for being so ungrateful, she sought for something cheerful to say.

'It was very kind of Loftus to put his carriage at our disposal.'

'It was indeed. It would have been a chilly ride in the gig.'

She heard the sigh in her father's voice. At times like these Papa felt the change in their circumstances. The tithes that provided a large proportion of his income as rector of the parish had diminished considerably since Arrandale Hall had been shut up and when their ancient coachman had become too old to work they had pensioned him off. Grace had persuaded her father that a carriage was not a necessity; they could manage very well with the gig and the old cob. And so they could, although she could not deny there were benefits to riding in a closed carriage during the colder months of the year.

Sir Loftus owned the manor house in the market town of Hindlesham. It was only a few miles, but Grace was thankful when they reached Arrandale village, for they would be home very soon. It was nearing midnight and most of the buildings were in darkness, no more than black shapes against the night sky, but light spilled out from the Horse Shoe Inn, just ahead of them. With her head against the glass Grace watched a couple of figures stagger on to the road without any heed for the approaching vehicle. The carriage slowed to a walk, the coachman shouting angrily at the men to get out of the way. From the loud and abusive response she was sure they had not come to harm beneath the horses' hoofs.

Grace was relieved her father was sleeping peacefully in his corner of the carriage, for he did not like her to hear such uncouth language. Dear Papa, he was apt to think her such a child! Smiling, she turned her gaze back to the window. They were level with the inn now and there was someone else in the doorway. As the carriage drove by, the figure turned and she saw it was Mr Peregrine.

There was no mistaking him, the image was embedded in her mind even as the carriage picked up speed. He was hunched, his coat unbuttoned and he was wearing a muffler around his throat rather than the clean linen she had taken the trouble to provide for him. His hat was pulled low over his face and it was the merest chance that he had looked up at just that moment, so that the light from the inn's window illuminated his face.

Why should he be skulking around a common inn at midnight? And had he recognised her? Grace drew herself up. She was not at fault. If he had seen her, then she was sure he would be at pains to explain himself. She was more than ever relieved that he was not sleeping in the house. When they reached the vicarage she gently roused her father and accompanied him indoors. She decided not to say anything to him about their guest tonight, but unless the man had a satisfactory explanation for his activities she would urge her father to tell him to leave.

The following morning she found their guest breaking his fast in the kitchen, freshly shaved, a clean neckcloth at his throat and looking altogether so at ease that for a moment her resolve wavered. But only for a moment.

'Mr Peregrine. When you have finished your breakfast I would be obliged if you would attend me in the morning room.'

Those piercing violet-blue eyes were fixed upon her, but he waited until Mrs Truscott had bustled out of the room before he spoke.

'You wish to see me alone?'

She flushed, but remained resolute.

'I do.'

'Is that not a little…forward of you, Miss Duncombe?'

Her flush deepened, but this time with anger.

'Necessity demands that I speak to you in private.'

'As you wish.' He picked up his coffee cup. 'Give me ten minutes and I will be with you.'

Grace glared at him. Mrs Truscott had come back into the kitchen so she could not utter the blistering set-down that came to her lips. Instead she turned on her heel and left the room. How dare he treat her thus, as if she had been the servant! If he thought that would save him from an uncomfortable interrogation, he was sadly mistaken.

Wolf drained his cup. The summons was not unexpected. It was unfortunate that Grace had seen him last night and it was his own fault. A carriage rattling through the main street at any time was a rare occurrence in Arrandale and he should have realised that it was most likely to be the Duncombes returning from Hindlesham. If only he had kept his head down, remained in the shadows, instead of staring into the coach window like a fool. Even now he remembered the look of shocked recognition on Grace's face. Well, he would have to brazen it out.

He made his way to the morning room where Grace was waiting for him, her hands locked together and a faint crease between her brows. She was biting her lip, as if she did not know quite how to begin. He decided to make it easy for her.

'You want to know what I was doing at the Horse Shoe Inn last night.'

'Yes. You are, of course, quite at liberty to go wherever you wish,' she added quickly. 'It was rather your appearance that puzzled me.'

'My appearance, Miss Duncombe?'

She waved one hand towards him. 'Today you are dressed neatly, with propriety. Last night you looked like a, like a…' He waited, one brow raised, and at last she burst out, 'Like a ne'er-do-well.'

He shrugged. 'I have always found it expedient to adapt to my surroundings. I had a sudden fancy for a tankard of home brewed and I did not want to make the other customers uncomfortable.'

It was not a complete lie. It had been a risk to go into the taproom at all, but the parson had told him the landlord was not a local man and would not know him. Wolf had hoped that with his untidy clothes and the ragged muffler about his neck no one would associate him with the Arrandale family.

Grace looked sceptical.

'Since the inn supplies us with our small beer I can only assume you had a sudden fancy for low company, too,' she said coldly. 'Forgive me if I appear uncharitable, but I think you have imposed upon our hospitality long enough.'

The door opened and the parson's soft voice was heard.

'Ah, Mr Peregrine, there you are.' Mr Duncombe came into the room, looking from one to the other. 'Forgive me, am I interrupting?'

Wolf met Grace's stormy eyes. 'Your daughter thinks it is time I took my leave.'

'No, no, my dear sir, there is no need for that, not before you have finished your business in Arrandale.'

Wolf waited for Grace to protest, but although her disapproval was tangible, she remained silent.

'Miss Duncombe is afraid I am importuning you, sir.'

'Bless my soul, no, indeed. I am very pleased to have you here, my boy.'

'But your daughter is not.' His words fell into a heavy silence.

'Perhaps, my son, you would allow me to speak to my daughter alone.'

'Of course.' As Wolf turned to go the old man caught his arm.

'Mark me, sir, I am not asking you to quit this house. In fact, I strongly urge you to stay, for as long as you need. You are safe here.'

'But if Miss Duncombe is not happy about it—'

'Let me talk with Grace alone, if you please. We will resolve this matter.'

Grace frowned. She did not understand the look that passed between the two men, but the stranger went out and she was alone with her father.

'Now, Grace, tell me what is troubling you. Is it merely that you think Mr Peregrine is imposing upon me?'

'I do not trust him, Papa.' She saw his look of alarm and said quickly, 'Oh, he has not acted improperly towards *me*, but—' She broke off, searching for the right words to express herself. 'Yesterday, when I was coming home after visiting Mrs Owlet, I came upon him in the Arrandale Chapel, and I saw him again last night, outside the Horse Shoe Inn when we drove past at midnight.'

'Ah.' The parson smiled. 'These are not such great crimes, my dear.'

'But you must admit it is not the behaviour of an honest man.'

'It may well be the behaviour of a troubled one.'

'I do not understand you.'

'No, I am aware of that. I am asking you to trust me in this, Grace.'

'Papa!' She caught his hands. 'Papa, there is something you are not telling me. Do you not trust *me*?'

He shook his head at her.

'My love, I beg you will not question me further on this matter. One day, I hope I shall be able to explain everything, but for now you must trust me. It is my wish that Mr Peregrine should remain here for as long as it is necessary.'

He spoke with his usual gentle dignity, but with a firmness that told her it would be useless to argue.

'Very well, Papa. If that is your wish.'

'It is, my child. Now, if you will forgive me, I am off to visit the Brownlows. They sent word that the old man has taken a turn for the worse and is not expected to last the day.'

'Of course. I must not keep you from your work.'

'Thank you. And, Grace, when you next see Mr

Peregrine I want you to make it plain to him that we want him to stay.'

With that he was gone. Grace began to pace up and down the room. Every instinct cried out against her father's dictum. The man was dangerous, she knew it, to her very core. So why was her father unable to see it? Grace stopped and pressed her hands to her cheeks. The image of Mr Peregrine filled her mind, as he had been that day by the pump, droplets of water sparkling on his naked chest like diamonds. That danger was not something she could share with her father!

There was a faint knock on the door. She schooled her face to look composed as Truscott came in with a letter for her. The handwriting told her it was from Aunt Eliza, but her thoughts were too confused to enjoy it now. She would saddle Bonnie and go for a ride. Perhaps that would help her to see things more clearly.

Wolf heaved the axe high and brought it down with more force than was really necessary. The log split with satisfying ease and even as the pieces bounced on the cobbles he put another log on the chopping block and repeated the action. It was a relief to be active and he was in some measure repaying his host's kindness. The vision of Grace's stormy countenance floated before him and he pushed it away. He wanted to tell her the truth, but Mr Duncombe had advised against it. He must respect that, of course, but there was something so good, so honest about Grace that made the deception all the more abhorrent.

The axe came down again, so heavily that it cleaved the log and embedded itself in the block. He left it there while he eased his shoulders. He had discarded his coat and waistcoat, but the soft linen of his shirt was sticking to his skin. It would need washing again. A reluctant smile tugged at his lips as he recalled Grace tripping out into the garden and seeing him, half-naked, by the pump. He remembered her look, the way her eyes had widened. She had not found his body unattractive, whatever else she might think of him.

The smile died. There was no place in his life for a woman, especially one so young. Why, he was her senior by ten years, and her innocence made the difference feel more like a hundred. No, Grace Duncombe was not for him.

There was a clatter of hoofs and the object of his reverie approached from the stable yard. Her face was solemn, troubled, but the mare had no inhibitions, stretching her neck and nudging his arm, as if remembering their last meeting. Idly Wolf put a hand up and rubbed the mare's forehead while Grace surveyed the logs covering the cobbles outside the woodshed.

'My father wishes me to make it clear that you are welcome to remain here as long as you wish.'

'Thank you, Miss Duncombe.'

She looked at him then.

'Do not thank *me*. You know I would rather you were not here.'

She went to turn the mare, but Wolf gripped the leather cheek-piece.

'Grace, I—'

The riding crop slashed at his hand.

'How dare you use my name?'

He released the bridle and stepped back. Fury sparkled in her eyes as she jerked the horse about and cantered away.

'Hell and damnation!' Wolf rubbed his hand and looked down at the red mark that was already appearing across the knuckles.

'Is everything all right, sir?' Truscott appeared, looking at him anxiously. 'I just seen Miss Grace riding out o' here as if all the hounds of hell were after her.'

Wolf's eyes narrowed. 'I need a horse. A fast one.'

Chapter Four

The frantic gallop did much to calm Grace's agitation, but it could not last. She had already ridden Bonnie hard for a couple of hours that morning and the mare needed to rest. She had returned to the stables, determined to carry out her father's instructions and speak to their guest. She thought that, perched high on Bonnie's back, she would be able to remain calm and aloof, but the sight of the man had caught her off-guard. The white shirt billowing about him accentuated his broad shoulders and sent her pulse racing. And when he fixed her with those eyes that seemed to bore into her very soul, she panicked. Her reaction to his presence frightened her and his hand on the bridle was the last straw for her frayed nerves. She had thought only of getting away. But now, as she slowed Bonnie to a walk, she was filled with remorse. She hated violence and was ashamed to think she had struck out so blindly. She would have to apologise.

With a shock Grace realised she was on the outskirts of Hindlesham. Having come this far she should carry on to the Manor and give her thanks for last night's dinner. Loftus might well be out on business but his mother would be there. The very thought had Grace turning and cantering back towards Arrandale. Mrs Braddenfield frequently urged Grace to look upon her as a parent, since her own dear mother was dead, but Grace could no more confide in her than a stranger. Besides, Mrs Braddenfield would agree that Papa was far too trusting, that this 'Mr Peregrine' should be sent away immediately and perversely Grace did not want to hear that. Oh, heavens, she did not know what she *did* want!

She eased her conscience with the knowledge that Mrs Braddenfield was not in want of company. The lady had told them herself that her neighbours were being very attentive during the absence of Claire Oswald, her excellent companion. No, Mrs Braddenfield did not need her visit and, in her present agitated state, Grace would be very poor company indeed.

* * *

Grace had reached Arrandale Moor when she saw someone galloping towards her. She recognised Mr Styles's bay hunter immediately, but the rider was definitely *not* the elderly farmer. He was tall and bare-headed and she thought distractedly that he looked as good on horseback as he did chopping wood. Her mouth dried, she had a craven impulse to turn and flee, but she drew rein and waited for horse and rider to come up to her, steeling herself for the apology she must make to the man calling himself Mr Peregrine.

It took all her nerve to keep Bonnie still, for it looked at first as if horse and rider would charge into her, but at the last moment the bay came to a plunging halt, eyes wild and nostrils flaring. The rider controlled the powerful animal with ease, his unsmiling eyes fixed on Grace.

'Sir, I must apologise—'

'You said you want the truth,' he interrupted her. 'Very well. Follow me.'

Without waiting for her reply he wheeled about and set off back towards the village. Intrigued, Grace followed him. They passed the vicarage and took the narrow lane that bordered Arrandale Park until they came to a gap in the paling. As soon as both horses had both pushed through they set off again, galloping towards the Hall. The pace did not ease until they reached the weed-strewn carriage circle before the house itself. Grace saw her companion throw himself out of the saddle and she quickly dismounted before he could reach her. He looked to be in a fury and even as she slid to the ground she wondered if she had been wise to follow him.

'Come along.'

He took her arm and escorted her up the steps, arriving at the door just as Robert Jones opened it. With a curt instruction to the servant to look after the horses, he almost dragged Grace inside.

She had never been inside the Hall before. She wanted to stop and allow her eyes to grow accustomed to the shuttered gloom, but her escort led her on inexorably, through what she could dimly see was a series of reception rooms to the narrow backstairs. Fear and curiosity warred within her, but for the moment curiosity had the upper hand.

'Where are we going?'

'You will soon see.'

He marched her up the narrow, twisting stairs to a long gallery that ran the length of the building. After the darkness of the shadowy stairwell, the light pouring in from the windows was almost dazzling.

'Why have you brought me here?'

A prickling fear was already whispering the answer.

'You will see.' He strode along the gallery and stopped at one of the paintings. Only then did he release her. Grace resisted the urge to rub her arm where his fingers had held her in a vice-like grip.

They were standing beneath a picture. A family group, an older man with powdered hair in a dark frock coat and a tall crowned hat, a lady in an elegant muslin dress with a blue sash that matched her stylish turban. Between them, in informal pose, stood their children, a fair-haired schoolboy and beside him, his arm protectively resting on the boy's shoulder, a tall young man dressed in the natural style that was so fashionable ten years ago, a black frock coat and tight breeches. But it was not the clothes that held her attention, it was the lean, handsome face and the coldly cynical gleam in the violet-blue eyes that stared out defiantly beneath a shock of thick, curling dark hair. She glanced at the man beside her and involuntarily stepped away.

'Yes, that is me.' There was a sneer in the deep, drawling voice. 'Wolfgang Charles Everdene Arrandale. Not-so-beloved son and heir of Arrandale. This was painted to celebrate my twenty-first birth-day. Not that it was much of a celebration, I was a rakehell even then, in true Arrandale tradition. Is it any wonder my father thought me capable of murder?'

'And the boy?' It was all she could think of to say.

'My brother Richard, seven years my junior. He could have inherited Arrandale. When I left England I deliberately cut myself off from the family, ignored letters and messages, even the news that my parents were dead. I wanted everyone to think I had died, too, but it seems Richard would not accept that. Consequently the miserly lawyers have held the purse strings at Arrandale and my foolish brother has dipped into his own pocket to pay for necessary maintenance work here.'

Surely a murderer would not say such things.

Grace needed to think, so she moved along the gallery, studying the portraits. There were signs of Wolfgang Arrandale in many of them, in the shape of the eye, the strong chin and in most of the men she saw that same world-weary look, but the lines of dissipation were etched deeper. Reason told her she should be frightened of this man, but she felt only an overwhelming sadness and an irrational, dangerous wish to comfort him.

At the end of the gallery she turned.

'Why have you come back now?'

'I learned I have a daughter.'

'You did not know?'

'No. I thought when I left England I had no commitments, no responsibilities. I had brought enough shame on the family and thought it best if I disappeared. Now, for my daughter's sake, I need to prove my innocence.'

She forced herself to look him in the eye. 'Are you a murderer?'

'I have killed men, yes, in duels and in war. *But I did not kill my wife.*'

He held her gaze. Grace desperately wanted to believe him, but she could not ignore the portraits staring down at her from the walls, generations of rogues, rakes and murderers going back to the time of good King Hal. Everyone in the parish knew the history of the family. Why should this Arrandale be any different to his ancestors?

Her legs felt weak and she sank down on to a chair, regardless of the dust. She should have known who he was. It made such *sense*, she should have known.

He began to pace the floor, his boots echoing on the bare boards.

'There is a warrant for my arrest and a price on my head. If I am caught, your father could be charged with harbouring a criminal. He did not want you to have that on your conscience, too. But he was afraid you might guess.'

'Why should I do that?' She was answering herself as much as him. 'I was at school when your wife died. By the time I came home to look after Papa it was old news and the Arrandales were rarely mentioned.'

'Except to curse the name for bringing hardship and poverty to the village.'

She heard the bitterness in his voice and said quietly, 'Will you tell me what happened?'

He stared out of the window.

'I do not know. We argued, I rode out to cool my heels and when I came back I found her lying at the bottom of the stairs.'

'Could she have fallen?'

He looked at her then. 'Judge for yourself.'

He strode off towards a door at the far end of the gallery. Grace knew this was her chance. She could go back the way they had come, escape from the house and from Wolfgang Arrandale. That would be the safe, sensible thing to do.

It took only a heartbeat for Grace to decide. She followed him out of the gallery and down a different set of stairs, wider and more ornate than the ones they had ascended.

'This is the grand staircase,' he said, as they reached the first floor. 'My wife's room was there, the first door on the far side of the landing.'

The lantern window in the roof threw daylight onto the cantilevered stone staircase. It incorporated two half-turns and landings, so that it occupied three sides of the square inner hall. Grace looked at the shallow steps and elegant balusters. There was a smooth wooden handrail that would provide a good grip for the daintiest hand. Grace imagined herself emerging from the bedroom to descend the stairs. Her fingers would be on the rail as she crossed the landing, long before she reached the top step. Her companion let his breath go with a hiss.

'I have had enough of this place. Let us go.' He put out his hand, but let it drop, his lip curling when Grace shrank away. 'No doubt you will feel safer if I go first.'

Silently she followed him down the stairs. When

they reached the bottom he stood for a moment, looking down at the flagstones as if reliving the awful sight of his wife lying there.

'You said you had just come in,' she said, trying to think logically. 'From the front entrance?'

'No, the garden door, that way.' He indicated a shadowy passage set beneath the stairs. 'I had taken the key with me. I was in a foul temper and wanted to avoid seeing anyone.' He looked down at the flags again. 'I found her just here, on the floor.'

Grace looked at the spot where he was standing, then she looked up at the landing almost directly above them.

'You are thinking, Miss Duncombe, that she might have fallen from the balcony, rather than tumbled down the stairs. I remember the injuries to her head were commensurate with such a fall.'

Grace put her hands to her mouth.

'That could not have been an accident.' She read agreement in his eyes and closed her own, shuddering. 'Oh, poor woman.'

'Quite.' He sighed. 'I beg your pardon, I have said too much. I never intended you to know the full horror of it. Come, let me take you outside.'

She did not resist as he caught her arm—more gently this time—and led her to the door. When they reached the front steps she stopped and dragged in a long, steadying breath. The sun still shone brightly, a few feet away Robert Jones was holding the two horses. It was only minutes since they had gone into the house, but she felt as if she had come out into a different world. When she spoke she was surprised at how calm she sounded.

'Thank you, Mr Arrandale, you may release me now, I am not going to faint.'

His hand dropped. 'I am glad to hear it.'

Grace set off towards the horses. Without a mounting block she had no choice but to allow him to throw her up into the saddle and she made herself comfortable while he scrambled up on to his borrowed mount. When he thanked Jones for holding the horses the servant lost himself in a tangle of words.

'It was nothing, Master—Mr Arr—I mean...'

'You may be easy, Jones. Miss Duncombe knows who I am now.'

The man looked as if a great weight had been taken from his shoulders.

'Well that's a mercy. I'll wish 'ee both good day, then, sir. Miss Duncombe.'

They trotted away. Grace's head was bursting. Speculation, arguments, doubts whirled about and they were halfway across the park before she broke the silence.

'If you are innocent, you should have stayed and defended yourself.'

'I know.'

'So why did you flee the country?'

'My father insisted I leave. He and my wife's cousin bundled me out of the house before I could think clearly. My father had…connections at Size-well who would take me across to France.'

'Do you mean smugglers?'

He nodded. 'The weather was bad so I remained at an inn on the quay for a few days. It gave me a chance to think it all through. I had just decided to turn back when word reached me that the dia-monds were missing and the Sawstons were bring-ing a prosecution against me for theft and murder. Thus I am as you see me, Miss Duncombe. A fu-gitive with a price on his head.'

They had reached the gap in the paling and Wolf stopped to let Grace go first. He wondered what she thought of him now. He was somewhat encouraged when she waited on the road for him to join her.

'Well,' he said, as they moved off towards the vic-arage. 'You now hold my life in your hands.'

She threw him a troubled look. 'Pray do not joke

about it, Mr Arrandale. It is not a responsibility I want, I assure you.'

She tensed and he looked up to see Sir Loftus trotting out of the vicarage drive. He nodded at Wolf before turning to address Grace.

'This is the second day in a row that I have missed you, my dear. If I were the suspicious sort I should think you were avoiding me.'

She laughed and replied with perfect calm, 'Now how can that be, sir, when I had no idea you were going to call today? I have been taking advantage of the fine weather to show our guest around the area.'

'Indeed? And how much longer do you intend to remain in Arrandale, Mr Peregrine?'

'Oh, I hardly know, a few days, a week.'

Wolf waited for Braddenfield to ask him the nature of his business here, but Grace gave the man no chance. She reached across and put a hand on his arm.

'It must be nearly dinner time, Loftus. Will you not stay and take pot luck with us? It will give me the opportunity to make amends for not being in when you called.'

Wolf held his breath. The last thing he wanted was to spend the evening in the company of a Justice of the Peace. Not by the flicker of an eyelid did he show his relief when Braddenfield declined the invitation.

'Another time, perhaps,' he said, patting Grace's hand. 'My mother is expecting me.'

'Of course.' Smiling, Grace gathered up her reins. 'Pray give her my regards.'

'That was close,' murmured Wolf, as they watched Sir Loftus ride away.

'Not at all,' she replied. 'I learned last night that his mother's companion is visiting her family and I knew he would not leave his mama to dine alone. It was quite safe to invite him.'

A laugh escaped Wolf. 'By Gad, then it was very coolly done, ma'am.'

Two spots of colour painted her cheeks.

'It was very badly done,' she retorted, kicking her horse on. 'Do not think I take pleasure in deceiving an honest man!'

It was at times such as this that Grace regretted they only had the Truscotts at the vicarage to help them. She would have liked to hand her horse over to a groom and disappear to her room; instead she had to stable Bonnie herself. In normal circumstances she did not object, Truscott already worked very hard and she could not expect him to look after her mare as well as the old cob they kept to pull the gig.

She had just finished rubbing down Bonnie when Wolfgang Arrandale came into the stable.

'I have brought a bucket of water for your mare.'

'Thank you, but there was no need,' she told him coldly. 'What have you done with Mr Styles's bay?'

'I have returned him and paid Styles handsomely for the loan of his horse.'

'And now you are back to plague me.'

'That is not my intention. I beg your pardon.'

She sighed. 'No, I beg *yours*, Mr Arrandale. You are my father's guest and I have behaved very badly to you.'

'That is understandable, if you think me a murderer.'

'Papa believes you are innocent.'

'But you do not, do you?

She eased herself out of Bonnie's stall only to find him blocking her way. She knew he would not move until she gave him an answer.

'I do not know *what* to believe. You...' She locked her fingers together. 'You frighten me.'

'I do not mean to.'

He took her hands. His grasp was gentle, but it

conveyed the strength of the man. Odd that she should find that so comforting.

'Believe me, Miss Duncombe, I mean you no harm.'

'No?' She looked up at him. 'But just your being here might harm us. Harbouring a criminal is an offence, I believe.'

'Is that why you said nothing to Sir Loftus?'

Was it? She didn't know any more.

He was still holding her hands and gazing down at her with no hint of laughter in his face. Her mouth dried. Suddenly everything seemed sharper, she was aware of the dust motes floating in the band of sunlight pouring in through the window, the soft noises from Bonnie as she munched the hay from the rack, the faint cries of a shepherd and his lad driving their sheep through the village.

Then everything around them faded into nothing. She was aware only of the man holding her hands, his powerful presence calling to something inside. It set her heart pounding so heavily she thought she might faint. His eyes bored into her and, fearing he could read her thoughts, she dragged her gaze away, but only as far as his mouth. Strong, unsmiling, sensual. She wondered what it would be like to have those finely sculpted lips fixed on hers. As if in answer his hands slid up her arms, pulling her closer and she leaned into him, her face turned up to receive his kiss.

It was no gentle, reverential salute, it was rough and demanding and Grace responded instinctively. She clung to him, her lips parted. Following his lead, she let her tongue dip and dance and taste. She felt intoxicated, an explosion of excitement ripped through her, leaving her weak, and when Wolf raised his head to drag in a deep, ragged breath she remained in his arms, her head thrown back against his shoulder, gazing up at him in wonder.

Fear rushed in. With a little cry of alarm Grace pushed herself free and ran from the stable. He overtook her as they reached the house.

'I frightened you, I am sorry,' he murmured, stepping past her to open the door.

She did not pretend to misunderstand him. 'I frightened myself.'

'Grace—'

She put up her hand and shook her head. Tears were very near. 'I am not free to, to *like* you!'

And with that she fled.

Wolf stood and watched her disappear into the house. *Like* him? Like was too mild a word for

what had passed between them and he cursed himself for allowing it to happen. He must concentrate
on clearing his name. There was no time for dalliance and certainly not with a gently bred vicar's daughter. What if she developed a *tendre* for
him? He glanced down at his hand. The weal where
her riding crop had caught him was still bright, a
testament to the passion he knew she possessed.
His mouth twisted. She was one who would love
fiercely and he had no wish to break her heart.

He exhaled, the breath whistling out. That would
be a dastardly way to repay all the kindness the
parson had shown him. No, he had learned all he
could in Arrandale and it was time he moved on
and forgot all about Miss Grace Duncombe. Closing the door carefully behind him, Wolf went in
search of his host.

Grace summoned Betty to help her out of her
riding habit. She was still shaking and her lips still
burned with the memory of that kiss. It frightened
her that she could lose control so easily. Perhaps
she was like those wanton women of the Bible such
as Jezebel or the daughters of Zion. A dispiriting
thought and it made her ask Betty to look out her
grey silk. It was her most sober dress, a plain, high-

necked gown with long sleeves and only a tiny edging of lace at the neck and cuffs. Even Papa had joked that it made her look like a nun.

Once she was dressed she dismissed Betty and sat down before her looking glass to re-pin her hair, but for some moments she did nothing but gaze at her reflection. There was no doubt she looked very severe. Some months ago Mrs Braddenfield had commented favourably upon the grey silk and in a rare moment of rebellion Grace had put it away, determined never to wear it again. However, this was a necessity, she thought, picking up her hairbrush and dragging it through her hair with quick, jerky movements. She needed to be covered from neck to toe from the glances of men, glances that could bring the blush not only to her cheeks but to her whole body.

Her hand stilled. No, it was not men in general. Loftus had never made her blush in that way. In fact, it had never happened before in all her four-and-twenty years. What was it about Wolfgang Arrandale that caused her pulse to race and the blood to sing in her veins?

'It is because he is so tall,' she told her reflection. 'Not since you were a child have you had to look up to a man. It is a novel experience, and you have allowed your fancy to run away with you.'

Yes, that was it. She finished brushing her hair and quickly pinned it up. It was the novelty of the man. He was so tall and dark and…

'And dangerous.'

Her words echoed around the bedchamber. She had so little experience of the world. Of men like Wolfgang Arrandale. She gave a sigh. Mama had died when she was a baby and Grace had never felt her lack, until now. Now she wished quite fervently that she had a mother to advise her. She glanced at the small writing desk in the corner, where she had tossed her aunt's letter before going out for her ride. Aunt Eliza had stood in place of a mother once, until she had married Mr Graham. Grace had felt bereft then, and a little aggrieved, but her aunt had never stopped loving her. And Aunt Eliza was so much more worldly-wise than Papa. That was the solution. Grace moved across to the writing table and sat down.

Grace went downstairs just in time to go in to dinner. The conversation was desultory while Truscott placed the last of the dishes on the table, but once they were alone Grace braced herself for the inevitable.

'So, Grace,' said her father. 'You know our guest's little secret.'

'Not such a *little* secret, Papa.'

'No, indeed, my dear. I would rather he had not told you, but perhaps you now understand a little better the need for secrecy.'

'I do understand it, Papa, but I could wish Mr Arrandale had not put such a burden upon you.'

'Believe me, Miss Duncombe, if I thought I could trust anyone in Arrandale half so well I would not have done so.'

Enveloped in her grey gown and the width of the dining table between them, Grace thought she might risk a glance at the speaker. A mistake. He looked dark and saturnine in the dim light. There was a pent-up energy about him, like a wild animal poised and ready to spring. Having raised her eyes to his, she found it difficult to look away.

Her father gave one of his mild exclamations.

'My dear sir, I am *glad* you came to me and, despite my earlier concerns, I cannot regret that Grace knows the truth.' He put out his hand to her. 'We have never had secrets from each other, have we, my dear?'

She reached for his fingers and gave them a squeeze.

'No, Papa, we have not. And that reminds me, there is something I have to tell you.' She paused as Truscott and Betty came in to clear away the empty dishes, but only for a moment. After all, what she was going to say was not really a secret. 'I have had a letter from Aunt Eliza.'

'My sister,' Papa explained to their guest. 'She kept house here and looked after us until Grace went off to school. Then she left to get married.'

'I remember Miss Eliza Duncombe from my visits to Arrandale as a boy,' he replied, when the servants had withdrawn again. 'How is she, sir?'

'My sister is a widow now, alas, although her husband provided for her very well. She has a house in Hans Place and lives there very comfortably, I believe.'

Grace nodded. 'Her letters are always cheerful, however I think she is a little lonely since Mr Graham's death a few years ago. You will know, Papa, that whenever she writes she invites me to visit. Indeed, you have been urging me any time these past twelve months to do so.' She took a breath. 'I have just now sent off a note, accepting her invitation. I plan to join her within the week. I hope you do not mind, Papa?'

Grace looked up, expecting surprise from her father and even a little regret that she would be leaving him. She had mustered her arguments: if he said he would be lonely she would point out that he had Mr Arrandale to keep him company, and if he expressed concern at her going away when they had a visitor she would have to explain that she could not be easy in her conscience, harbouring a fugitive.

In the event, her preparations were unnecessary. Papa looked surprised, but only for a moment, then he gave a wide smile.

'Why, that is excellent news, my love. I am delighted for you.'

She gave a sigh of relief. 'I thought perhaps you would wonder at my going now...'

'Not at all, my dear, not at all. In fact, the timing could not be more propitious. You see, Mr Arrandale is off to London, too, so you may travel together.'

Chapter Five

Wolf almost laughed at the look of horror upon Grace's face.

He said drily, 'I think you will find Miss Duncombe's intention in leaving Arrandale is to remove herself from my presence.' He added with a touch of bitterness, 'She does not share your belief in my innocence, sir.'

'That may be,' said the parson, 'but I am sure Grace is as keen as I am to see justice done.'

'Yes,' said Grace. 'Of course, Papa, but...'

'It would be quite ridiculous for you to travel to London separately. Why, you would be following one another within a matter of days, and what is the sense in that? And, Grace, I would be much happier to know you had a gentleman to escort you to your aunt's door.'

'Not if that gentleman is wanted for murder!'

Grace looked shocked by her outburst and said immediately, 'I beg your pardon, but I do not need a gentleman to escort me, Papa. I thought I might take Betty.'

The parson laid down his knife and fork. 'And how, pray, do you expect the poor child to get back? Why, she has less sense than a peahen.'

Wolf watched as Grace opened her mouth to protest, then closed it again. He felt a certain sympathy for her.

'I understand your concerns, Miss Duncombe, but your father is right, I had already decided to go to London within the next few days. In fact, we were discussing the matter before dinner. However, I shall not inflict my company upon you if it is so abhorrent.'

'Thank you, sir, but Papa is correct,' came the stiff reply. 'It would be sensible to travel together.'

'Then perhaps a private chaise might be in order.' Wolf saw her brows go up and added coldly, 'The burden for this extravagance would not fall upon your father, my funds are more than sufficient.'

Her response was equally chilly.

'You must excuse me if your dress and your manner of arrival caused me to doubt that.'

'When I landed in England I wanted to attract the

least possible attention. Thus I travelled as a gentleman of middling fortune, and with only one portmanteau. Going to London is another matter.' She
looked sceptical and, goaded, he went on, 'Be as-
sured, madam, I could hire a dozen private chaises
to convey me there if I so wished!'

Wolf clamped his jaws together. He thought
he had learned to govern his hot temper, but this
woman brought out the worst in him. He wondered
if he should apologise to his host, but the parson
was unperturbed and helping himself to another
portion of lamb from the dish at his elbow.

'Where will you stay, my son? I am sure my sister would put you up.'

'But, Papa, Hans Place is very out of the way.
Even Aunt Eliza admits it is not convenient for the
fashionable shopping areas such as Bond Street.'

'Do I look as if I wish to shop in a fashionable
area?' Wolf retorted. Those dark eyes flashed with
anger, but she made no response. He said stiffly,
'Thank you, sir, but I shall arrange my own accommodation when I reach town.'

'As you wish, my boy, but I shall send an express
to Eliza, so she may expect you. She would never
forgive me if she learned you had been so close and
had not visited her.' He sat back. 'Now, if we have

all finished shall we retire to the drawing room? I will ask Truscott to serve our brandy there and we can discuss the details of your journey.'

Grace put down her napkin. So she was to be allowed no respite. If only she had not been so precipitate! She had dashed off her reply to her aunt and asked Truscott to send one of the village lads to Hindlesham with it, to catch the night mail. It would look very odd if she were to cry off now.

'Miss Duncombe?'

She heard Wolf Arrandale's voice behind her and realised he was waiting to escort her from the room. There was nothing for her to do but rise and put her fingers on his sleeve.

'This has put you in an awkward situation,' he said as they entered the drawing room. 'If I had not agreed the whole with your father before dinner I might have told him I needed to remain here a little longer.'

'And if I had not been so quick to write to my aunt.' She gave a little smile as she released his arm and walked to a chair beside the fire. 'I fear Fate has conspired against us, sir, and I for one am not disposed to fight it any longer.'

'Will you cry friends with me, then?'

She said cautiously, 'Not friends, but not enemies, either.'

'That will do for me.'

He held out his hand and instinctively she put up her own. She stared at the red mark across his knuckles and said remorsefully, 'That looks very sore.'

'I do not notice it, I assure you.'

'You did not deserve that. I am sorry.'

'Not then, perhaps, but later…'

Grace felt the heat burning up through her again.

'What happened in the stables was not entirely your fault,' she admitted. 'I fear we bring out the worst in each other, Mr Arrandale.'

She thought he was about to agree, but her father walked in and the moment was lost.

Truscott brought in the decanters and they talked of innocuous matters until each had a full glass, brandy for the gentlemen and madeira for Grace. Papa looked askance when she requested it, but she felt in need of something stronger than ratafia to get her through the evening. As soon as Truscott closed the door upon them her father turned to her.

'Now, my dear,' he said, his eyes twinkling. 'We must decide how best to get you two to London. I would not want Sir Loftus to think you were running away like star-crossed lovers.'

Lovers! A shiver of excitement scurried through Grace at the thought. She swallowed and tried to concentrate.

'Indeed not, Papa,' she agreed. 'And, sadly, I do not think we can take Loftus into our confidence.'

'Good heavens, no. A very worthy man, but he is, after all, a magistrate.'

She said awkwardly, 'He has been pressing me to order my wedding clothes, so he will not object to my going to town for that purpose.'

'Have you set a date then, Miss Duncombe?' asked Wolfgang politely.

'No, but Loftus is keen to do so.' She wrapped her hands around the wineglass and stared down at it. 'I shall tell him we will be married as soon as I return from London.'

'An excellent suggestion,' agreed Papa. 'If you will forgive me saying so, my dear, you have kept the poor man waiting quite long enough.'

Grace continued to stare into her glass. She had expected to feel nervous at the thought of getting married, but not this sick, unhappy dread.

Do not think of it, then. Concentrate instead upon getting safely to London.

Wolfgang's deep voice interrupted her thoughts. 'If you will tell me where I can hire a travelling chaise, I will arrange everything.'

'If I might suggest...' She looked up. 'I think we should take the mail coach. Loftus is bound to enquire and he will not expect me to travel by private chaise.'

'Will he not want to escort you himself?'

'I was about to ask that myself.' Papa turned his gaze upon her. 'Is that not a possibility, Grace?'

'Yes. But we could travel on Friday. Loftus will be engaged at Hindlesham market on that day. And...' She paused. 'Perhaps Truscott could drive us to Newmarket. I know the mail picks up from Hindlesham after that, but we need not alight, so there is less chance that anyone would see us, or think that we were travelling together.'

'You are a born conspirator, Miss Duncombe.'

The admiration in Wolf's voice only flayed Grace's conscience even more. Her father declared it an excellent plan and the two men discussed the final arrangements. However, when everything was settled and their guest had retired, Grace remained seated, gazing into the fire and twisting her hands together.

'Something is troubling you, my child.' Her father

drew a chair up beside her and reached out to take her hands. 'You do not like this business, do you?'

She shook her head.

'No, Papa, I do not like it. My conscience is not easy. And after what happened to Henry...'

'That is why I was loath to share Mr Wolfgang's secret, my love. I am convinced of his innocence, but I knew for you it would bring back painful memories of Henry's tragic death.'

She shuddered and he gave her hands a comforting squeeze.

'I know it is difficult for you, my love, but when Wolfgang Arrandale came to me for help I could not refuse him.'

'And you truly believe he is innocent?'

'I do, Grace. Even more, I fear someone has deliberately put the blame on him. The tragic events of Mrs Wolfgang's death might have been used to cover the theft of the necklace, but it could be something much more sinister.'

A cold chill ran down Grace's spine.

'He showed me the spot where he found her. Papa, it was directly beneath the balcony. What if...what if he lost his temper with his wife and pushed her over the balcony? It *is* possible, is it not, Papa?'

'Yes, it is possible,' he replied. 'But he has returned here to prove his innocence. Surely that is in his favour?' He gripped her hands. 'He asked for my help, Grace, and I cannot deny him.'

No more can I.

Grace felt a band tighten around her heart. Papa was such a good man he would not think ill of anyone. She was far less sure of her own reasons for wanting to help Wolf Arrandale.

'No, of course not, Papa.' She kissed his cheek. 'Tomorrow I shall see Loftus and tell him I am going to London.'

Grace was not looking forward to her visit to Hindlesham and she delayed it as late as possible the following morning by taking baskets of food to the needy. The last of the baskets was for Mrs Owlet, the widow who had broken her leg. The visit was not strictly necessary and Grace admitted it was an attempt to learn more about the Arrandales, but if she was hoping for reassurance then she was sadly disappointed. When Grace broached the subject the widow was scathing in her condemnation of the family.

'The old man was a villain,' she said, almost spitting with hatred. 'Dying like that and leaving us all to fend for ourselves.'

'He could hardly be blamed for that,' said Grace, recoiling a little from such vehemence.

'His sons are as bad. Rakes, both of 'em. The whole family is damned.'

It was not what Grace wanted to hear.

'Oh, surely not,' she murmured, preparing to take her leave.

The old woman clutched her arm, fingers digging in like claws. 'And the oldest boy, the wife-murderer, well, he's turned out worst of all. He walks with the devil.'

Grace made her excuses at that point and hurried back to the vicarage, but however much she told herself Mrs Owlet was embittered because the Hall had closed and she had lost her position, the words haunted her.

The visit to Hindlesham could be delayed no longer. Grace changed into her riding habit and went to the stableyard, where she found Wolfgang leading out Bonnie.

He walks with the devil.

'You have been busy, so I saddled the mare for you,' he said. 'I thought you would go in the gig, but your father told me you would prefer to ride.'

'He sees no harm in my riding alone here, where

I am so well known. Besides, Truscott needed the gig to go to Newmarket and book our places on the mail.'

She allowed him to keep the mare steady while she used the mounting block and he held Bonnie while Grace arranged her skirts.

'Thank you.'

She gathered up the reins, but he did not release the mare.

'No,' he said quietly. 'Thank *you*, Miss Duncombe. I appreciate what you are doing for me.'

'For my father,' she corrected him. She glanced around to make sure they were alone. 'He believes you are innocent.'

'And you do not?'

His look sent the butterflies fluttering inside again. She knew where this man was concerned her heart was ruling her head. The only defence she could summon up was anger.

'I would rather not think of you at all, Mr Arrandale!'

He nodded and stepped away from the mare's head. 'Do not tarry, Miss Duncombe. It looks like rain.'

Grace trotted out of the yard, resisting the temptation to look back. One more day and she would not have to see Wolfgang Arrandale again. A few weeks in London with Aunt Eliza, then she would return and marry Loftus. Safe, dependable Loftus. The marriage settlements had been agreed: they would secure her future and that would be a great comfort to Papa.

It would be a comfort to her, too. It had to be. Her betrothal was a promise to marry and she had been raised to believe a promise was sacred.

Once they reached open ground, Grace set Bonnie galloping, but for once the exhilaration of flying over the moor did not banish everything else from her mind. If Wolfgang was innocent, as her father believed, then she prayed he would be able to prove it. But what then? Would he return to his old rakehell life, or would he marry and settle down at Arrandale? That would be an advantage for the parish and it was what her father wanted, so she should want it, too. After all, it could make no difference to her. She would be married to Loftus and living at Hindlesham.

As if conjured by her thoughts the manor house appeared ahead of her and she was momentarily daunted by the necessity of explaining her sudden departure to her fiancé. Grace sat a little straighter in the saddle. It must be done, there was no going back now.

* * *

Upon her return to the vicarage Grace ran upstairs to change before going in search of her father. She found him in his study with Wolfgang. They rose when she entered, her father exclaiming in some alarm, 'My dear, never tell me you rode back from Hindlesham in this rain?'

'I was obliged to do so, Papa, unless I wanted to remain at the manor all day.' She smiled. 'Do not fret, sir, Betty has taken my riding habit to dry it in the kitchen and apart from my hair still being a little wet, I am perfectly well, I assure you.'

'Nevertheless, you should sit by the fire,' said Wolfgang, vacating his chair for her.

'Yes, you must,' agreed her father. 'I cannot have you catching a chill. How did you get on at the manor?'

Grace sank down gratefully and held her hands out to the flames.

'Fortune favoured me,' she said. 'Loftus has gone to Cambridge and will not be back until late, so I spoke to his mother. I did not rush away, Papa, I was not so impolite. Miss Oswald, her companion, has returned from visiting her sister in Kent and we spent a pleasant hour conversing together.'

'Oswald?' Wolf looked up. 'Dr Oswald's daughter?'

'Yes. She kept house for her father, but when he died several years ago she was left with very little to live on. Papa knew Mrs Braddenfield was seeking a companion and he suggested Claire for the post,' Grace explained. 'Miss Oswald virtually runs the manor and is sincerely attached to her employer. They deal extremely well together. Much better than I shall ever do!'

She ended with a rueful laugh, but her father did not notice.

'There was some speculation that she and Sir Loftus would make a match of it when his wife died,' he said. 'But instead he turned his attention to Grace.'

'Does she resent you?' Wolf asked her.

'I hope not. She is a sensible woman and we get on very well.'

'I am glad,' he said. 'She could make life uncomfortable for you when you are married. I would not like to think of you being unhappy.'

Grace looked up quickly. The idea that he should care about her future was unsettling. She pushed herself out of the chair.

'If you will excuse me, I had best go and pack.'

'Would you not like to sit by the fire a little longer?' asked her father. 'Your hair is still damp.'

Grace shook her head. Much as she liked the warmth of the blazing fire she needed to be away from Wolfgang Arrandale. She needed to decide how best to deal with him and the confusing feelings he aroused in her.

Wolf noted that Grace was subdued at dinner, and as soon as the meal was over she announced that she was going out.

'Must you?' Mr Duncombe glanced towards the window. 'Your hair is barely dry from this morning's soaking.'

'It is not raining very hard now, Papa, and there is a visit I must pay. Perhaps Mr Arrandale would escort me.'

The parson's brows went up, but he was not nearly as surprised as Wolf. It was the last thing he expected, but he rose at once.

'Of course,' he said. 'Give me a moment to fetch my greatcoat from the garret.' He hurried away, returning moments later to find Grace waiting for him at the door, her heavy cloak about her shoulders. He said, as they stepped outside, 'I have taken the liberty of borrowing your father's umbrella. It is sufficiently wide for two.'

He offered her his arm, noting the tiny pause before she rested her fingers on his sleeve. The rain was little more than a fine drizzle as they set off and since there was no wind the umbrella kept them both dry.

'Where are we going?'

She lifted the spring flowers she was holding in her free hand. 'To the church.'

The High Street was deserted. Doors were closed against the chill of a damp spring evening and the smell of woodsmoke pervaded the air. Wolf felt a definite lightening of his spirits. She had invited him to come with her. How normal it seemed to be walking along with Grace at his side, how *right*.

'You are standing too tall, sir. Do not give yourself away!'

The urgent whisper reminded him that he was a fugitive with a price on his head. Every hint of pleasure fled as bitterness and regret welled up. He wanted to rail against the world for the injustice of it but really, who was there to blame but himself? He had been a wild youth and the world was only too ready to believe he had capped his misdemeanours by murdering his wife.

Turning that around would take a miracle and Wolf did not believe in miracles.

It did not take them long to reach the churchyard. Grace dropped his arm and went before him, taking a narrow path between the graves. It was barely raining now and Wolf closed the umbrella. She had stopped beside one of the headstones when he came up to her.

'Your mother,' he said, reading the inscription.

'Yes. I never knew her, she died when I was a babe, but I come here to pay my respects, especially if I am going away.'

She stooped to lay a bunch of flowers at the base of the stone and paused for a moment, resting her gloved fingers on the carved lettering. Wolf was silent, unwilling to intrude upon what was clearly a private moment and wondering why she had invited him to join her. When she rose he noticed that she was still carrying flowers.

'Two bunches, Miss Duncombe?'

'Yes. This way.'

She led the way to a far corner of the graveyard where a small, square stone marked a plot beneath an ancient yew tree, whose overhanging branches made the twilight so deep that Wolf had to bend close to read the inscription.

'"Henry Hodges. Curate of this parish. Twenty-six years."'

'My fiancé.' She placed the flowers on his grave and straightened. 'He died five years ago. We were going to be married at Christmas, on my nineteenth birthday.'

Wolf knew he should say something consoling. Instead he found himself asking her how he had died. She did not answer immediately, she was staring fixedly at the grave and he wondered if she had heard him.

'Violently,' she said at last, her voice very low. 'Henry was on his way home late one evening after visiting a sick parishioner. He saw a w-woman being attacked, robbed. Henry intervened and… and was stabbed.' She shook, as if a tremor had run through her. 'He was brought to the vicarage, but we could not save him. He died in my arms.'

Wolf struggled not to reach out to her. He said curtly, 'And the man who killed him?'

'Hanged. Not that I wanted that.'

'You could forgive him, after what he had done?'

'Not forgive, no. But I did understand.' She took a deep breath. 'My father spoke for the man at the trial. He was one of our parishioners and Papa said he had been a good man, a stable hand at the Hall until it closed. Since then years of poverty and want had driven him to despair.'

'Is that why you wanted me to accompany you? That I might more fully appreciate the harm my family did by closing the Hall?'

'No. You are not responsible for that. As I understand it your father's profligate ways had long made the estate's downfall inevitable.' Her dark, troubled gaze was fixed on him. 'I wanted you to understand that my heart is here, with Henry. Anything else is just...just earthly desire.' She turned and began to retrace her steps, saying over her shoulder, 'That k-kiss. It should not have happened. I should not have allowed it.'

So that was it. She was warning him off. Not that there was any reason to do so, he had already decided Grace Duncombe was a complication he did not need in his life.

'Sometimes these things catch one out,' he replied lightly.

'Apparently so.' She glanced at him. 'I wanted to explain, before we set off for London tomorrow. I do not hold you wholly responsible for what occurred in the stable, and…and I want to think no more about it.'

'Consider it forgotten, Miss Duncombe.' A few fat drops of rain splashed on the path and he raised his umbrella again. 'Shall we go back now?'

Grace took his arm and Wolf led her back to the vicarage, wondering why he did not feel more relieved that she was in no danger of losing her heart to him.

It was almost twenty miles to Newmarket and Grace spent the journey squeezed between Wolfgang and Truscott, in a gig only intended for two people. Wolfgang rested one arm along the back of the seat to make more room for her, but it felt to Grace as if he had his arm *around* her. She tried not to lean against him, but it was impossible to sit bolt upright for the whole time, and as the gig bowled along the road through the early morning darkness the rocking motion made her sleepy. At one point she awoke to find herself snuggled against him. When she tried to sit up his arm pulled her gently back against his shoulder.

'Hush now,' he murmured into her hair. 'Truscott needs room to handle the reins, even though the horse sees the road better than he does.'

And Grace allowed herself to believe him. She sank back against his convenient shoulder and dozed contentedly until they reached their destination.

A grey dawn was just breaking when they alighted at the inn, but even at that early hour the place was bustling. Grace was thankful that they could go into the dining room, where a few coins soon procured them two cups of scalding coffee.

It put new heart into her, so much so that she could almost forget her embarrassment at having virtually slept in Wolfgang's arms. She looked up to ask him what time the mail was due in and found he was gazing at her. A slow, lazy smile curved his lips.

Two thoughts raced through her head. She could not remember him smiling, really *smiling* before. And how much she wanted to smile back. That would never do, one could not share smiles with a suspected murderer!

She said crossly, 'Pray sir, why are you laughing at me?'

He immediately begged pardon but that only made her glare at him.

'What were you thinking?' she asked suspiciously.

'That no other woman of my acquaintance has ever looked as neat as you do at this ungodly hour.'

'Any woman of sense would be in bed at this hour.'

'There is that, of course.'

Grace had answered without thinking, but his response made her choke on her coffee and a blush of mortification burned her cheeks.

'You should not say such things,' she told him, wiping coffee from her lips.

'Why not? I was complimenting you on your appearance.'

She was not deceived by his innocent reply, but decided it would be wiser not to pursue the subject. She heard the laugh in his voice when he spoke again.

'I know you are trying to maintain a dignified silence, but you have coffee on your cheek. Here, let me.'

He reached across, cupping her chin with his fingers and drawing his thumb gently across her cheek. Grace wanted to close her eyes and rest her face against his hand. When she looked at Wolfgang there was no mistaking the heat in his gaze.

Her breath stopped. She could not look away, his eyes were violet-black in the lamplight and they seemed to pierce her very soul.

'London mail!'

The landlord's strident call broke the spell. Grace looked up to find the dining room had emptied.

'You'd best be quick,' the landlord warned them, standing by the door. 'The mail don't wait for no one.'

Wolf rose and put his hand under her elbow. 'Come along, Miss Duncombe.'

She would have liked to shake him off but really, she was not at all sure that her legs would support her.

There were only two places left in the mail coach. Grace took the window seat and Wolf climbed in to sit beside her. She pulled her cloak about her. At least she could lean into the corner of the carriage. There would be no need for her to fall asleep on his shoulder, as she had done in the gig.

Soon they were rattling over the open road, swaying and jolting so much there was no chance for Grace to rest, she was afraid her head would crash against the window.

'This 'un's a bone-shaker and no mistake.' A

motherly woman sitting opposite grinned at her. 'Never you mind, dearie, the road is a vast deal better on t'other side of Hindlesham, you wait and see.'

Grace nodded. She hoped so, for she had no idea how she would endure a whole day's travel.

By the time they reached Hindlesham the sun was creeping over the horizon. As they clattered through the streets, two of the passengers began to gather up their things ready to alight at the Golden Lion. The coach swept into the inn yard and even before it stopped the ostlers came running to change the horses. The early morning sun was low enough to shine through the arch and on to the side of the coach where Grace was sitting, illuminating her through the window. She decided that as soon as the passengers had alighted she would change seats, but even as the motherly woman heaved herself out of the door Grace spotted Claire Oswald standing in the yard and knew she had been recognised. It would be pointless to move now. Claire waved and came up to the open door.

'I wondered if you would be here, Miss Duncombe. When I did not see you in the coffee room I thought perhaps I had been mistaken and you were catching the night mail.'

Claire was looking rather fixedly at Wolfgang and Grace sat forward to block her view.

'Good morning, Miss Oswald.' She glanced around the yard, hoping she did not sound as anxious as she felt. 'Is Sir Loftus with you?'

'No, he is busy in the market. Mrs Braddenfield had a letter for the mail and I said I would deliver it.'

The ostlers had finished their work and the shout went up to stand clear. Miss Oswald stepped back.

'I wish you a good journey, Miss Duncombe.'

The door slammed and Grace waved through the glass as the coach began to pull away.

'Well, that was unfortunate,' murmured Wolfgang. 'I presume that was Claire Oswald.'

'Yes.'

The other passengers were busy making themselves comfortable and did not appear to be taking any notice, but Grace was wary of saying more.

She and Wolfgang passed the rest of the journey in near silence and when they eventually alighted at Bishopsgate the sun had already set. Grace stood in the yard with her small trunk at her feet and feeling bone-weary.

She said, trying to be cheerful, 'I would not have

believed sitting down all day could make one so tired.'

'We have a little further to go yet,' Wolf warned her. 'Wait here while I find someone to take us to Hans Place.'

'There really is no need for you to accompany me across London,' she replied. 'You had much better find yourself lodgings.'

'I promised your father I would see you safely to your aunt's house.'

There was a note of finality in his voice and Grace did not argue. If truth were told she was too tired to make the effort. However, as she waited for him to find a cab she remembered something that had been nagging her at the outset of the journey and once they were in the hired carriage she asked him the question.

'The lady we saw at Hindlesham, Miss Oswald. Can you remember meeting her when you were at Arrandale? She looked at you most particularly.'

He frowned.

'I do not think so. I was rarely at Arrandale before my marriage. My father decided that the future heir should be born at the Hall. Having chosen my wife for me, he thought he was entitled to rule my life.'

'Chosen? Did you not have any opinion?'

'Oh, yes, I had far too many opinions! But I always knew I would have to knuckle down some time. Florence Sawston came from a good family and brought a fortune with her. It was a provident match and approved by both families. When it was clear she was carrying our child it seemed sensible to move to Arrandale and acquaint myself with my inheritance, but Father and I had never dealt well together. It was a disaster. He saw my attempts to familiarise myself with the running of the estate as interference, every suggestion was scorned. I was a dissolute wastrel with no idea what was due to my name.' His lip curled. 'And that from a man who had lived for years on the profits of Arrandale, squandering his money on mistresses, gambling and high living. It was clear almost as soon as I moved in that we could not work together. We could never meet without arguing.'

'That must have been very uncomfortable for your wife,' she murmured.

Wolf gave a bark of laughter, but there was little humour in it.

'Florence thrived on conflict. She was an expert at stirring the coals, setting me even more at odds with my father. Sometimes I think it was a match made in hell.'

'And your mother, did she not support you?'

'My mother was only interested in her own comforts. Richard and I had learned long ago not to worry her with our concerns.'

'I am sorry. I cannot imagine how it must be to live in a house of strife.'

'Do not pity me, madam. It was a bed of my own making. Arrandales are masters of it, we go through life raking hell, so we should not complain when we get burned.'

Grace wanted to reach out to him, to comfort the lonely boy he must have been and the angry, wayward young man growing up without a parent's love. She gripped her hands tightly together in her lap. Ten years in exile had made him bitter and he would not want her comfort, or her sympathy.

And whatever Papa said, she was not even sure that he deserved it.

They came to a halt and by the light of the streetlamps Grace could see they were in a square surrounded by terraces of tall, new buildings. As they alighted from the cab the door of one of the houses was thrown open and Aunt Eliza came flying out.

'Dear Grace, how happy I am to see you and in such good time, too. I have been looking out for you this past hour, but I really did not expect you to arrive so soon. Come in, my dear, come in. And Mr Peregrine, too. Come in, sir, we cannot welcome you properly while we are standing on the street!'

Wolf thought it was like being taken up by a small whirlwind. Mrs Graham ushered them inside, talking all the time and never pausing until they were in the welcome warmth of her elegant drawing room.

'Now then, a little refreshment. Jenner, fetch the tray, if you please.'

'Thank you, ma'am, but I will not stay,' said Wolf. 'I came only to see Miss Duncombe delivered safely to you. The cab is waiting.'

'Nonsense, Mr...Peregrine.' She was smiling and looking at him with a decided twinkle in her sharp eyes. 'My brother mentioned that you were an old acquaintance and I see it now. Yes, I remember you very well, sir, and I will not allow you to go anywhere else tonight. You shall stay here, as my guest. No, not another word. I insist. Jenner, send Robert to pay off the cabbie and fetch in Mr Peregrine's bags. He is to take them to the blue room, if you please, and do you bring in the refreshments. Wine, I think, and a little bread and butter. Unless you would like Cook to find you something hot for supper?'

Wolf shook his head and Grace said politely, 'Thank you, no. We dined on the road.'

'Oh, I should have had Jenner take your greatcoat, sir, but never mind, take it off and throw it over the chair over there, with Grace's cloak, then come and sit by the fire, do.'

The lady was already pulling Grace down on to a sofa beside her, so Wolf took a chair opposite. He glanced at the door, to make sure it was firmly shut.

'So you know me, Mrs Graham?'

'Lord bless you, sir, I remember you very well,' came the cheerful reply. 'You were always in a scrape as a boy and it seems to me that nothing has changed.'

'I fear this time it is more than a scrape, ma'am—' He broke off as the butler returned.

'Yes, well,' said his hostess, 'we will discuss everything as soon as we are settled comfortably. Thank you, Jenner, that will be all. I shall ring when I need you again.' She paused just long enough for the butler to withdraw before saying, 'Now, why has my niece brought you to London, Mr Wolfgang?'

'I did not bring him, Aunt!'

'I have come to find my late wife's dresser,' he said, when Mrs Graham waved aside Grace's indignant protest. 'I believe she may be able to help me discover the truth about my wife's death and the theft of the Sawston diamonds.'

'And about time, too.'

'You believe he is innocent, Aunt?'

Wolf winced at Grace's surprised tone. It was clear what she thought of him.

'Those of us acquainted with Wolfgang Arrandale as a boy know he is no villain, my love.' Mrs Graham turned her eyes towards him and added drily, 'However, from what I heard of the situation at the Hall ten years ago, I could understand if you *had* murdered your wife.'

'You are frank indeed, madam! I did not do so, however.'

'And how do you intend to prove it?'

'I need to find out what happened to the necklace. Its loss was reported by my wife's dresser. I know Meesden came to London after my wife's death and set herself up in a little shop. She could not have done so on the salary my wife paid her.'

'And where is this shop?' asked Mrs Graham. 'Perhaps we could help you find this woman.'

'Aunt, no!' exclaimed Grace.

'Thank you, ma'am, but your niece came here to get away from me,' said Wolf.

'I am sorry, sir, if I appear unfeeling, but—'

'Not at all, Miss Duncombe, I understand that I have put you in a difficult situation.' He turned back to Mrs Graham. 'I will accept your hospitality for tonight, ma'am, but only for tonight.'

'My dear sir—'

He cut off the widow's protests with a shake of his head.

'You are very kind, madam, but your brother has already put himself at considerable risk to help me. I must pursue my enquiries alone.' He glanced at Grace, who was stifling a yawn. 'I fear we have exhausted Miss Duncombe. We have been travelling since dawn, you see.'

As he had hoped, Mrs Graham was immediately distracted.

'Oh, of course. Poor Grace, you have scarcely eaten a crumb. You must be ready for your bed. I will take you up immediately and send Robert to show our guest to his room.'

Wolf rose to bid the ladies goodnight and when they had left the room he sank wearily back in his chair. Mrs Graham's unquestioning belief in his innocence had lifted his spirits, but now he felt exhausted and not just from the physical exertion of the journey. It had been a trial to maintain the polite, distant friendliness with Grace in front of their fellow passengers. Several times they had started a conversation, only to break off the moment it became interesting, aware that they were not alone. Which was a pity, because they had much in common, if only they could talk. He closed his eyes. The only time he had spoken freely was in the cab to Hans Place. For a moment he had let down his guard and given her a glimpse of his early life. He should not have done so, because if there was one thing he was certain of, it was that he did not want Grace Duncombe to pity him.

Grace followed her aunt to a pretty yellow guest chamber at the front of the house. A good fire burned in the hearth and Aunt Eliza left her with Janet, the maid appointed to attend her, promising to look in a little later, to make sure she had everything she required. Grace felt herself relaxing. She had fulfilled her own and her father's obligations to Wolfgang Arrandale. She could let him go with a clear conscience. And she had no duties here. All that was expected of her was that she should enjoy herself. She was determined to do so; she would take a little holiday before she returned to the vicarage and her wedding to Sir Loftus.

* * *

When her aunt knocked softly on the door a little while later Grace was propped up against the bank of pillows, reading one of the novels thoughtfully provided for her entertainment.

'May I come in, my love? I wanted to make sure you were comfortable.'

'Extremely comfortable, Aunt, thank you.'

'Good, good.' Aunt Eliza shut the door and came across to stand by the bed. 'I am so pleased that you are come to stay at last. But I was a *little* surprised at the speed of your reply. I hope there is nothing wrong at home?' She added quickly, 'I know your father must be in good health or you would not have left him. But…is all well between you and Sir Loftus?'

'Why, yes.' Grace carefully placed a bookmark on her page and closed her book. 'In fact, that is the reason for my coming to London, to buy my bride clothes. Will you help me?'

'Nothing would give me greater pleasure, my dear.' Aunt Eliza fell silent. She sat on the edge of the bed and plucked at a loose thread in the embroidered coverlet. 'What Mr Wolfgang said, about you coming to London to escape him…'

'When I learned his identity I was uneasy about

his presence at the vicarage,' said Grace. 'There is a reward offered for his capture, you know.'

'Yes, I did know that, my love. It must have been very difficult for you, engaged as you are to Sir Loftus.'

Grace nodded. 'Papa is convinced of Mr Arrandale's innocence, but you know my father is so good he cannot believe ill of anyone.'

'Titus is so unworldly I wonder more people do not take advantage of him,' replied Mrs Graham frankly. 'However, in this instance I agree with him. Wolfgang Arrandale was always a wild boy, but I think it was more an attempt to gain his parents' attention rather than any inherent wickedness. His father was much worse in his day and, unlike dear Titus, Mr Arrandale could never see *good* in anyone, even his own sons. As I understand it he was convinced Wolfgang had murdered his wife and shipping him off to France only helped to confirm the boy's guilt.' She sighed. 'It is very commendable of Mr Wolfgang to come back now and try to find out the truth, but it was all so long ago. I fear he is unlikely to succeed.'

'I pray that he does, Aunt,' said Grace earnestly.

'Yes, I hope so too, my love, but if not…well, we must not let it concern us overmuch. These great families all have their trials and tribulations.' She leaned forward to kiss Grace's cheek. 'Now, you must rest and in the morning we will decide just what bride clothes you should have!'

Chapter Six

The noise from the square woke Grace. Carriages rattled on the cobbles, hawkers shouted and there was the faint ring of hammers. She smiled. Aunt Eliza's letters had mentioned the incessant building work taking place as London expanded.

She dressed quickly and made her way downstairs, where she found her aunt at breakfast. She was not alone, a pug dog with an incongruous collar of sparkling gems was on the floor beside her, eating pieces of ham and chicken from a silver dish. Aunt Eliza smiled when she saw Grace.

'Meet Nelson. I bought him as a companion when dear Mr Graham died. He is named after our heroic admiral.'

Grace looked at the overweight little dog snuffling in the dish and wondered if the heroic admiral would consider it a compliment.

'Mr Peregrine was up betimes and is even now preparing to leave,' her aunt continued, with a warning glance towards the butler. 'I was a little concerned that the poor young man might be a little, indigent, but he assures me he has sufficient funds. One would never think it, to look at him.'

Grace was silent while Jenner served her with coffee and bread rolls.

She said, as the door closed behind him, 'He paid for everything on the journey here, ma'am, including the tickets. I believe he made his present fortune abroad, although it might be unwise to enquire too closely into his methods of acquiring it,' she added darkly.

'Very true! The boy was always a scapegrace. My dear, what is the matter? You are looking very censorious.' Aunt Eliza put down her cup. 'Pray do not say you have grown into one of those disapproving females who finds no fun in anything.'

Grace waved her hand, unable to express herself. How was she to explain the confusion she felt about Wolfgang Arrandale? There was a darkness about him. It was like an aura. She had felt it from the first moment they had met. He had lived outside the law for so many years that perhaps he no longer knew the difference between right and wrong. He reminded her of an animal, a panther, lithe, alert and ready to spring. He was dangerous, she knew it in every fibre of her being. He fascinated her and that was dangerous too.

Her aunt sighed.

'You were such a lively little girl, Grace. You were forever climbing trees and tearing your gown, reading books full of knights and princes, always looking for adventure. What happened to that love of life, my dear?'

'I grew up,' Grace replied stiffly. 'And I am now engaged to a Justice of the Peace.'

When she had finished breakfast Grace took her reading book into the drawing room, but she left the door open, and as soon as she heard Wolfgang's deep voice in the hall she went out.

'So it is time for you to leave us, sir.'

'It is.' He turned to her. 'I am very grateful to your family for your hospitality. You need not be polite and say it was nothing. I am aware it was a great deal.'

'No more than any Christian would do,' she murmured. 'Shall we see you again?' The enormity of the task he had set himself filled Grace with dread and she had to ask, 'What will you do, if you are not successful?'

He shrugged. 'Go abroad again. Make a new life elsewhere.'

She put out her hand. 'I wish you good fortune in your endeavours, sir.'

'And I wish you good fortune in your marriage, Miss Duncombe.'

She watched as he raised her fingers to his lips, a last chance to memorise every detail of that darkly handsome face, then he was gone.

Wolf heard the door behind him close as he walked away. It was a sound he had heard many times in his career, physically and metaphorically. As a wild young man, respectable mamas had shut their doors on him to protect their daughters, even though those daughters were only too eager to fall into his arms. Friends of his schooldays had turned their backs on him when his exploits became too outrageous, so he had entered doors that were never closed to a rich young man, those belonging to ladies who lived in discreet little houses in Covent Garden, the less reputable gambling dens and the dingy drinking taverns, where the night invariably ended in a bloody brawl. The only one that had ever hurt was the door to his father's study, resolutely shut upon his sons unless they were hauled in for a reprimand. Even the beating that regularly ensued was preferable to the cold indifference his parents usually showed him. They saw him as a commodity, a means of continuing the family name, and Wolf was mostly referred to as a confounded nuisance. And his father believed him capable of murder.

Wolf felt the familiar black depression creeping over him. It had overwhelmed him during those early years in exile when his innocence seemed far less important than the shame he had brought on the family. He had decided then that it was his turn to shut the door. He made it clear he wanted to hear nothing more about England and the Arrandales. He had gone his own way, survived, prospered by fair means or foul and had expected to spend the rest of his life wandering through Europe as Monsieur Georges Lagrasse. Until last winter, when he had learned he had a daughter.

Florence. Named after her mother. Did she look like her namesake, or was she a dark, thin child, as he had been? Was she happy? It was most likely she did not know what had happened to her mother, for she was only a child, but that would change. When she grew up and took her place in society the gossip mongers would not hesitate to drag up all the sordid details of her parents' tempestuous marriage and its tragic end.

When he had learned of his daughter's existence he had realised it was impossible to shrug off all responsibility for the past. He must prove his innocence. If he could not do so then she, too, would find that many doors were closed to her, save those of generous, kind-hearted people like the Duncombes.

The thought brought him back to Grace. She would not close her door to his daughter, he was sure, but he wanted her to know he was innocent, too. The thought took hold; he imagined how it would be to have her trust him. Perhaps even to like him. He remembered when she had come upon him washing himself at the kitchen pump, the hectic flush that had disturbed her calm serenity. Even now the thought made him smile. She was such an innocent he doubted she had ever seen a naked chest before! She had been shocked, but not frightened.

He had wanted to pull her against him then and there, so she could feel his skin against her breast while he kissed that luscious mouth. And later, in the stable, he had allowed himself to give in to temptation. Why, he had no idea. She was not his type at all, far too tall and willowy for his taste. And far too respectable. Dammit, he didn't *like* good women!

But there was no denying that he wanted her approval. Wolf gave a little grunt of annoyance. It made no sense. She was about to be married to a man as good and respectable as Wolf was bad. But he could not bear the thought of her thinking ill of him.

Wolf emerged on to Sloane Street and moved his portmanteau to the other hand, looking for a cab to hire. He must not allow thoughts of Grace Duncombe to distract him, nor could he afford to give in to the melancholia that had paralysed him for those first few years in France. He needed to find out the truth of what had happened at Arrandale Hall ten years ago. He had to right some of the wrongs that had been caused by his long absence.

A battered hackney carriage slowed in response to his signal. He gave the driver directions to his lawyers' offices in the city and climbed in. His investigations could take months and it might all come to nought. He must forget all about Miss Grace Duncombe and her family.

* * *

Two weeks later he was back in Hans Place, pacing up and down on the expensive Aubusson carpet in Mrs Graham's drawing room and anxiously chewing his lip. This was hard. He had sworn he would not return, but he needed help and could think of no one else.

When Jenner came to tell Grace that 'Mr Peregrine' was waiting downstairs in the drawing room, she could not stop the sudden, soaring elation. She had tried to put Wolf from her mind, but he was there, at her shoulder every waking moment. Even in her dreams. She had known him such a short time, but it felt like for ever. In the two weeks since she had last seen him she had gone over and over every moment they had spent together, every look, every word and now she was quite certain he had not killed his wife. Such certainty was quite unreasonable, but in her defence, Papa and Aunt Eliza were both convinced of his innocence, too, and they had known him for much longer. After ten years there was only the smallest of chances he could clear his name, so she had to reconcile herself to never seeing him again, but it was very hard.

Not that they could ever be anything other than

friends. She was about to become Lady Braddenfield and as such, even if Wolf did clear his name
and return to Arrandale, they would rarely meet.
But for the moment, just the thought of seeing him
again was enough to raise her spirits. She ran to her
looking glass and patted her hair, but what she saw
there gave her pause. She must not show Wolf this
glowing face. He might misunderstand and think
that she cared for him, that she could offer him
more than friendship. Schooling her countenance to
show only cautious reserve, she went slowly downstairs.

Wolf's heart lurched when Grace entered the
room. She looked more beautiful than ever in a
pale-blue redingote over her cream gown. A matching bonnet swung from its ribbons held in the fingers of one hand. She did not smile at him and her
dark eyes still held that wary look.

'I am afraid my aunt is out, *Mr Peregrine.*' Jenner had deliberately left the door open, but after a
brief hesitation she closed it before turning to look
at him. 'You have not yet succeeded, then.'

'No.' He took another turn across the carpet and
came back to stand before her. 'I need help.' Her

brows rose a fraction. 'I need the help of a lady,' he explained. 'A lady of unimpeachable reputation.'

She stared at him for a moment, then walked back to the door. She was going to refuse. She was going to ask him to leave. Why should he be surprised? He had no right to expect more help from her.

'Then to preserve my unimpeachable reputation we should not remain in here alone. I was about to take my aunt's dog for a walk. Will you join me?'

'Of course.'

He followed her into the hall and watched her place the straw bonnet over her curls, tying the ribbons beneath one ear in a jaunty bow, quite at variance with her solemn look. The tip-tap of clawed feet on the marble floor made him turn. A wooden-faced footman was leading a small and very ugly lapdog into the hall.

'Thank you, Robert.' Grace took the lead from the footman. 'Come along, Nelson, it is time for your walk.'

'Nelson!' Wolf could not help the exclamation.

'Yes.' There was a definite twinkle in her deep-blue eyes now. 'Shall we go?'

They stepped across the road to the railed garden in the middle of the square.

'As you can see, the gardens are very new,' she

said. 'Once all the houses have been built I am sure it will become much busier, but presently there are very few of us who use this area. It is ideal for walking Nelson. I like to bring him out for an airing at least twice a day. My aunt indulges him dreadfully.'

He glanced down at the little pug waddling beside her.

'So I can see,' he muttered.

'He was much fatter than this when I arrived and wheezed most horribly. My next task is to convince my aunt to exercise him. I think it would be beneficial to them both.'

'You have changed.'

'Changed, sir? I should think so. My aunt has been spoiling me, buying me I do not know how many new gowns.'

'No, it's not that.' He frowned. 'You are less…' *Repressed,* he wanted to say. *Not so starched up. Not so prim and proper.* Impossible. 'You are more cheerful.'

'Perhaps that is because I no longer have a wanted man under my roof.'

'Is that it? Did you feel the weight of my presence so very much?'

She shook her head, a smile lilting on her generous mouth.

'No, that is not the whole of it, but I could not help teasing you a little. As you teased me, did you not?'

'I did and I point to this as proof of how different you are. You never laughed at me in Arrandale.'

'No.'

'Has being in London made you so much happier?'

'I was not unhappy in Arrandale,' she said quickly. 'Merely in need of a holiday.'

'Are you regretting your betrothal to Sir Loftus?'

'Not at all.'

Her answer was a little too quick. He said, 'But you do not love him.'

'You know I do not. But there is affection and respect. That is a good foundation for a happy marriage.'

Perhaps, thought Wolf. It was certainly something he had never had in his own marriage.

'You said you needed my help,' she prompted him.

'Yes.' Where to begin? Now it came to the moment he was loath to continue, to embroil her in his sordid affairs.

'We are alone here, sir, you can speak freely now.

Perhaps you should start by telling me what you have been doing for the past two weeks.'

'Perhaps I should. The day I left you I went first to the city, to see my lawyers. Old Mr Baylis was on the point of retiring when I married. His son has now taken over and he is a very different character, I could see that the moment I walked into his office. He would not have acknowledged me, but his two clerks recognised me instantly. He has sworn he will not inform upon me, but I do not know if I believe him. However, I am still a free man at the moment and I have instructed him to draw up papers giving my brother power of attorney. I shall also write to Richard, telling him of the matter, so the rascally lawyer cannot worm out of it.'

They stopped while the pug relieved himself against a convenient bush.

'So three more people now know you are in England.'

'Many more than that. As soon as I arrived in town I looked up my old valet, Kennet. His brother owns a tavern in Bench Lane so he was not difficult to track down. Fortunately he was unhappy with his current situation and delighted to give notice and join me. I also discovered my tailor and my barber are still in business and visited them, but I am confident they will not give me away.' He glanced down at Nelson, who was sniffing at his new Hessians and leaving a slobbery trail across their shiny surface. 'The bootmaker was a different matter. The staff there were all unknown to me, so I thought it prudent to be Mr Peregrine, a rich gentleman from the country, intent on cutting a dash in town.'

And he will certainly do that, thought Grace as they began to stroll on again. Today she had hardly known him for the same man. With his cutaway coat that fitted without a crease across his shoulders, pale pantaloons, tasselled Hessians and a tall beaver hat set at a rakish angle on his head, he looked the epitome of a man of fashion. She had seen any number of them in town, but in her opinion none had looked quite so handsome. She was glad that in the transformation he had not allowed his barber to cut his thick dark hair into the famous Brutus crop, she liked the way it curled over his collar.

Grace quickly pulled herself up. What was she thinking? His appearance was nothing to her. Just as her new style of dress could mean nothing to him. She had objected strongly when Aunt Eliza had taken her to the fashionable modistes in Bond

Street, but her aunt had been very persuasive, telling her that it was her duty to look her best.

'A man wants to be proud of his wife, Grace. Soon you will no longer be the parson's daughter, but Lady Braddenfield, a prominent member of the local society. Your neighbours will expect you to bring a little town bronze to Hindlesham. You must not disappoint them.'

To every argument Grace put forward her aunt had an answer and to her final protest, that Aunt Eliza should not be spending her own money on such finery for her niece, she had responded with a clincher.

'And what else should I spend it on, pray? I give generously to charity and I am a great supporter of the Foundling Hospital, but it is not the same as having *family*. You will be doing me a kindness, my love. I have no children of my own to spend my money on, no one except Nelson, and there are only so many diamond-studded collars one can buy for a pug.'

Grace pulled on that diamond-studded collar now as she dragged her attention back to the reason she was walking here with Wolfgang Arrandale.

'And how does your turning into a man of fashion affect me, sir?'

'It doesn't. At least, I needed to smarten myself up. A fashionable gentleman attracts little attention in Bond Street. From the servants at Arrandale I had learned that my wife's dresser, Annie Meesden, bought a milliner's shop there. She told them her uncle had died and left her some money. No one knew quite where the shop was and it took me a week to discover that she is no longer there. The shop failed within a year and Meesden was forced to find work again as a lady's maid. Luckily the registry office that she approached keeps very good records and I was able to trace her to a house in Arlington Street, the home of an elderly widow, one Mrs Payne.

'The problem is, Miss Duncombe, I have been unable to learn anything more. Mrs Payne's staff are very tight-lipped. None of them will impart any information at all, either out of loyalty or for fear of losing their position. Short of keeping vigil outside the house in the hopes of seeing Meesden I am at a stand.'

'Could you not write to this Mrs Payne, or ask your lawyer to do so?' she suggested.

'I did. I sent a letter, posing as Mr Peregrine, which received a terse reply to the effect that Mrs Payne does not correspond with unknown gentlemen and to approach her son, who deals with all her household affairs. I duly wrote to the fellow, only to receive a note from his secretary, saying he is on business in Scotland and will be out of town for several months.'

'And this is why you require a lady of, er, unimpeachable reputation. To contact Mrs Payne.'

'You have it precisely, ma'am.'

'No doubt your acquaintance with such ladies is limited,' she murmured.

'Very limited,' he replied frankly. 'There is no one else in town I can trust with this task, saving yourself. Or your aunt.'

They walked on in silence while Grace considered everything he had told her. She could of course decline to help him. Aunt Eliza would be only too pleased to step into the breach, but her aunt was so garrulous who knew what she might let slip?

Do not make excuses, my girl, you want to do this. Admit it, you have had enough of shopping and paying visits to Aunt Eliza's friends. You want a little adventure before you settle down.

Grace ignored the demon who whispered such scurrilous things in her ear. It was her duty to assist a fellow creature in need. Papa would understand, he would never refuse a plea for help. Neither should she.

'So, Miss Duncombe. Will you help me?'

'I will, sir.' She looked across the square. 'I think that is my aunt's carriage at the door now, which is excellent timing, for we have completed two full circuits of the gardens, sufficient exercise for Nelson, and we may now return to the house. Will you come in and take tea with us? Then you may tell me all I need to know.'

Grace went to Arlington Street the following afternoon, but her call proved fruitless. In her efforts to look as respectable as possible Grace took her maid with her, but even this did not help. The old lady was every bit as irascible and uncooperative as Wolf had led her to believe and after less than ten minutes Grace found herself being shown to the door. As she paused in the hall to collect her muff and umbrella from her maid, the tomb-like silence was shattered by a series of yaps and a lively little brown-and-white spaniel dashed up to Grace and began to fawn about her.

'Lottie, Lottie, come here, you *naughty* dog!'

A flustered maid appeared, saying breathlessly, 'I am ever so sorry, ma'am. She's ready for her walk, you see, and that always makes her so lively that she can't help herself.'

'That is no trouble at all,' said Grace, stooping to fondle Lottie's ears. 'I am sorry if my visit to your mistress has delayed their walk.'

'Oh, no, ma'am, I always takes Lottie out.' The maid tucked a grey curl back under her cap and bent to scoop up the little dog.

'You are very fortunate to have the park so conveniently close,' said Grace, smiling.

'Oh, yes, ma'am, that we are. I takes Lottie there twice a day. Every morning, afore breakfast and then again about now, so she will sit quiet with the mistress for an hour afore dinner.' With a bob of a curtsy the maid retreated to the nether regions of the house and Grace made her way back to Hans Place. Her aunt pounced on her almost as soon as she walked through the door.

'Well, have you found Meesden?'

'No. All I could discover was that Meesden left Mrs Payne's service two years ago. More than that the lady would not say.'

'Oh, that is annoying,' exclaimed Aunt Eliza. 'I was hoping we would be able to further Mr Wolfgang's investigations. He will be so disappointed to find we have learned nothing.'

'But all is not yet lost,' said Grace. 'I am not prepared to give up yet. Tomorrow I shall take Nelson walking in Green Park!'

Early the following morning Grace lifted the little pug from Aunt Eliza's carriage when it drew up at the edge of the park. She had no idea what time Mrs Payne took breakfast and in preparation for a long vigil she had put a thick cloak over her redingote to keep out the cold and the threatened showers. Nelson was also wearing a woollen coat. Grace thought it made him look like a cushion on legs, but her aunt had insisted that May had not yet begun and Nelson, too, should be protected from the inclement weather.

They were strolling along the Queen's Walk for the second time when Grace saw a small figure in a red flannel cloak emerge from a gate in the wall just ahead, and she had a little brown-and-white spaniel with her.

Fortune favoured Grace, for the maid was walking towards her. Despite Nelson's new exercise regime, she knew that if her quarry had been heading away from them the pug's short legs would never have been able to catch up. Nelson was showing little interest in his surroundings, but the spaniel was very inquisitive and as they drew closer she made prancing overtures towards the pug. Grace feigned a start of surprise and stopped squarely before the maid, blocking the path.

'Oh, surely that is Mrs Payne's little dog. Lottie, is it not?'

'Why, yes, ma'am.'

The maid bobbed a polite curtsy and Grace turned and fell into step beside her, saying with a little laugh, 'How strange that we should meet again so soon. Do you mind if I walk with you? Poor Nelson would be glad of the company, I am sure.'

'Poor Nelson' was doing his best to ignore the spaniel's friendly overtures, but the maid was clearly dazzled by the pug's sparkling collar and could not deny any request his owner might make.

Grace marvelled as she listened to herself chattering on, drawing the maid out by degrees, until she admitted that she had been in Mrs Payne's service for nigh on twenty years.

'Indeed? Then you must be a very loyal and trusted servant,' said Grace. 'Your mistress is fortunate to have you.' She dropped her voice a little. 'In fact, you may be able to help me. You see, the reason I called upon Mrs Payne yesterday was to learn information about her lady's maid. Mrs Meesden.'

'Annie Meesden? Why she's been gone from this house these two years or more.' The maid clapped a hand over her mouth. 'Not that the mistress likes us to talk about these things.'

'I quite understand,' Grace responded smoothly. 'However, Mrs Meesden has applied to me for a position. Mrs Payne made it quite clear to me that all such matters are dealt with by her son, but you see, my dresser has given notice very suddenly and I am *desperate* to replace her. Mrs Meesden seems quite perfect for the role, but she has no references and I should so like to hear some good word of the woman, before I take her into my household.'

The maid had her lips firmly shut and Grace gave a little sigh.

'Your mistress is quite right to insist that you do not give away any secrets, so I will not ask you to say anything. But I am sure you understand my anxiety. Being unmarried and alone I am very anxious to avoid taking on someone who may prove unreliable.' She then turned the subject, talking about such innocuous topics as the weather and the trials of running a house in town.

Goodness, Grace Duncombe, you sound very much like a lonely spinster, desperate for company!

She finally ran out of words and fell silent. Nelson

and Lottie chose that moment to move to one side of the path to investigate some interesting smells at the base of a tree. Grace and the maid both stopped and after a moment the maid let out a hiss of breath, as if she had been searching her conscience and had come to a decision.

'I don't see what harm it can do for me to tell you, ma'am,' she burst out. 'Mrs Meesden was turned off, you see. That's why she has no reference from Arlington Street. Rude to Mr Payne, she was, and although the mistress said she was an excellent dresser, she couldn't allow insolence towards her son.'

'No, I should think not,' said Grace, shaking her head. 'Very bad indeed.'

'Well, from what I heard in the servants' hall afterwards, it wasn't the first time she'd been turned off. And she was never married, neither, even though she called herself "Mrs".' The maid was in full flow now and Grace let her talk, she would sift out the important points later. 'Seems she couldn't abide men. Well, that's understandable.' The maid sniffed. 'Being in service can be hard for a woman, ma'am. Some of the tales I've heard would make your hair stand on end and that's the truth. Not that there's anything of that sort at Mrs Payne's house, which is why I've stayed so long. She's a strict mistress and she don't allow no goings on.'

'I am very glad to hear it,' Grace said warmly. As they began to stroll on again she said casually, 'Do you know what became of Mrs Meesden?'

The maid shook her head.

'Bad business, ma'am. I heard she couldn't get another position and is now taking in sewing.'

'Oh, the poor creature,' exclaimed Grace, thinking how far the woman had fallen since being lady's maid at Arrandale. She said, in perfect sincerity, 'I do hope her fortunes can be improved.'

'Ah well, ma'am, p'raps they can be, if you was to take her on, you not having a gentleman in the house for her to take against.'

'Where is she living now, do you know?

'That I don't, ma'am, but Mrs Payne must know, because she sometimes sends gowns to her for mending.'

'That is very charitable.'

The maid gave a snort. 'Not her! It's more that Meesden's the best needlewoman she's ever known. The mistress ain't the charitable sort, for all she's patron of the Foundling Hospital. The Lord helps them as helps themselves, she says.' She looked up guiltily. 'You won't tell the mistress I told you any o' this, will you, ma'am?'

'No, of course not,' replied Grace. They had reached the southern end of the Queen's Walk and she could see her aunt's carriage in the distance.

'Thank you for the information, you have been most helpful.'

The maid was gazing round-eyed at the silver coin Grace had pressed into her hand. 'Ooh, ma'am, I shouldn't—'

'Nonsense, that is for allowing Nelson to have Lottie's company on his morning walk, nothing more,' said Grace, thankful that the two animals were actually walking together quite amicably.

'Yes, yes, of course.' The maid nodded. She added ingenuously, 'But I shan't tell anyone who gave it to me, ma'am.'

'No, that might be best,' said Grace, stifling her conscience. 'You could merely say a lady pressed it upon you, when you gave her directions.'

With another friendly smile Grace scooped Nelson into her arms and set off briskly for the waiting carriage, pleased with her morning's work.

Chapter Seven

Wolf left the premises of Baylis & Thistle and paused on the flagway to pull on his gloves. There was a chill wind blowing and he decided to walk back to town rather than take a cab. The exercise would warm him up after sitting in his lawyer's cold offices for so long. It was not only the building that was cold, he thought grimly, the lawyer's greeting was only marginally warmer than at his first visit two weeks earlier. He knew he should expect nothing else. After all, both the original partners were long dead and young Mr Baylis knew him only as a fugitive from justice. However, the fellow had drawn up the power of attorney as instructed and it was signed now, so whatever happened to him, his brother would be able to administer the estate. He must write to Richard and tell him.

He tensed when he saw a fashionably dressed

gentleman approaching. There was no mistaking Sir Charles Urmston, his dead wife's cousin. Wolf cursed under his breath. There was no point in turning away, Urmston had seen him. The man's start of surprise was followed very quickly by a delighted smile.

'My dear sir, I had no idea you were back in England.'

Wolf had no option but to stop.

He said coolly, 'It is not generally known.'

'Ah, quite, quite.' Urmston's smile disappeared and he shook his head. 'Bad business, very bad business. Poor Florence.'

Wolf would have walked on, but Urmston put up his hand.

'Pray, sir, do not think I ever blamed you for her death.' Wolf could not hide his look of disbelief and Urmston hurried on. 'Good heavens, no. I admit it was a shock, when I first saw you leaning over her, but I think I know you better than that! But we cannot part again without some discussion.' He turned and slipped his arm through Wolf's. 'Let us drink coffee together.'

Wolf fought down the instinct to pull free. He had never liked Urmston, but the man might have some useful information and he had learned precious little so far. Urmston suggested a nearby coffee house. Wolf would have preferred them to be a little further away from the city, for the place was full of clerks and lawyers, but at least there was little chance of anyone recognising him here.

They found an empty table and Urmston ordered coffee before sitting down opposite Wolf.

'So, my friend, what brings you back to England?'

Urmston's florid countenance showed only a look of innocent enquiry, but Wolf was cautious.

'I needed to see my lawyer.'

'About what?' When Wolf did not reply Urmston sat back, spreading his hands. 'Surely you know you can trust me, my friend.'

'Can I? You were damned eager to hustle me out of the country.'

'No, no, that was your father's doing, I assure you. He thought if you remained you might be clapped up. He was adamant about it and it seemed a sensible idea, to get you out of the way until things calmed down.'

'The consequence of which is that everyone thinks I am guilty,' retorted Wolf.

Urmston shook his head. 'If it had not been for the diamonds going missing at the same time...'

'I did not take them.'

'No, I believe you,' muttered Urmston, chewing his lip. 'I think Florence's dresser took them.'

'But she was devoted to her mistress.' Too devoted, thought Wolf. He had caught her out on more than one occasion lying to protect Florence.

'Have you seen Annie Meesden?' enquired Urmston, staring into his coffee cup. 'Have you spoken to her?'

Wolf had lived by his wits for the past ten years and they were screaming at him now not to trust this man. He answered one question with another.

'Do you know where I might find her?'

Urmston shook his head. 'No, she has given me the slip.'

'Then you *have* been looking for her.'

For the merest instant Urmston looked uncomfortable, as if Wolf had caught him out. Then he was smiling again.

'Naturally, at the beginning. I would have done anything to prove your innocence.'

Lies, thought Wolf. Urmston would not go out of his way for anyone but himself. If he wanted anything it was the necklace.

Wolf took another sip of his coffee. 'What can you tell me about the night Florence died?'

'Why, nothing,' said Urmston. 'I was out on the terrace and came in only when I heard your mother shrieking. I rushed into the hall and there you were, crouched over Florence's body.'

'And you thought I had killed her.'

'Never!'

Wolf looked at him steadily. 'You said I had allowed my temper to get the better of me.'

'Did I? I was upset. Upon reflection I realised you were innocent.'

'And the reward for my capture?'

'That was Sawston's doing. If I had gone to see him immediately I might have prevented that, but I had business in Newmarket. By the time I returned to Arrandale a week later, my uncle had offered a reward for your capture.' Urmston leaned forward, saying in an urgent under-voice, 'Trust me, Arrandale, I only want to help you. If there is anything I can do, you only have to ask it.'

'Thank you.'

Wolf rose, but his companion put a hand on his arm.

'At least tell me where you are staying!'

Wolf looked down at him.

'If you need to contact me, a message for Mr

Peregrine at the Running Man in Bench Lane will reach me.'

With that he turned on his heel and walked out.

Wolf went quickly back to his lodgings, packed up his bags and paid his shot. He was taking no chances, he did not believe that Urmston had *just happened* to bump into him. He hailed a cab, then another to take him across town, making sure he was not followed before he set about finding himself fresh rooms. By the time he had secured new lodgings in Half Moon Street the day was well advanced. He remembered Mrs Graham's invitation to call and take pot luck at any time and he decided to do that. After all, he needed to see Grace, to find out if she had been able to discover anything about Annie Meesden. Not just need, he admitted. He wanted to see her.

His welcome at Hans Place was as warm as ever. Mrs Graham ordered another place to be laid at the dinner table and invited him to sit down and take a glass of wine.

'Grace is still in her room, but I expect her any moment.'

Wolf nodded and studied his wine rather than

face the twinkle in his hostess's eye. He felt a spurt of irritation. The lady knew what he was; she could not possibly condone any connection between him and her niece. Even if everything went his way and it was proven that he was neither a thief nor a murderer, he was no match for Grace Duncombe. She was too good, too sweet.

She came into the room at that moment and the sight of her in a simple cream dress with her golden hair glowing like a halo about her head confirmed his thoughts. She was virtue incarnate. He rose and braced himself to greet her. Confound it, why could she not remain by the door and give him a cool and distant nod? But it seemed any reservations she had about him had been swept away. She was positively glowing with excitement and came forward, holding out her hand to him as if they were the best of friends.

'Good evening, sir.' Her soft musical voice had an added note, as if it incorporated her smile. 'Has my aunt told you about my visit to Mrs Payne?'

He kissed her fingers with punctilious politeness, but for the life of him he could not let her go. Instead he held on to her hand as he raised his head and looked at her. There was a faint blush on her cheek, but it could not be because of him. Rather, it was because she was happy. It radiated from her. With an effort he released her and moved away.

'She has told me nothing, so you had best sit down and do so.'

He had not intended to be so curt, but the sunshine in her smile was destroying the armour he had put around his heart. Desperately he tried to shore it up. He could not afford distractions and Grace Duncombe was most definitely a distraction. She sank down on to a sofa and folded her hands in her lap, apparently not offended by his abrupt manners.

'It was not very successful,' she admitted. 'When I called upon the lady yesterday she told me very much the same as she had written to you, that I should talk to her son and not bother her with matters of staff. However, I managed to speak to one of the housemaids.'

'Grace took Nelson to Green Park where a maid walks Mrs Payne's lapdog every morning,' put in Mrs Graham. 'Once the dogs were acquainted the maid could hardly avoid speaking to her. Was that not ingenious?'

'It was, if it persuaded the maid to talk to you.'

'It did.' Grace sat forward, her eyes shining. 'She

told me the dresser was turned off two years ago, but Mrs Payne still sends sewing work out to her.'

'And you have her direction?'

Grace shook her head. 'Not yet, but I feel sure we will have it very soon.'

'How so?' Wolf frowned, trying not to think how alluring Grace looked with that gentle smile and her eyes twinkling with mischief.

Mrs Graham gave a little tut. 'Pray do not keep poor Mr Wolfgang in suspense, my love.' She turned to him. 'There is a ball tomorrow night to raise funds for the Foundling Hospital and since Mrs Payne is a patron, I feel sure she will attend. I had been disinclined to go. These affairs are always the same, no matter how many donations one has made in the past one feels obliged to pledge more. However, it will be a perfect opportunity to talk to Mrs Payne, so I have purchased tickets for us to attend.'

'How fortunate that you insisted I buy a new ball gown, Aunt!'

Grace's light-hearted laugh caught Wolf off guard. It hit him like a wave, battering against him, breaking down the last of his defences. Something in her was calling to him, like a kindred spirit. A companion in adversity.

'You are enjoying this,' he said.

It was more of an accusation than a statement, but she merely lifted her shoulders and let them fall again.

'I confess it is a little more exciting than the life I have been used to.'

He frowned. 'I would not have you put yourself in danger.'

Again that merry laugh, clear and bright as a bell.

'What danger can there be in attending a ball? Unless I trip and sprain my ankle.'

Dinner was announced and they said no more on the subject, but the change in Grace fascinated Wolf. A few weeks in her aunt's house had transformed her. It was not merely that she had left off the soft greys she had worn at the vicarage and was dressed more fashionably, she looked more alive, her eyes sparkled, her generous mouth had an upward tilt, as if a laugh was never far away, and her light gold hair was piled loosely about her head with the odd little curl escaping to rest like a kiss upon her neck. He imagined that if he pulled just one pin from those heavy tresses they would cascade over her shoulders like a waterfall.

It was a beguiling image and it stayed with Wolf throughout dinner. Grace at her dressing table, dragging a brush through those golden locks. Grace undressed.

Grace undone.

His fork clattered on to the plate and he muttered an apology. He signalled to the hovering waiter that he might remove the dishes. Thank heaven there was only the dessert course to endure, then the ladies would retire and leave him in peace for a while. He was uneasy in polite society. He had forgotten how to behave.

Sitting in solitary state and enjoying brandy from Mrs Graham's excellent cellar, Wolf calculated how long he would have to remain before he could leave without giving offence. Ten minutes, would do it, he thought. Long enough to thank his hostess for her hospitality. But when he returned to the drawing room he found himself wrapped in a cocoon of domestic comfort. The fire was blazing cheerfully, candles cast a golden glow over the room and the two ladies were at their ease, Mrs Graham flicking through a copy of the *Ladies' Magazine* and Grace with an embroidery frame in her hand.

Mrs Graham put aside her magazine to make him welcome. She ushered him to a chair by the fire, sat down opposite and proceeded to talk to him about

Arrandale as she remembered it. Wolf answered her politely, but only half his mind was on the subject. From his seat he had a good view of Grace, who continued to set neat stitches in her embroidery, joining in very little with conversation. Even when her aunt left the room she did not look up from her work. He watched her in silence for a while.

'The last time we met I said you had changed,' he remarked. 'Now you are different again.'

The needle hovered about the cloth.

'My aunt is giving me what she calls a little town bronze.'

'That is not it. You are more at ease in my company. Why is that?' She began to ply her needle again, but Wolf could not let it go. 'Do you, can I hope you no longer think me guilty?'

She bent her head even lower over her embroidery.

'My father and aunt are convinced you are not guilty, so I am willing to give you the benefit of the doubt.'

She answered very quietly, but her words lifted a weight from Wolf's shoulders. A weight he had not been conscious of until now. When had her opinion become so important to him? She picked up a pair of silver scissors to cut her thread, then began to pack away her sewing.

'That is the only reason I am helping you to find Mrs Meesden.'

'Admit it, you are enjoying yourself.'

'There is a certain satisfaction in it.' He saw the faint but unmistakable upward curve of her mouth. Her eyes lifted to his, but only for a moment. 'It is part of my holiday, before I go home. To my fiancé.'

'And will you tell Sir Loftus what you have been doing in London?'

She raised her head at that.

'Of course,' she said. 'I shall tell him everything.'

Grace had replied with a touch of hauteur but later, when Wolfgang had gone and she had retired to her bed, she admitted to herself that it was not true. She could not tell Loftus quite everything. Not the way her pulse jumped whenever she saw Wolfgang, nor how the days seemed to drag when he was not with her. She certainly could not tell Loftus about the inordinate rush of happiness she had felt when she learned Wolf was to take dinner with them that evening. And certainly not the trembling excitement she felt whenever he looked at her.

No, she thought sleepily. Those were memories

to be locked away, along with childish dreams of adventure and knights in armour.

'Mrs Graham, welcome. How good of you to support our little ball.'

Grace stood by silently as her aunt returned their hostess's greeting. Lady Hathersedge was a cheerful lady with a determined gleam in her eye that said she would be asking for large donations of funds from her guests before the end of the evening. When Grace was presented she felt obliged to explain that her father was a mere country parson.

'Indeed?' Grace could almost see Lady Hathersedge writing her off. 'It is a pleasure to have you with us, Miss Duncombe.'

'Goodness,' murmured Grace, as she accompanied her aunt into the drawing room. 'I feared for a moment I might be turned out of doors when she realised I am as poor as the proverbial church mouse.'

'Not at the price we paid for the tickets,' muttered Aunt Eliza behind her fluttering fan.

'*You* paid, Aunt. I feel quite guilty about asking you to spend so much.'

'Nonsense, what else were we going to do this evening? No, I am delighted to be helping you and

Mr—our friend,' she corrected quickly. 'Now, if you will point out Mrs Payne to me, I will do the rest. Heavens, but it is a crush in here. Thank goodness you are so tall, my love, you should be able to spot our quarry if she is here.'

Grace laughed, in no way offended by this frank reference to her height. She was accustomed to being the tallest person in the room.

That is why you are so attracted to Wolfgang Arrandale.

Grace gave her head a little shake. It was unworthy of Papa's daughter to like a person for their physical attributes such as their height, or the width of their shoulders. One should like a person because of their character, because of their kindness and goodness, not because they made one feel dainty and petite. And alive.

'Mrs Payne is over there.' She touched her aunt's arm, forcing her thoughts back to the present. 'The lady in the black bombazine.'

'Ah, yes, I see her. And I am slightly acquainted with the lady beside her, so that will give me an introduction. You had best let me deal with this alone, my love. Off you go and enjoy yourself.'

With that she sailed away to confront Mrs Payne, leaving Grace slightly bemused. How was one to enjoy oneself in a room full of strangers? The orchestra were striking up for the first of the country dances, but one could not dance without a partner.

However, Grace had not been her father's hostess for years without learning a degree of self-sufficiency. She watched the first dance and when the music began again she made her way slowly around the room, smiling vaguely whenever anyone looked her way. The reception rooms were very grand and had a number of smaller apartments leading off, the largest of which was set out in readiness for supper. Grace had made a full circuit when a flurry of activity near the main entrance doors attracted her attention. She was close enough to hear a stentorian voice announce, 'Mr John Peregrine!'

Her heart leapt to her mouth when she recognised the tall figure in the doorway, but it was with fear rather than any warmer emotion. He was so tall, so distinctive, his dark hair curling over the collar of his black coat and providing a stark contrast to the snow-white shirt and neckcloth. She glanced around, wondering why no one was staring at him, surely they would recognise Arrandale of Arrandale, even after ten years? But to her relief the music was starting again and everyone was bustling and pushing towards the dance floor. A nervous laugh shook her. What effrontery, to stand there for all the world to look at him while he lifted his quizzing glass and cast an arrogant and slightly weary eye over the assembly.

He should not be here, courting danger so brazenly. The quizzing glass stopped at Grace and as he moved towards her she lost all desire to laugh. Her nerves were on edge and she was afraid she might do or say something to betray him.

'Mr Peregrine.' She held out her hand.

'Miss Duncombe. I thought I might find you here.'

'What are you doing here?' She hid her words behind a smile as he bowed over her fingers. 'What if you are recognised?'

'In this company? There is little chance of it. My family is not renowned for supporting good causes. Although in the past we might well have added a few foundlings to the hospital.'

His eyes glinted with wicked humour and she felt the tingle of excitement running through her. It was quite reprehensible.

'Pray do not try to shock me,' she retorted in a

low, angry under-voice. 'I cannot believe you would put yourself in such danger.'

'I am flattered by your concern. Where is your aunt?'

'Over there, by the window. Talking to Mrs Payne.'

'Ah, yes, I see.' When she tried to pull away his grip tightened on her fingers. 'Are you as friendless here as I am? Perhaps you would like to dance.'

'And attract even more attention? No, I thank you!'

'Then we shall take a stroll about the room.' He placed her hand on his arm. 'I shall keep you company until your aunt is free.'

'I wish you would not,' she said, unable to hide the note of desperation in her tone.

'Very well, if you prefer, I shall take you in to supper.'

She gave a little sigh of exasperation. 'I cannot think it is safe for you to be here at all.'

'Miss Duncombe, after so many years, do you think anyone will—'

'Hush,' she hissed at him. 'Our host is bearing down upon us.'

'Ah, Mr Peregrine! Forgive my not being at the door to greet you.' Lord Hathersedge bowed and introduced himself. Almost without pausing he said, beaming at them both, 'So you have met Miss Duncombe? Capital! Perhaps you are acquainted with her aunt, too? Mrs Graham is one of our most generous supporters.'

'I do indeed know her, my lord.' Wolf inclined his head, wondering if the twenty guineas in his pocket would be enough to make the fellow go away. He wanted to talk to Grace. She was the reason he had come here this evening. He wanted to see her in her finery. And by heaven she did look fine, her blonde hair sprinkled with tiny pearls and an apricot silk gown that somehow gave her clear skin a golden sheen, as if she had been kissed by the sun. She took his breath away.

'My lady tells me you are new in town, sir.' Their host had planted himself before them, barring their way. Wolf could see he was determined to say his piece before he allowed them to escape. 'Perhaps you are not familiar with the sterling work of the Foundling Hospital.'

'Oh, I am aware of it, my lord. My family have been great contributors over the years.'

Wolf heard Grace's sudden intake of breath, felt her fingers pinch his arm. He wanted to be alone with her, to dance or drink wine. Perhaps he might even feed her peaches and cream and make her blush by telling her they could not bear comparison to her lovely complexion.

He said, 'Believe me, my lord, first thing in the morning I shall instruct my bankers to send a hundred guineas to you.'

'A hundred guineas!'

Wolf waved a languid hand. 'Is that not enough? Let it be two hundred then. I feel sure you can put it to good use.'

I must be dreaming, thought Grace.

This was not how people in her world behaved. She wanted to laugh out loud at Wolf's cool assurance. Lord Hathersedge was staring at him, goggle-eyed, and Wolf put out his hand to gently move him to one side, murmuring apologetically that he wanted to take his partner in to supper. They had moved only a step when Grace noticed that their way was blocked again, this time by a gentleman in a blue coat and his fair-haired lady coming out of the supper room. What held Grace's attention was their height. The gentleman was easily as tall as she was, the lady a little less, but they made a strikingly handsome pair and there was something familiar about the gentleman, the way he walked, the world-weary look about his eyes. The man stopped, a look of shock upon his face. At the same time she heard Wolf bite off a muttered exclamation.

To Grace everything was frozen, like a tableau. Wolf and the man were staring at one another while Lord Hathersedge stood beside them, a look of bemusement on his ruddy countenance. Then the gentleman in the blue coat put out his hand.

'By heaven! Wol—'

Immediately Grace gave a little cry and lurched against Lord Hathersedge.

'Oh, do forgive me, I feel a little faint.'

'What? Oh, oh, my heavens!' He patted Grace awkwardly on the shoulder as Wolf quickly put his arm about her and pulled her back against him, holding her close.

Grace sagged against his arm and gave a little moan. 'Mr Peregrine, perhaps you could take me somewhere a little quieter…'

The fair-haired lady sprang forward, as if released from a spell.

'Yes, yes, sir, let us do that. Lord Hathersedge, is there not a room where we may be quite private?' She directed a look towards her host, who started, frowned, then nodded.

'Yes, yes, of course. That door over there, madam,

you will find it leads to a sitting room. It should be quite empty.'

'Excellent.' The lady moved beside Grace. 'We will take her there immediately. Richard, my love, you will fetch a little wine, if you please, and bring it to us. Richard?'

From beneath her lashes Grace could see that the man was staring open-mouthed at Wolf. A little push from his lady made him start and he lounged away. Grace directed a wan smile at Lord Hathersedge.

'I beg your pardon for being such a nuisance, my lord, but you can see I am in good hands now. You may safely leave me and return to your other guests. I know you have much to do.'

She was obliged to repeat her assurances before her host would leave her, but at last he allowed Wolf and the lady to bear Grace away from the ball room. They found the sitting room empty, candles glowing in the wall sconces and a good fire in the hearth. The lady released Grace and gave a little sigh of relief.

'This is perfect,' she said. 'We shall be able to talk in here quite freely.'

It was only then that Grace realised how tightly Wolf was holding her. She put one hand against his chest. 'Thank you, sir. I am very well now, I assure you.' He was still pale and when he looked at her his eyes were oddly bright. She said gently, 'The gentleman is your brother, is he not?'

'Yes,' said the lady, when Wolf remained silent. 'He is Richard Arrandale, and I am his wife, Lady Phyllida.' She chuckled. 'I vow I have never seen two men so dumbfounded.'

'Nor I,' murmured Grace.

The door opened and Richard Arrandale came in, kicking the door closed behind him.

'I thought we might all need to be revived,' he said, nodding at the tray in his hands. It held a decanter and four glasses.

Lady Phyllida went across to take the tray from her husband, murmuring, 'I will deal with this while you greet your brother in a more fitting manner.'

Grace eased herself free of Wolf's arm and stepped away. For a moment the two men stared at each other before coming together and embracing silently. Lady Phyllida caught Grace's eye and smiled.

Wolf cleared his throat. 'By George, Brother, this is the last place I expected to find you. Atoning for past sins, Richard?'

They were sitting opposite one another, a glass in hand. Emotions were running high, and Wolf kept his tone light. Richard answered in the same vein.

'It is my wife's doing. I am a reformed character.' He smiled and put out his hand to Lady Phyllida.

'How long have you been in England, Mr Arrandale?' she asked as she sat down beside her husband.

'Pray, ma'am, call me Wolf,' he said. 'I have been in the country just over a month.'

'A month!' exclaimed Richard.

'I want to prove my innocence. I wrote to you two days ago, but I sent the letter to Brookthorn Manor. By heaven, Richard, when I met Cassandra in Dieppe last autumn she said you had just become a father. I did not expect you to be jauntering to London so soon!' He added awkwardly, 'I should congratulate you.'

'You should indeed. We have a healthy son, who I hope is sleeping peacefully in his crib in Mount Street. We had business in London and did not intend a long visit, but we did not wish to leave little James behind us.' The soft look fled from Richard's eyes and he frowned again. 'You have been in England for *a month*, Wolf, and you did not think to inform me before yesterday? I don't doubt it will be another week before your letter reaches us in Mount Street!'

'I told no one, save Miss Duncombe's father.'

'And Miss Duncombe, apparently.' Richard exhaled, as if reining in his temper. His blue eyes moved to Grace and a smile flickered. 'Forgive me, ma'am. I am a little acquainted with your father, but you and I have never met before tonight. I have no doubt Mr Duncombe would prefer to keep you away from the infamous Arrandales.'

'No, sir. It was his wish that we should help your brother prove his innocence, if we can.'

Wolf glanced up at Grace, who was standing beside his chair. She was on his side, supporting him. He felt a sudden tightening of his chest at the thought, but there was no time now to consider if it meant anything.

'You recognised Richard?' he asked her.

'I did, sir. At the same moment your sister-in-law recognised you.'

'And your quick thinking put us to shame, ladies,' said Richard, smiling and raising his glass in salute.

'I hope no one else made the connection,' Grace murmured.

Richard shook his head. 'I made a point of speaking to Hathersedge again when I fetched the wine.

He was still congratulating himself for extracting such a generous pledge from Wolf. Two hundred guineas, Brother. Are you good for it?'

'I am, but I pray you will not ask me where I acquired my funds.'

'No. I shall ask you instead how you plan to clear your name.'

'By finding out what happened to the Sawston diamonds. I feel sure they hold the key to my wife's death.'

'Talking of Florence, I saw her cousin last week,' said Richard. 'Sir Charles Urmston. He stopped me in St James's Street and asked after you. Coincidence, do you think?'

'I doubt it.' Wolf frowned. 'He was hovering about when I came out of our lawyer's offices yesterday. If you didn't tell him I was in England—'

Richard scowled. 'Since you had not deigned to tell me you were here I could hardly do so!'

'Well, someone told him I was in England,' said Wolf. 'He asked me about Annie Meesden, my wife's dresser.'

'Perhaps he thinks she knows something,' suggested Grace.

'It is possible, I suppose,' agreed Richard. 'I saw her soon after she had moved to London and she appeared to be genuinely distressed about the death of her mistress. She blamed you for it, Wolf.'

'That does not surprise me.'

'If you did not do it, could it have been an accident?'

Wolf shook his head. 'The more I have thought of it the more certain I am that someone pushed her over that balcony. Florence hated carrying my child, she was always complaining of her swollen body, and how ungainly it made her, but I do not think she would have taken any risks. And I think Urmston is involved in this somehow. His coming up to me yesterday was just too convenient.'

'Well, I never liked the fellow,' stated Richard. 'I suspected him at the start, especially when I discovered he had come into a fortune within a week of the necklace going missing.'

'Did he now? That is something I did *not* know, and it sounds very promising.'

Richard raised one hand. 'Sorry to disappoint you, but it appears there is nothing in it. I made my own enquiries into the matter. Oh, I know it was some years later, but the facts are indisputable. The day after the tragedy Urmston left Arrandale and went to Newmarket. He met a young man there, a Lord Thriplow. He had just inherited the title and arrived in Newmarket eager to spend his money. Urmston took his whole fortune in one sitting. Poor boy blew his brains out the next day, but that didn't worry Urmston. It's an unedifying tale, but there are plenty of witnesses to it.'

Wolf grimaced. 'Yes, people remember that sort of thing.'

'Thriplow's money did not last him very long,' Richard continued. 'Urmston soon gambled it away, as he did his wife's dowry.'

Wolf's brows rose. 'So he married, did he?'

'Aye, but his wife died soon after the wedding,' said Richard. 'Rumour has it he mistreated her. One thing is certain, he has no fortune now.'

'And he told me he thought Meesden had taken the diamonds.' Wolf frowned. 'Perhaps he is not our villain after all.'

'Or he and Meesden were in it together and she tricked him,' suggested Richard.

Lady Phyllida shuddered. 'I do not know Sir Charles Urmston well, but I never liked him, and not merely because he wanted to seduce my step-daughter. I could easily believe he would steal from his own cousin.'

'And at the time he did not *know* he was going

to win a fortune at Newmarket, did he?' Grace reasoned.

'That is true,' Wolf conceded. 'But if Meesden did hoax him, why wait until now to find her?'

There was a soft tap on the door and Mrs Graham peeped in.

'Grace, my love. Lord Hathersedge told me you had been taken ill.' She came in, carefully closing the door behind her.

Wolf jumped up. 'Pray be easy, ma'am, your niece is very well. Her *malady* was a ruse to throw our host off the scent of what could have been an embarrassing meeting.'

Mrs Graham's anxious look disappeared as he made the introductions.

'I would not have recognised you,' she said, smiling at Richard. 'But then, I have not seen you since you were a schoolboy. I hope you will be able to help your brother, sir.'

'Aye, if he will let me.'

'I would rather none of you were involved in this,' declared Wolf quickly.

'Pho,' cried Richard. 'That is uncharitable of you, Brother.'

'None of you seem to appreciate the danger of associating with a felon.'

'You have not yet been proven guilty.'

Grace's gentle reminder did nothing to alleviate the black mood that was gathering like a storm cloud over Wolf. Richard had a wife and baby now. What right had he to involve him in his problems? It was bad enough he had already involved Grace.

'Well, I have news about Annie Meesden,' declared Mrs Graham. She hesitated and looked at Wolf. 'Perhaps you would rather wait until we are away from here.'

'By no means,' said Richard firmly. 'Tell us now, ma'am. You may depend upon our discretion.'

Wolf sighed and put up his hands in a gesture of defeat. 'Very well. What did you learn, Mrs Graham?'

The widow sat down on a chair, beaming widely.

'I think I managed it very well,' she said. 'I talked to Mrs Payne about the hospital, pledged a little money then discussed with her the difficulties of finding a clever needlewoman to do one's mending these days. As I hoped, she immediately suggested Mrs Meesden. It appears the woman has sunk very low and lives in a single room in Leg Alley, off Long Acre, north of Covent Garden. A very insalubrious area, but it seems one of the reasons Mrs Payne uses the woman is that not only is her sewing excellent, but she charges very little.' Her mouth turned down in a little grimace of distaste. 'I was shocked at her nip-farthing ways, but I thought it best not to say so.'

'No, indeed, Aunt,' said Grace. 'And how clever of you to find out her direction so adroitly.'

'Yes, thank you, ma'am,' said Wolf. 'I am in your debt. I shall call in Leg Alley first thing tomorrow.'

'You should lie low and let me go,' offered Richard.

'You do not know the woman, Brother. No, I must speak with her.'

'But you should not go alone, sir,' said Grace.

'Of course, alone.' Wolf gave an impatient huff. 'It will not be the first time I have ventured into such a place.'

She shook her head at him. 'That is not what I mean. When I talked to the maid she told me Mrs Meesden dislikes men. She was turned off for insolence towards Mr Payne. I do not think she will talk to you.'

'Wolf will make her talk,' said Richard grimly.

'I am sure he could do that,' murmured Grace. 'But will it achieve the result we want?'

Wolf scowled. 'Then what do you suggest, Miss Duncombe?'

'Let me come with you. She does not know me, but she will know my father, from her months at Arrandale, and she may be more willing to talk to me.'

Wolf acknowledged the truth of this. Even after ten years he could still remember the dresser's barely concealed contempt for him. She was un-likely to fall upon his neck and reveal all. He might use threats or bribes, but even then he could not be sure she would tell him the truth.

'Very well,' he said at last. 'We will go to see her together.'

'You must take my carriage,' put in Mrs Gra-ham. 'And I shall send a footman. No, two. Those alleys around Covent Garden are little better than rookeries.'

Grace looked at Wolf. 'Come to the house tomor-row at ten, sir, and we will set off from there.'

Mrs Graham sighed. 'Oh, dear, perhaps I should not let you go, my love. What your father would say if he knew of it I do not like to think.'

Grace laughed. 'It was his idea that I should help Mr Arrandale, ma'am, so he could hardly com-plain!'

* * *

The carriage drew to a halt at the entrance to a grim little alley. It was so narrow Grace doubted the sun ever reached the lower windows.

'You do not have to do this,' muttered Wolf.

She squared her shoulders. 'Nonsense. We are agreed.' She picked up the package beside her. 'I have brought one of my old gowns that needs mending. It is the perfect excuse for seeking out Annie Meesden.'

Filth and detritus covered the cobbles and blocked the gutter that ran through the centre of the alley. Grace wrinkled her nose, thinking how much worse the place would smell in high summer. A slatternly woman with a baby at her breast was sitting in a doorway and Wolf asked her if she knew of Mrs Meesden.

'She is a mending woman,' added Grace, indicating the package in her hand.

The woman sniffed and jerked her head.

'Next door but one. Top floor.' She grabbed the coin Grace was holding out to her and a sly look came in her bloodshot eye. 'Thank 'ee, madam. That'll buy some milk for the babe, but if you could spare a few more pennies, I ain't eaten fer a week.'

Wolf pulled Grace away.

'It will only go on gin,' he muttered.

'I know.' Grace sighed, glancing back at the woman, who was already making her way unsteadily along the alley. 'I thought we had suffering enough in Arrandale, but it is nothing to this.'

She followed him to the house where they hoped to find Annie Meesden. The door was open and they went in. If there was a landlady she was nowhere in sight.

'At least the stairs have been swept,' Grace remarked. 'That is a good sign.'

There were two doors on the top floor, one stood open to reveal a wretched woman sprawled on the bed and snoring loudly. Wolf looked at the woman's face, then knocked at the closed door. A female voice demanded to know who was there. Wolf nodded to Grace.

'Mrs Meesden?' she called. 'I have some mending for you.'

The door opened a fraction to reveal a small, thin woman in a white cap. Her eyes widened when she saw Wolf and she tried to close the door, but his arm shot out and stopped her.

'What's wrong, Annie?' he drawled, pushing his way in. 'Are you not pleased to see me?'

The woman stepped back as he moved into the room. Grace followed him.

'What do you want?'

The woman retreated behind her little table, hissing like a wildcat. Grace closed the door.

'Please, Mrs Meesden, we mean you no harm. I am Grace Duncombe. You may remember my father, he is the vicar at Arrandale.'

Grace noticed a worn Bible on a shelf by the bed and she hoped the information would reassure the woman. Meesden spared her no more than a quick, contemptuous glance before turning her attention back to Wolf.

'How did you find me?'

'That is not important. I want to know the truth about what happened to my wife.'

The woman glared at him and Grace was chilled by the hatred in her eyes.

He said again, 'How did she die, Annie?'

'It's your fault,' she spat. 'If she hadn't married you she would be alive now.'

'But I did not kill her, Annie, so who did?'

'If *you* didn't, then it must've been an accident.'

The woman sat down on a chair, her mouth stubbornly closed.

'And what happened to the necklace?' Wolf demanded. When she did not reply his fist banged on the table. 'Did you steal it and use the money to set up your milliner's shop? If so, you were sadly duped. It was worth more than enough to keep you living comfortably for the rest of your days.'

'No, I didn't take it,' she said, goaded. 'Like I told 'em, my uncle died and left me money to buy the shop.' Her face twisted into a look of disgust. 'Only it wasn't enough to keep it going through the hard times. Still, it was more than I got from the Arrandales. My mistress never left me a penny, not that she was expecting to die so early, poor lamb.'

'Mayhap you thought the necklace would recompense you for that.'

'I tell you I didn't steal it.'

'But you know who did.'

'I don't know anything. Miss Florence dismissed me early on the night she died, but when I left her the necklace was in her jewel box. I saw it. The next time I went to her room it was missing. 'Tis the truth.' She waved her hand at them. 'You can leave now. I've nothing else to tell you.'

Wolf shook his head. 'You know more than you are saying, Annie.'

'No, I don't.' She wrapped her arms around her

skinny frame. 'I told you, I don't know anything. Now go away and leave me in peace.'

She sniffed, staring doggedly at the floor.

'Very well, we'll go.' Wolf hesitated, his fingers tapping thoughtfully on the table. 'My lawyer is presently arranging pensions for staff at Arrandale who were turned off when the house was closed up. I will instruct them to add you to the list.'

Her eyes flew to him, a mixture of hope and suspicion in her ravaged face.

'Are you trying to bribe me?'

'You will not be paid one penny until you have told me the truth about the night my wife died.'

'Let him help you, Mrs Meesden,' Grace urged her, coming up to the table.

'What's it to you?'

The question was flung at her with such malice that Grace flinched, but she kept her voice calm as she replied.

'I want to see justice done and I would like to see you move on from this place.'

'Justice? That won't bring my mistress back. And you...' her hate-filled eyes fixed on Wolf again '...you are as guilty as anyone. No.' She hunched on her chair. 'My mistress's secrets will go with me to the grave.'

'Even the name of her killer?' said Wolf.

Grace saw a flicker of fear in the woman's eyes.

'And what of the necklace?' he went on. 'Who stole your mistress's diamonds?'

With a cry that did not sound human the woman flew out of her seat.

'No one stole the diamonds!' She stood behind the little table, her thin chest rising and falling with each angry breath. 'Get out before I screams the house down. That wouldn't look good for you and Miss Charitable Duncombe here, now would it?'

'Think it over, Annie.' Wolf moved to the door. 'I know you could help me and you would. You can leave a message for me at the—'

'I'll see you hang first.'

'Surely you do not mean that,' exclaimed Grace and felt the full force of those malevolent eyes turned upon her.

'Oh, yes, I do. Miss Florence never loved him. She shouldn't have married him. She would've been happier with—' Her voice broke and she dragged up the corner of her apron to wipe her eyes. 'A curse on all men! Go away, the both of you. Get out.'

Grace reached into her reticule.

'I hope you will reconsider Mr Arrandale's offer,'

she said quietly. 'But whatever you decide, this may help.'

She placed a silver coin on the table and the woman stared at it. Grace stepped away, wondering whether she had offended her even more.

Annie Meesden nodded to the parcel Grace was carrying. 'What's that?'

'A gown for mending,' said Grace. 'It is only a torn hem, but I thought it might allay suspicions if I brought something.'

The woman put out her hand.

'If you leave it I'll see to it, in exchange for your half-crown.' She added, when Grace gave her the parcel, 'Come back the day after tomorrow and I'll have it ready. Now get out.'

Without another word Grace and Wolf left the room.

Grace and Wolf did not speak until they were in the carriage and on their way back to Hans Place, then Wolf let out a long breath.

'You were right when you said she dislikes men.'

'And you in particular.' Grace clasped her hands together. 'Will she help, do you think?'

'Perhaps, when she has thought it over.'

Grace frowned, going back over everything she

had seen and heard in Leg Alley. She said slowly, 'She is frightened, but I do not think she stole the necklace.'

'Then how did she find the money to set up her own business? Unlike Urmston, there is nothing to verify her story.'

'I do not know, but you saw that rather than accept charity she has taken my gown to repair. Her appearance, too, is in her favour. Despite the squalor of the house her room was clean, and her cap and apron were spotless. I find it hard to believe she is dishonest. And besides, she said no one had stolen the necklace. That was an odd thing to say, do you not agree?'

'There is that.'

Grace sighed. 'Whatever the truth of it, I do not like to think of her living in such penury. Could you not instruct your lawyers to pay her a pension immediately?'

'And if I do that, how am I supposed to persuade her to confide in me?'

'You forget, she said she would see you hang, first.'

'She may well do so.'

Grace flinched at his savage laugh.

'Pray do not jest about that.'

He reached out and covered her hands for a moment with one of his own. It was large and strong and she had to resist the temptation to cling on to it.

He turned his head to look down at her. 'You would have me pay an annuity to a woman who clearly hates me?'

'Your wife left her nothing. That was not kind.'

'My wife was never kind. Very well, I will visit Baylis in the morning and instruct him.' His brows went up. 'Now what is the matter, madam?'

'We have the carriage at our disposal, should we not do it now?'

'No. Emphatically not. Your aunt is anxious enough about your coming here today without delaying your return.'

'You could drop me at Hans Place first. I am sure my aunt would not object to you using the carriage for such a good cause.' She paused a moment before adding, 'It would then be done, sir, and you need not worry about it.'

A moment's silence then his breath hissed out and he gave a ragged laugh.

'By heaven but you are persistent, Miss Duncombe! Very well, I will impose upon your aunt's kindness and borrow the carriage to call at the offices of Baylis & Thistle today. There, will that do?'

'Why, yes, sir, that will do very well.' She could not help smiling. 'And perhaps you would like to join us for dinner, afterwards?'

'Thank you, but I am engaged to dine with my brother and his wife. We have a great deal to catch up on.'

'Oh, of course. That is perfectly understandable.'

Grace tried to keep the wistful note from her voice as she enquired when they might expect to see him again.

Wolf did not reply and she felt the sudden tension in the air, as if harsh reality must be faced.

He said at last, 'It would be safer for you and your aunt if I did not call again.'

'We are too involved now for you to leave us without a word.'

'Then I shall contact you, when I have any news.' He turned away to look out of the window. 'Have you ordered your wedding clothes?'

'Not all of them. My aunt is taking me to Bond Street tomorrow.'

'And when do you return to Arrandale?'

'In two weeks.' Grace bit her lip, thinking of the latest letter from Hindlesham. It was polite, cheerful and expressed Loftus's wish for her speedy return, but there was nothing of the lover in the carefully penned lines and his news seemed dull and colourless compared to the past few weeks in London.

'I shall be glad to go back,' she remarked, as much to convince herself as her companion. 'I fear too much time spent in the metropolis could be injurious to one's character.'

As could too much time spent in Wolf Arrandale's company.

The carriage turned into Hans Place and drew up at Aunt Eliza's door. Wolf leapt out.

He said, as he handed her down, 'I do not believe you are in danger of being corrupted by the metropolis, Miss Duncombe.'

She stumbled and his grip tightened on her fingers. To steady herself, Grace put her free hand against his chest, it was hard as rock beneath the silk of his waistcoat. He was so close she could smell him, an alluring trace of scents that made her want to cling to him. Or to run away.

'On the contrary, sir, I think I am in very great danger of being corrupted!'

Oh, heavens, had she really said that? The heat rushed to her face, she dared not look at him, but snatching her hand from his grasp she picked up her skirts and fled.

* * *

Grace went directly to her room. She did not ring for Janet, but paced the floor, confused by the conflict warring inside her. Wolf Arrandale was dangerous, but there was no doubt she enjoyed his company. When he looked at her she found it was all too easy to bury any doubts about his innocence. But even though she believed he was no criminal he was not a good man. He drew her like a moth to a flame and there was only one way that could end.

And she could not ignore the price on his head. The longer she and Aunt Eliza continued to assist him, the deeper they were drawn into the dangerous world of subterfuge. With a little cry of frustration she made a very unladylike fist and punched it into her palm. Before meeting Wolf she had been a truthful, respectable parson's daughter. She had never lied, never been kissed.

Never lived.

'No!' She stopped her perambulations, head up, a new determination building inside her. She had a good life waiting for her. As Lady Braddenfield she could continue her father's work of looking after the poor, nursing the sick. She could be a wife and mother. It was what she had been born and bred to be. A good woman.

* * *

Grace made her way to dinner that night, resolved upon her course of action. This new restlessness, this longing for excitement and adventure, it would pass, given time. Naturally, she hoped Wolfgang Arrandale would find a way to prove his innocence, but she would play no further part in his life. However, when Jenner brought her a note and she saw her name written in a bold scrawling hand she knew it was from Wolf and she almost snatched it from the tray.

The message was short, merely telling her that a small regular pension would be paid to their mutual acquaintance and that the lawyer was writing to the recipient to inform her of the details.

I would she could know that she has you to thank for this kindness, but that is not possible. Not yet.
W.

She looked at the single letter that passed for a signature. There was no address, nothing incriminating and no polite meaningless phrases of the writer being hers to command. Nor was there any indication that he would write again. She folded the note carefully and tucked it away. It was very likely the next she heard of Wolf Arrandale would be through the newspapers.

Wolf enjoyed the evening with his brother and sister-in-law more than he had expected. Richard was eager to learn how he had lived for the past ten years, but he took the little information that Wolf offered and asked for nothing more. They discussed politics, family, the lusty baby boy sleeping peacefully upstairs in the nursery. And the future of Arrandale.

'You talk as if you will never be master there,' Richard objected, when Wolf told him of the measures he wanted to see put in place. 'I know I have your power of attorney, but that is only a temporary measure, until you can clear your name. In fact, we should start on that immediately. We will find the best lawyers to represent you. And our great-aunt Sophia, Lady Hune, will help us, I am sure. She has connections.'

Wolf gave a faint, derisory smile.

'Do you tell me you have not already tried to prove my innocence?'

'You know I have, but that was before we had your testimony.'

'And what good do you think that will do?' Wolf replied bitterly. 'No, I have considered everything. The only witnesses to Florence's death are those who heard us arguing on the night she died and then saw me kneeling over her body with her blood on my hands.'

'But you have found your wife's maid, have you not? Perhaps she knows something.'

'I am sure she does, but whether her testimony would acquit or damn me I cannot say. I will have to talk to her again.'

Lady Phyllida had been sitting silently beside her husband, but now she leaned forward.

'You must have a care, sir.'

'I am always careful.'

'Not careful enough.' She handed him a folded newspaper. 'There is a piece here about you.'

Wolf read the report, his frown deepening.

'It claims you have been sighted in town,' said Richard. 'It also says the reward still stands. With such an incentive to find you, it can only be a matter of time before posters for your arrest are seen on the streets again.'

'You are quite right.' Wolf threw the paper aside. 'My guess is that Urmston has a hand in this. For all his weasel words to me I believe he wants me hanged.'

'What will you do?' asked Phyllida.

Wolf shrugged. 'If it was not for my daughter I would return to France now.'

'And leave Arrandale without a master?'

'You could fulfil that role, Richard.'

'Dam—dash it all, Wolf, I do not want it!'

Phyllida laid a hand on her husband's arm as she turned to address Wolf.

'Let us help you, sir, for your daughter's sake.' She added quietly, 'Little Florence is a lovely child and she looks a great deal like you.'

'You have seen her?' said Wolf eagerly.

'Yes.' Phyllida nodded. 'We have been to Chantreys to visit the Davenports.'

'And…' Wolf bit his lip '…is she happy?'

'She would be happier if she knew her papa, I am sure.'

Wolf stared at his sister-in-law. He did not want to involve them, but what choice did he have? At last he nodded.

'Very well, Richard. Write to Lady Hune, let her contact her lawyers, but if they say there is no hope then I will leave England. I would prefer to end my life in exile than on the gallows.'

* * *

It was gone midnight when he left Richard's house and hailed a hackney coach. He instructed the driver to drop him on the corner of Bench Lane. Halfway along the narrow passage the lights of the tavern were still burning. Muffled in his greatcoat and with his hat pulled low over his brow, Wolf entered and sought out the landlord. A short while later he was making his way to his lodgings, a folded note in his pocket and the first stirrings of hope that his luck was about to change.

Chapter Eight

Grace planned to spend the next day shopping for bride clothes with her aunt. She was obliged to remind Aunt Eliza several times that gowns such as those described in the society pages were not at all suitable.

'I am marrying the squire of Hindlesham, ma'am, not the Prince of Wales,' she declared over breakfast, when her aunt was once again poring over the latest newspaper to be delivered. 'You have already squandered enough of your money on me and I would not have you waste more buying gowns I will never wear.'

'Oh, very well.' Aunt Eliza sighed, closing the newspaper and placing it on the table beside her. 'But you must have a new silk for the wedding day, then you will need bonnets and reticules and a new redingote. Not to mention nightclothes.'

Grace concentrated fiercely on her breakfast. She did not want to think about nightclothes. She was resolved to do her wifely duty, but the idea of being intimate with Loftus was quite, quite different from the excitement she felt when she thought of Wolfgang. She closed her eyes. It could not last, this foolish infatuation that she had conceived. She did believe that. She did.

Grace was suddenly aware that a silence had fallen over the breakfast room. Opening her eyes, she saw her aunt staring in consternation at the newspaper.

She said sharply, 'Aunt Eliza?'

Silently her aunt passed the paper across the table. Grace looked at the closely printed words and felt a chill as one paragraph stood out from the others. It was slyly phrased, calling Wolf 'Mr W— A— of A—le', but there could be no mistake. There could not be many men charged with murdering their wife ten years ago and stealing a valuable necklace. And a reward. Two hundred guineas in exchange for a man's life.

'Oh, my dear.' Aunt Eliza's anguished whisper brought Grace's head up.

'What can we do?' she asked bleakly. 'I do not even know how to reach him.'

Grace wanted to stay at home, in the hope that Wolf might call and she could warn him, but her aunt did not agree.

'We are not expecting him and your nerves would be in shreds by the end of the day, my love. Let us instead write a note for Mr Peregrine. Jenner will see that he gets it, should he call. Trust me, my love, we are much better distracting ourselves in Bond Street. Now, you take Nelson for his morning walk and I will order the carriage.'

Grace wondered how Aunt Eliza could think of shopping at such a time, but a little reflection persuaded her that there was nothing to be gained by remaining in Hans Place. However, it was difficult to concentrate on silk or muslin or lace when she was constantly looking about her in the hope of seeing a very tall, dark gentleman on the street.

They returned to Hans Place to discover there had been no callers during their absence. Grace tried to hide her anxiety as she and her aunt went over their purchases, checking to see if there was anything else she required.

'We have done very well,' declared Aunt Eliza, ticking another item from her list. 'The gowns we have ordered should be ready for you to take back to Arrandale with you. Indeed, we have ordered so much I wonder if we should hire a second carriage to carry it all. Grace?' She put down her pen and paper. 'Dearest, I do believe you have not heard a word I have said!'

'I beg your pardon, Aunt. I was thinking that perhaps we should seek out Mr Richard Arrandale. I remember him saying they were in Mount Street.'

'Grace, my love.' Aunt Eliza reached out and put a hand on her arm. 'If someone is searching for Mr Wolfgang they will be watching his brother's house, too. If you begin sending urgent messages to him it may well alert the watcher to *us* and whoever it is might well begin to ask questions about a certain Mr Peregrine. Mr Wolfgang did not give you his direction because he did not wish to involve you.'

'I know, but if he is in danger—'

'I have no doubt that he is aware of what is in the newspapers and is taking extra care.'

'Do you really think so, Aunt Eliza?' Grace looked at her doubtfully.

'I do, my love, but if we have heard nothing by the morning I will pay a call upon Mrs Richard Arrandale. After all, there would be nothing untoward about that, since we met at the Hathersedges' ball the other night.'

* * *

Grace agreed and tried to be content, but there was no denying the relief she felt when her aunt received a letter, just as they finished dinner. As soon as they were alone Aunt Eliza tore open the sheet and confirmed that it was from Mr Wolfgang. She read it quickly.

'Well, I am very encouraged by his cheerful tone.'

'What does it say?' demanded Grace, trying to read over her shoulder.

'Meesden has agreed to talk to him. He says they are to meet in Vauxhall Gardens at eleven o'clock tonight.' She gave a little laugh. 'Listen, my love, "…that she is willing to pay the admission price tells me she is not quite so lacking in means as she would have us believe!"'

'Or perhaps she has learned of the pension he has settled upon her.' Grace smiled. 'He went back to the lawyers yesterday especially to arrange it…' Her smile faded. 'May I look, Aunt?'

She took the letter and scanned it, a tiny crease settling between her brows.

'What is it, my love? Is this not good news?'

'I do not know,' said Grace slowly. 'He writes that she sent him word last night, but how?'

'He gave her his direction, naturally.'

'No, he did not.' Grace shook her head. 'I was with him when he tried to tell her how she could reach him. I remember it distinctly because I thought that I should discover it, too, but she cut him short.' She handed back the paper. 'Oh, Aunt, I very much fear that this is some sort of trap!'

Wolf kept his domino close about him as he climbed out of the coach at Vauxhall. The Season had only just begun, but already the gardens were thronging with crowds and that made him uneasy. He had not been here for over ten years and ticket prices had increased significantly, but it appeared to have made no difference to the popularity of the gardens.

He pulled out his watch as he made his way towards the Italian Walk. It wanted but fifteen minutes to eleven and Meesden might already be waiting for him. He thought it odd that she should want to meet south of the river, but perhaps she was as keen as he not to be recognised and that was definitely easier amongst this vast, masked crowd. An avenue of trees led to the Italian Walk, a series of arches and pediments built in the Roman style with statues placed at intervals along its length. Lamps twinkled from the trees and between the pillars.

By their dim light Wolf strode on, looking for the statue of Minerva. Had Meesden known, when she chose the venue, that the goddess was said to have conferred upon women the skills of sewing and spinning? He had not thought her so well educated.

The statue he sought was set in a recess at the very end of the Walk, where there were plenty of people, but not the crush to be found around the orchestra and the supper boxes. Several couples were strolling along and a chattering group of ladies and their escorts tripped past as he stepped off the path.

A sudden breeze carried away the noisy chatter and set the leaves rustling on the thick bushes that enclosed three sides of the recess. Wolf had a sudden premonition of danger. He heard a cry and turned as a cloaked woman staggered from the bushes, her hands reaching out before her. It was only as she collapsed against him that he felt the hard projection of the knife handle beneath her ribs. Quickly he laid the woman on the ground, her cloak falling away as he did so. The lamplight showed him it was Annie Meesden, a stain blooming around the knife and spreading over the front of her gown like a huge, blood-red flower. Wolf pulled the knife from her with one hand while with the other he drew his handkerchief from his pocket and pressed it over the wound, although he knew it was too late. There was no life in the sightless eyes that stared up at him.

'Murder, murder!'

Wolf heard the cry and looked up to find a crowd gathering on the path, staring at him in horror. Four men jumped forward to lay hands on him.

'Not me,' he cried, struggling against them. 'Her killer is back there, in the bushes. Quickly, go after him!'

'Oh, no, you won't trick us with that one!' Leaving three of his comrades to hold Wolf, one of the men knelt by the stricken woman. 'She's dead.' He looked up. 'And here you are, with the knife in your hand and her body still warm.'

The commotion had drawn more people. There was no escape and Wolf could hear their voices clamouring for the constable to be fetched.

His eyes returned to the bloody body on the ground and with a sickening certainty he knew he had been tricked.

From the far side of the walk Grace watched in horror as the crowd grew around Wolf, their cries and shrieks like the baying of hounds.

'No. No!'

She wanted to run towards him, but Richard held her back, saying, 'There is nothing we can do for him here.'

'But they will kill him!'

'No, they won't. They have sent for the constable.'

'Can we not go to him?'

'No,' said Richard. 'He is incognito. If I rush to his support it is very likely someone will make the connection.'

'If only we had come earlier!'

'You came to Mount Street as soon as you realised the danger,' muttered Richard. 'I am only thankful that we were at home.'

Grace nodded. They had arrived at Vauxhall in time to see Wolf heading for the Italian Walk. There had been no mistaking his tall figure, even in the black domino.

'I do not understand,' she said now, trembling with the shock of it. 'The arbour was empty when he stepped into it. And the next moment he is kneeling over a body.'

'There is a certain familiarity with that scenario,' drawled Richard.

Grace turned to stare at him. 'You do not believe he murdered her?'

'Do you?'

'No.' She shook her head emphatically. 'No, I do not. I was watching closely. She was not there when he walked in and I did not see her enter from the path.'

Her companion relaxed just a little.

'That is what I thought, too,' he said. 'It's damned suspicious. Come on, we need to know if the woman is Mrs Meesden.' He took her arm and led her to the edge of the crowd. 'What is going on here?'

The authority in Richard's voice caused some of the onlookers to move aside. He pushed into the crowd, Grace close beside him. It was impossible to get to the front, but Grace was tall enough to see Wolf being held by two burly individuals. A sudden shifting of the crowd gave her a glimpse of a woman's body lying on the ground. Grace forced herself to look at the dead woman's face. There was no mistaking Annie Meesden's gaunt features. Pressing her handkerchief against her lips, Grace nodded to Richard.

'It is her.'

'What has happened?' he demanded, loudly enough for his brother to hear.

Wolf looked towards them and briefly met Grace's eyes.

He said, as if addressing his captors, 'The woman was stabbed before she came out of the bushes behind the statue. Her killer must have been back there.'

A large woman in a mob cap and torn coat laughed scornfully.

'A likely tale!' she scoffed. 'The poor besom fell foul of her beau, plain as day.'

Several constables had arrived and were pushing their way through the crowd to take charge.

Grace pressed Richard's arm. 'Let us look around the back and see if there are signs that anyone has been there.'

It was much darker away from the main walk. Richard unhooked one of the lamps and led the way. It was too much to expect to find anyone lurking behind the little recess, but the lamplight showed them where the smaller branches had been snapped off and the ground was trampled.

'The bushes are much thinner here,' observed Grace. 'It would not be difficult to get through.'

'I think you are right,' muttered Richard. 'The killer stabbed her here, then pushed her forward. I can even see through to the path.' He stepped back. 'One of the constables is coming around here to look for himself. We must go.'

'What about Wolf?'

'There's nothing we can do for him at present. We will find out where they are taking him and I will go to see him in the morning. You need not be anxious about my brother, Miss Duncombe. They will lock him up securely, but I have no doubt it isn't the first time he has spent the night in a prison cell.'

Wolf was marched away and bundled into a carriage for the short journey to the prison. He cursed himself for being so easily fooled. He had let down his guard, allowed himself to believe that Annie Meesden truly wanted to help him. Had she conspired with the killer to lure him to the gardens? If so she had paid for it with her life. His jaw clenched. How foolish he had been to believe she wanted to meet him. He thought of seeing Grace and Richard in the crowd; she must have read his note and rushed here to support him, bringing Richard with her as the only man she could trust. He hoped, nay, he was sure his brother would realise there was some deep game afoot, but what would Grace think of him now that she had seen him in that incriminating situation? A chill went through him. Henry Hodges, the love of her life, had died from a stab wound. What had it done to her, seeing him there with a bloody knife in his hand? As the carriage rattled on his thoughts were as gloomy as the dark streets. It was too much to expect her to believe he was innocent now.

New Gaol in Horsemonger Lane was less than twenty years old and rose like a solid black square against the darkness. As the carriage pulled up Wolf was surprised to see the double doors were open. He frowned.

'I thought I'd be in a lock-up until I had seen the magistrate.'

'He's waiting for you,' was the gruff response. 'Just your misfortune that it's Hanging Hatcham on duty tonight!'

The constables roughly manhandled him out of the carriage on to the cobbled yard of the prison. He was escorted into a reception room where a portly figure in a powdered wig was sitting at a desk.

'I am Gilbert Hatcham, magistrate here.' The man introduced himself. 'I was told I might expect you this evening, Mr Wolfgang Arrandale.'

'You are mistaken,' said Wolf coolly. 'My name is Peregrine. John Peregrine.'

The magistrate gave a fat chuckle.

'Is that what you are calling yourself?' He lifted a

printed sheet from the desk and glanced at it. Even in the lamplight Wolf could see that it was creased and yellow with age. The only word he could read from this distance was the one in large thick letters stretched across the page. 'Reward'.

Hatcham continued to scan the sheet. 'It says a tall man, six feet five inches, near black hair and violet-blue eyes.' He came around the desk and stared up into Wolf's face. 'Well, I can't see the colour of your eyes in this light, but I think the description is sufficiently close. Put him in a holding cell.'

'Will you not grant me bail?' demanded Wolf as the constables began to hustle him from the room.

'You are wanted for the murder of your wife and the theft of her diamonds, and now you have been caught red-handed taking the life of another poor wretch. No, sir, you will not be granted bail!'

Wolf woke up in near darkness, feeling parched and uncomfortable. He was wrapped in his black domino and lying on bare boards that ran the length of the cell, but they were several inches short of his height, so he was not able to stretch out. His ribs hurt, too; his captors had been none too gentle in their treatment of him. The only sources of light were the grille in the door and a hole in the ceiling, too high and small for a man to climb through, but within minutes of his waking he discovered it was large enough for the guards to pass down a flask of small beer and a crust of bread for him to break his fast. A short time later the door opened and a guard appeared, a black outline against lamplight from the corridor.

'You have visitors. Upstairs.'

'I am glad you do not expect me to receive them here.'

Wolf took time to fold his domino and put it on the boards before he accompanied his gaoler up the stone steps. Above ground the sun flooded in through the windows and he blinked uncomfortably in the light. His escort ushered him into a small panelled room, sparsely furnished with a square wooden table and four chairs, where he found his visitors waiting for him; his brother and a tall veiled lady that Wolf knew immediately was Grace. His spirits leapt, but plunged again when she lifted her veil. She looked so pale and drawn he guessed she had not slept and it was as much as he could do not to reach out for her. His frustration manifested itself in a scowl.

'You should not have brought her here, Richard.'

It was Grace who replied, saying quietly, 'I insisted upon it.'

Wolf's scowl deepened. 'You were at Vauxhall—can you doubt the evidence of your own eyes and believe me innocent?'

'Your brother and I were watching more closely than the others. You did not stab that woman. Your past may be very dark, sir, but you are no murderer.'

He was shaken by his sense of relief. It flared like a torch, but he could not bring himself to admit to it. He responded gruffly.

'I still say you should not be here. You should not be alone with any Arrandale!'

Richard scowled back at him. 'You need not concern yourself with the propriety, Wolf, Phyllida accompanied us. She is waiting in the carriage.'

'Trying to distance herself from her wicked brother-in-law,' said Wolf bitterly.

'No, she is trying to spare you embarrassment, you ungrateful cur!'

Wolf put up his hand, at last acknowledging his ill humour.

'I beg your pardon,' he said. 'Forgive me, Richard. I am grateful, truly.'

'Aye, well,' growled Richard, rubbing his nose. 'It isn't only that. She is in a delicate condition.'

'Then I am obliged to her for coming even as far as the gates with you,' exclaimed Wolf. He gripped his brother's hand. 'I felicitate you, Richard, and I am even more grateful that you should be here. But I am surprised. I expected to see my rascally lawyer.'

'I sent word to Baylis to come as soon as he can,' Richard replied shortly. 'We have just had a most unsatisfactory interview with the magistrate.'

'Gilbert Hatcham?'

'Yes. He refused bail for you.'

'He told me as much last night.' Wolf glanced to check that the door was closed and that they were alone before inviting them to sit down. 'How much did it cost you for this meeting?'

'Enough. This may be a new model prison, but a few pieces of silver can still achieve a great deal. Although not your freedom, Brother.'

Wolf grunted. 'Hatcham said he was expecting me. He had an old poster on his desk. Odd, do you not think, that he should have a ten-year-old notice so readily to hand?'

'Damned suspicious,' muttered Richard.

'How are they treating you?' asked Grace.

Wolf shied away from the concern in her voice.

'As you would expect them to treat a murderer,'

he replied lightly. 'They barely gave me time to wash the poor woman's blood from my hands before they hustled me into a cell.'

He knew they must both have seen the dried blood on his clothes, although no one mentioned it.

Richard said, 'You were lured to that meeting, Wolf.'

'Yes, and I think I know by whom, although I cannot prove it while I am locked in here.'

'Then we must do it for you,' declared Grace.

Her vehemence touched him, but he hid it behind a rueful smile and a light word.

'I fear I have led you woefully astray, Miss Duncombe. What would your fiancé say if he knew you were here?'

'He would want justice, as I do.'

'But not at the expense of your reputation.'

'At any expense!'

She looked so resolute that his heart swelled.

'Why were you both at Vauxhall last night?' he asked.

'Miss Duncombe suspected a trick.'

A tinge of colour stole into Grace's cheeks. 'Your note said Annie Meesden had sent you word, but I distinctly remember she cut you off before you could tell her how to contact you.'

'Yes, I realised that, too, but only later, after I was locked up. A stupid error on my part.'

'So who did know how to contact you?' asked Richard. 'Apart from myself?'

Wolf met his eye. 'Sir Charles Urmston. I foolishly thought he might have information that could help me, so I told him how to reach me.'

'By Jove, that makes perfect sense!' exclaimed Richard. 'But how did he know where to find the woman?'

'I am not sure,' said Wolf slowly. 'I know he was looking for Annie Meesden, because he asked me if I knew anything of her. I did not tell him and I made sure we were not followed when we went to see her the other day. So either he picked up her trail or—'

He broke off, but it was too late.

'Or someone told him her direction,' said Grace. She put her hands to her face, a look of horror shadowing her eyes. 'If only I had not pressed you to set up a pension for her.'

Richard looked from one to the other. 'What is this?'

'After we had seen Meesden I persuaded your brother to arrange a small annuity for her,' explained Grace. 'For that he had to tell his lawyer where she was living.'

'There is nothing to say Baylis passed on that information,' said Wolf quickly.

Grace shook her head. 'You said yourself this man, Urmston, first came up to you directly outside the offices of Baylis & Thistle and at that stage—apart from Aunt Eliza and myself—the only person who knew you were in London was your lawyer. Perhaps it was inadvertently done.'

'Whatever it was I think the Arrandales will be finding themselves another lawyer,' exclaimed Wolf wrathfully.

'Yes, well, I have been thinking that myself,' said Richard. 'I have suspected for years that Baylis has been creaming off the profits from your estate but nothing could be proved, and with you still nominally head of the family I couldn't turn him off, either. I will deal with him, don't worry, but for now we need to get you out of here.'

'You won't do it. Hatcham as good as told me last night I am here until my trial.'

And he expects me to hang.

He stopped himself from saying the words aloud and he met Richard's eye, sending him a silent message not to give Grace any more reason to worry.

His brother nodded. 'We shall make enquiries on your behalf, Wolf. Our first call will be Meesden's lodgings. Miss Duncombe has a gown to collect and we shall see if we can learn anything there.'

'Good,' said Wolf. 'You had best find Kennet, too. He will be at my rooms in Half Moon Street. Tell him what has occurred and ask him to bring some money. At least I may buy some comforts in this hellhole.'

He was giving them directions when a burly turn-key came in to tell them their time was up.

Wolf rose. He nodded to Grace, not trusting himself to go near her. Then he turned and gripped his brother's hand. 'Do what you can for me, Richard, and you had best engage another lawyer with all speed!'

Grace pulled her veil over her face and accompanied Richard Arrandale from the building. Her legs felt very weak and she was relieved when they were once more sitting in the carriage with Lady Phyllida. The sight of Wolf, unshaven, his eyes troubled and still wearing his bloody evening clothes, had shaken her to the core. Until then his predicament as a wanted man had seemed a distant threat, but as they drove away her eyes were drawn upwards to the roof of the prison and the black timbers of the scaffold, outlined against a lowering sky.

'We cannot let him hang.'

She did not realise she had spoken the words aloud until Richard replied.

'He won't, you need not worry about that. The Arrandales have had plenty of practice at cheating the gallows.' When her eyes flew to his face he added quickly, 'We will do the thing by fair means, if we can, but if not—'

She put up her hand.

'Please, do not tell me anything more.'

'I agree,' said Phyllida. 'Pray do not burden us with unnecessary conjecture, Richard.' She turned to Grace. 'Would you like to go back to Hans Place now? We can collect your gown for you, if you would rather not be mixed up further in this affair.'

Grace clasped her hands together and stared out of the window, but all she could see was Wolf's haunted eyes.

'I do not have any choice,' she murmured, almost to herself. 'I must see this through.'

They drove quickly to Half Moon Street to speak to Wolf's valet and then went on to Leg Alley. It was just as grim and daunting as it had appeared at

Grace's first visit. Richard insisted his wife remain in the carriage while he and Grace picked their way through the rubbish to the house. The door was closed, but Richard's firm rap upon the weathered boards brought a plump, sharp-eyed woman in a grubby apron to open it. She declared she was the landlady and demanded to know their business.

'I have come to collect a gown from Mrs Meesden,' Grace explained.

The woman shook her head.

'She's dead. Murdered.' She said it with such relish that Grace did not have to feign her look of horror.

'Good heavens, when was this?'

'Last night. She went off to Vauxhall with her man friend and never came back. He's been arrested for her murder.'

Richard's brows went up. 'The fellow came here?'

The landlady leaned against the wall and folded her arms.

'Aye. I told the constables as much. He called late in the afternoon and they stayed upstairs 'til about nine o'clock. *She* said she had work to finish, but if you ask me they was carousing, for she was so drunk she could hardly get down the stairs when they left. He almost carried her out.'

'How dreadful, but I should still like to retrieve my gown,' said Grace. 'It is a yellow muslin with green embroidery at the hem. Perhaps I might step in and look for it?'

Richard held out a coin. 'I assure you, madam, we want only to collect the lady's property.'

The landlady's hand darted out to take the coin.

'Aye, well, I don't suppose it will do any harm if I takes you up there now.'

She waddled away and they followed her up to Annie Meesden's tiny room. Grace tried to take in as much detail as possible. It looked more untidy than she remembered, a chair was tipped over and on the table stood two glasses and an almost empty bottle that Richard picked up and held to his nose.

'Was the lady in the habit of drinking brandy?'

'Not that I knew of. If she had been I'd have sent her packing long ago. This is a respectable house.'

'And the man who came to see her, was he a regular visitor?' he asked.

'Never seen him before, but then I don't see everyone who comes and goes. As long as my tenants is quiet and pays their rent I don't interfere.'

'But you saw the man who called yesterday,' Richard pressed her. 'Was he as tall as I am? Taller, perhaps?'

The landlady regarded him with her sharp eyes but said nothing. Richard pulled another coin from his pocket. 'Well?'

'No, sir, he wasn't as tall as you.' The money disappeared into her pudgy hand. 'Fashionable swell, though. Handsome. Black shiny hair and a fine set o' whiskers.'

'And you would be willing to swear to this in court?'

Immediately the woman looked wary and Richard said impatiently, 'Surely the constables asked you to describe the fellow?'

'No, sir. They said there was no need. They said her killer was locked up right and tight. Now, is that your dress on the table, madam? Yellow muslin with green stitching, you said. Mrs Meesden was working on it when I showed her gentleman friend upstairs.'

'Yes, that is it,' said Grace.

The gown was neatly folded and weighted down with Meesden's Bible.

'Well, you should take it and go. I've got to clear this room today, I've another tenant wanting to move in.'

The landlady ushered them out of the room and down the stairs, closing the door behind them with a bang. Richard took Grace's arm and escorted her back to their carriage.

'Well,' demanded Phyllida as they set off. 'What did you learn?'

Grace said slowly, 'Meesden's visitor was not your brother-in-law.'

Richard agreed. 'The description the landlady gave us *does* fit Charles Urmston, though. I think he wrote the note to Wolf, then came here to take Meesden to Vauxhall, where he killed her.'

Grace frowned. 'That is a serious allegation, Mr Arrandale.'

'I know but I believe he would do it.'

'Perhaps, if the dresser knew things that would implicate him in your sister-in-law's murder.'

'My thoughts exactly, Miss Duncombe.'

She sat upright and said with sudden decision, 'We must talk to Wolfgang again.'

'Now?' Richard looked at his watch. 'The day is well advanced. Your aunt will be expecting you.'

Wolf's image swam before Grace's eyes and she clasped her hands together, as if in supplication. 'I have the strongest feeling we should tell your brother our suspicions. Immediately.'

Phyllida touched her husband's arm. 'We have two footmen up behind us, my dear. One of them could be sent to inform Mrs Graham that we will be delayed.'

'But is it not too much for you, love?' he asked her. 'We have been gadding about all day.'

Phyllida smiled. 'I have been sitting at my ease in a coach, Richard. I am not at all tired, I promise you.'

With a nod Richard jumped out to issue instructions to his servants and Grace gave Phyllida a grateful look, then was immediately assailed by doubt. Was she allowing her growing attraction to Wolf Arrandale to cloud her judgement? Perhaps she just wanted to see him again. It was late, she should go home, but the feeling persisted that they should talk to him. She comforted herself with the fact that the others had not argued strongly against it and soon they were crossing the river again, heading for the prison.

They travelled in silence, each lost in their own thoughts, but as they were approaching the Sessions House Richard sat up, staring out of the window.

'I think we might have to revise our plans.'

There was something in his voice that alerted Grace and she followed his glance. Coming out of the coffee house on the corner of the street was the magistrate, Gilbert Hatcham, accompanied by a fashionably dressed gentleman. They stopped on the pavement to take leave of one another and the gentleman removed his hat to display his thick black hair and a fine set of whiskers. A cold chill settled over Grace.

'Is that Sir Charles Urmston?' she asked, her throat growing dry.

'It is indeed,' muttered Richard. 'And he looks to be on the best possible terms with the magistrate.'

Chapter Nine

The officers in the prison were surprised to see Grace and Richard back again so soon, but a few coins slipped into waiting palms gained them immediate access. This time they were escorted to the cells, ranged along a corridor with numerous heavy wooden doors on one side, each with a small grille through which the prisoner might be observed.

'Welcome to my new abode,' said Wolf, when they were shown in and the door firmly locked behind them. 'Did you see Kennet on your way in? He left only a short time ago.' He looked about him. 'An excellent valet. He brought me fresh clothes as well as my purse, which has purchased me this cell. It isn't a palace, but at least it has a window and blankets on the bed. And I have a table and chair, so pray be seated, Miss Duncombe. Perhaps I could see if they can provide tea…'

'Stop playing the fool,' said Richard impatiently. 'We do not have time for this.'

'No, of course.' Wolf sobered immediately. 'Did you discover anything at Meesden's lodgings?'

Wolf listened intently to his brother's recital of what they had found and at the end his countenance was forbidding.

'I am more than ever convinced that Urmston is behind all this,' he muttered.

'I am certain of it,' retorted Richard. 'We have just seen him coming out of the coffee house with the magistrate. They looked as thick as thieves.'

'Well, that explains why he lured me to Southwark to meet Meesden,' said Wolf. 'He wanted me delivered up to Hatcham, whom he could trust to keep me locked away until the trial. That way I have little chance to prove my innocence.'

'Then we must do so,' said Grace. 'We could advertise, put up bills asking for witnesses to the murder, offer a reward.'

'I doubt you would have any success,' Wolf replied. 'We would need nothing short of a full confession from the real killer for a jury to find me not guilty.'

'We are pretty sure who it is, so I will extract one from the villain!' was Richard's savage response.

Wolf shook his head. 'Urmston will have thought of that. He will be on his guard, ready to use any attempt to intimidate him as further evidence of my guilt. By heaven, I begin to think it will take a miracle to extricate myself from this fix!'

Richard laid a hand on his shoulder. 'We shall get you out of here, Wolfgang, never fear. I expect our great-aunt Sophia to be in London very soon.'

'That is good news,' declared Grace. 'The support of the Dowager Marchioness of Hune can only help our cause.'

She looked so much more cheerful that Wolf kept silent, but he doubted even Lady Hune's money and influence could help him now.

'If only we knew who stole the diamonds,' he exclaimed. 'That would be one less charge to contend.'

'But Meesden said they were *not* stolen,' Grace reminded him.

'Aye, so she did.' Wolf paced the small cell, his brow furrowing as the thoughts chased through his head. 'Perhaps…'

'Perhaps they are still at Arrandale,' said Grace, her face lighting up.

'But if Meesden knew where, Urmston may have forced her to tell him,' argued Richard.

'There is that,' said Wolf. 'But he won't have had a chance to get them. Richard, you must go to Arrandale immediately. Urmston will remain in town until his tame magistrate has committed me for trial, but once he knows I am safely locked up he will go in search of the necklace.'

Richard shook his head. 'I need to be here with you. I'll ask Lady Hune to go directly to Arrandale.'

'By heaven, Richard, you cannot do that, Sophia is an old lady.'

'But she is indomitable, Brother, and she has a large and impressive retinue to protect her. If I explain everything, she will keep the villain out.'

The distant chime of a clock floated in through the unglazed window. Wolf looked up.

'Is Phyllida waiting in the carriage, Richard? You should go. Do not worry about me, there is nothing more to be done tonight.'

Grace rose and held out her hand. It fluttered like a wild bird in his grasp.

'I shall come back tomorrow, sir.'

'You would be advised to stay away.' He saw the obstinate set of her mouth and added, 'Truly, such attention would give rise to speculation. I would not have you become the subject of such gossip.'

Her head went up. 'I will take that risk.'

Wolf knew he should forbid her to come, but for the life of him the words would not pass his lips. She was the one glimmer of light in his sorry, sordid history and he could not bear to lose it. Not yet.

When they had gone Wolf sat for a while, thinking over all they had told him, and when the warder arrived with his dinner he gave him a message for the magistrate.

Kennet brought Wolf's breakfast the following morning, together with the latest newssheets and more fresh clothes. Once he was washed and dressed, Wolf dismissed his man and settled down to await his visitor. Noon passed, then one o'clock. Two. Wolf was lying on his bed staring at the square of blue sky through the little window when at last the door of his cell opened. He sat up.

'Good of you to call, Sir Charles.'

Urmston sauntered in, a monogrammed handkerchief clutched in his hand. The cloying scent that wafted into the cell with him suggested he had soaked the linen in perfume as protection against the noisome odours of the prison. He glanced about him, a look of distaste on his florid features.

'Hatcham said you wanted to see me. I had an

appointment with my tailor and could not come this morning. However—' he gave a mocking smile '—I knew you were not going anywhere.'

'Aye,' growled Wolf. 'Thanks to you I am incarcerated in this cell and likely to be here for some time.' He decided to go directly to the attack. 'Why did you give Hatcham that poster for my arrest?'

Sir Charles spread his hands.

'My dear Arrandale, I merely brought it to his attention, as any law-abiding citizen would do.'

'Law-abiding?' Wolf's lip curled. He rose, towering over the man. 'You killed Meesden, did you not?'

Urmston stepped back, but his cold, humourless smile did not falter.

'*You* were caught with the knife in your hand and her blood all over you. No one will believe you did not murder her.'

'But we both know I did not do it. And what about my wife?' asked Wolf. He glanced at the closed door. 'Come, man, now I am safely locked up, will you not tell me the truth?'

'I will tell you nothing!' Urmston spat out the words, his usual mask of urbanity slipping, but only for a moment. He looked down, tracing a crack in the floor with his silver-topped cane. 'Is this why you wanted to see me, to try to foist the blame for your crimes upon me?'

'I am innocent and you know it.'

'But who will believe you?' purred Urmston. 'There are at least a dozen witnesses to testify against you and I am sure by now some of them even believe they saw you plunge the knife into that poor woman. And what could any character witnesses say on your behalf? You were hardly a model of propriety before you fled to France, were you? No, Arrandale, you will hang. And soon, I promise you. Now, if that is all I am off to my dinner.' He lifted his cane to rap upon the door, then paused to say with studied indifference, 'By the by, when you called on Meesden, did she tell you what had happened to the Sawston diamonds?'

'Did she not tell you, before you killed her?'

Urmston's eyelids flickered, but he gave a little shrug.

'If you did not steal them, then I feel sure it was your wife's maid. But that need not concern you, Arrandale, the theft will be laid at your door.' Urmston called for the warder to let him out before he turned back to Wolf for one parting shot. 'That, added to the two murders, will be more than enough to hang you.'

Alone again, Wolf sat on the bed. So Urmston did not know where to find the diamonds. That was encouraging, but it was not enough to save him from the gallows. Frustration gnawed at him, he wanted to be out of this place, instead he had to rely on his brother and an aged aunt to search for the necklace and try to build a case for his defence. If they could not—well, he would find a way to escape and go back to France, but somehow the life of an outcast no longer appealed to him. He wanted to remain in England with his family. With Grace.

He pushed the thoughts away and went back over everything Urmston had said, looking for any little clue that might help. He was so engrossed in his thoughts that he did not hear the approaching footsteps, nor did he move when the key grated in the lock of his door. It wasn't until the tall figure in a cloak and veiled bonnet stepped into the cell that he looked up.

He was on his feet in an instant.

'You should not be here.' He tried to mean it, but his heart was drumming erratically against his ribs. He could not take his eyes off Grace as she put back her veil.

'I told you I would come.'

'Yes, and *I* told you it was dangerous. Urmston has just left me. Did he see you?'

'Yes, unfortunately. He was talking to Mr Hatcham when the warder was taking my details for the register.'

'The devil he was! Grace, it was bad enough that you should visit me with my brother, but to come alone—'

She was unmoved by his fury.

'I told them you are one of Papa's parishioners and it is my duty to visit you on his behalf. Sir Charles heard it, too, but he barely noticed me, I think I was very convincing as a reluctant and disapproving prison visitor.'

'Surely this is not the same lady who berated me so soundly for involving her father in this matter?'

He was shaking his head, but Grace saw that he was smiling. There was a mixture of admiration and disbelief in his look and she knew a tell-tale blush was not far away. Resolutely she fought it down.

'As I told the constable, one should never shirk from one's Christian duty, however unpleasant.' She nodded towards her basket, saying shyly, 'I am more used to taking food baskets to the poor, but I know you have funds and your man will fetch your dinner later, so I thought I might bring you books instead.'

'Thank you.'

Wolf's dark eyes were fixed upon her, unfathomable but disturbing. To cover her confusion she began to empty the basket.

'They are from my aunt's library. I have brought you some poetry, the *Gentleman's Magazine* and the last two volumes of *Udolpho*.' He had come closer and her skin prickled with awareness of him. She was trembling and her throat was dry, but she chattered on as she lifted the final book from the basket. 'I knew the guards would search the basket so I felt obliged to bring you a Bible, too, although I doubt you will read it.'

'Grace.'

His hand covered hers as she laid the Bible on the table. She had removed her gloves to sign the visitor register and his touch was like a spark on dry tinder. The shock of it set her heart hammering against her ribs. She fixed her gaze on the holy book lying beneath their hands and her mind was suddenly filled with thoughts of the marriage ceremony, of clamouring bells and bouquets of spring flowers. With a gasp she tried to pull away, but

Wolf's grip tightened. He drew her fingers against his chest, forcing her to turn towards him. Grace kept her eyes lowered, staring at the top button of his embroidered waistcoat. Thoughts flashed through her mind with lightning speed. He was not wearing his coat and that was most improper. She thought how white his shirt was, how well his waistcoat fitted him, how it enhanced the flat stomach and narrow hips.

How much she wanted to put her arms about him.

'Grace, look at me.'

She heard his soft words but dared not obey. If she raised her eyes she would see the broad shoulders made even wider by the billowing sleeves of his shirt, the lean jaw, shadowed now with a fine, dark stubble, the sensuous mouth that only had to smile to send all sensible thoughts flying. She swallowed nervously and gave her head a tiny shake. She must not look into his eyes or she was lost.

Wolf growled. She felt the rumble against her hand, still captive on his chest. He caught her chin, gently but inexorably pushing her head up. She tried to close her eyes and pull away, but her traitorous body would not obey and she found herself gazing into his eyes. They were the violet-blue of an evening sky.

'I…' She ran her tongue over her dry lips. 'Must not.'

He was lowering his head and she could resist no longer. She had tasted his kiss before and was desperate to do so again. With a tiny cry she threw her free arm around his neck and reached up to kiss him. It was a fierce, reckless embrace and she felt clumsy, inexperienced, but only for a moment. Wolf's mouth was working over hers and her whole body shuddered with delight. His arms went around her, holding her tight as the kiss deepened. Her lips parted and his tongue darted and delved, drawing a response from deep in her core. She was melting against him while his muscled body only seemed to grow harder. He was like a rock and she clung to him as waves of desire swept over her, leaving her weak.

Wolf raised his head, gasping like a drowning man. His body was shaking with the powerful hunger that coursed through him. It was the second time he had held Grace in his arms. She leaned against him, eyes half-closed and a delicate flush on her cheeks. But even now the languorous glow was fading. She lifted her head, a tiny crease of dismay already furrowing her brow. Soon she would be pushing him away, as she had done before. He could not bear to wait for her rejection so he released her and walked across to the window, rubbing one hand over his face.

'Now do you see why it is so dangerous to come here alone?' he demanded harshly.

When she did not reply he turned around. Grace was staring at the floor, clasping and unclasping her hands in front of her.

'I have been fighting and fighting against this,' she muttered, as if to herself. 'It means nothing, save that I have been too many years alone. It *cannot* mean anything. Once Loftus and I are married all will be well.'

'Will it?' Wolf shook his head, as much to clear his thoughts as to contradict her. 'You are deluding yourself if you think Braddenfield will arouse such passions in you.'

She put her hands to her head, pushing her fingers against her temples.

'You misunderstand me,' she said slowly. 'I do not *want* him to arouse me in that way. I had hoped to share those appetites once, with Henry, my first, my only love, but, but *carnal* desires have no place in my life now.'

He could not allow that, not when she had been in his arms, matching him kiss for kiss.

'Well, they *should* have a place!' He reached out and caught her hands. 'Desire is not a sin, Grace, it is natural and you should not marry a man you do not desire.'

'No!' She backed away from him, crossing her arms over her breast. 'Henry and I loved each other, we longed for the day when we could consummate our love and when I lost him it was unbearable.'

'How old were you when he died? Eighteen, nineteen?'

She sank down on the edge of the bed, hunched over as if in pain.

'I was nineteen. We were very much in love. We were made for one another. I knew it, even though we had known each other for less than two years. Can you understand that?'

'Yes, I can.' He knew now it was possible to fall in love in less than two months.

'Henry was my life,' she said simply. 'When he was taken, a part of me died, too.'

'But *only* a part of you,' he said. 'For the past five years you have been afraid to live. You have been afraid to allow yourself to *feel* anything. Even your engagement to Braddenfield is a safe and sensible choice.'

'You make it sound like a crime.'

'It is, when you could do so much more with your life.'

'How dare you criticise me,' she retorted, stung. 'I was very happy, until I met you!'

'If I have made you feel again then I cannot regret it, Grace. Oh, I know I am not the right man for you, I have lived for too long with the devil at my shoulder, but there are other men, good men, who would love you and make you happy, if you would give them a chance. You are too young to bury yourself away in a loveless marriage. You should be out in the world, living. Loving.'

'I do not *want* that!'

Her anguished cry silenced him.

She dragged the back of her hand across her eyes.

'When you came into my life I knew you were dangerous, someone even said you walk with the devil, but I did not want to believe it. Papa was keen to help and I, well, I thought a little adventure might be enjoyable, but it isn't. Not at all. It has cut up my peace most horribly, not least because I know I will not be able to tell Loftus and one should not have secrets from one's fiancé. I shall have to live out my life with that on my conscience, but I am promised to Loftus and I shall stand by my vow. I *want* to marry him. I shall be situated near my father and my future will be secure. That will please Papa.'

'And will it please you, too?'

'Yes.' She took out her handkerchief to wipe a stray tear from her cheek. 'I want a safe, quiet existence. I beg your pardon if my actions just now made you think otherwise, but that part of my life is buried with Henry.' She raised her solemn, resolute gaze to his. 'Henry was a paragon of goodness. He is the yardstick by which I measure all other men.'

Wolf had always known she was too good for him and now she had told him that her previous love was a saint. Very few men would match up to such a standard and certainly not an Arrandale.

He sighed. 'If I have caused you unhappiness I am very sorry for it and I beg your forgiveness. Believe me, you have done nothing for which you need reproach yourself. Go home and forget me, Miss Duncombe.'

Grace felt as drained and empty as the basket Wolf pushed into her hands. He hammered on the door and shouted for the warder. As the key grated in the lock she rose and he reached out to pull the veil over her face.

'Thank you for your kindness, ma'am, and allow me to wish you every happiness.'

Without a word Grace left the cell and made her way up the stairs. When she reached the office her hand was shaking so much she could barely write her name to sign out. Janet was waiting in the carriage, but although Grace could respond calmly to her anxious enquiries she kept her veil down, knowing that tears were not far away.

Grace had never told anyone how she had felt about Henry Hodges, the unfulfilled cravings and desires that had haunted her dreams. She had never even told Henry, when he was alive. She had always assumed he felt the same, but now she wondered. Henry's most daring move had been to kiss her cheek and when, on one occasion, she had tried to put her arms about him he had held her off, saying gently that there would be time for all that once they were married. In fact, there was no time at all. Within the month he was dead. A tear slipped down her cheek. She had loved Henry so much. No one could take his place. No one, least of all a man like Wolf Arrandale.

All the way to Hans Place Grace wondered what

she should do. To stay away from Wolf, to abandon him to his fate, seemed like the coward's way out. She had thrown herself at him in a most shameful way and she must now atone for it. Wolf had been surprised into reacting, but *he* was the one who had pushed her away. And he had told her quite plainly that he was not the man for her, so it was not as if her lustful feelings were reciprocated. She must show him and the world that she was strong and compassionate, a suitable wife for a magistrate. Wolf might not want her in *that* way, but her visits would help to break up the long days of his incarceration. She would be doing her duty. Dear Henry had died doing his.

And what she felt for Wolf Arrandale would fade. Did not Papa say often and often, *'Blessed is the man that endureth temptation?'* She must face this temptation and overcome it.

She quelled the tiny, traitorous voice that suggested that she *wanted* to see Wolf, that the tug of attraction was too great to resist.

By morning Grace had convinced herself that she was making too much of what had happened at the prison. She had been overcome by the horrors of Wolf's situation and had wanted to comfort him, nothing more. Good heavens, if Daniel could walk into a lion's den and survive overnight, surely she could spend an hour visiting an innocent man in his prison cell.

Mrs Graham looked up from her breakfast to smile as Grace came in.

'What an energetic girl you are, my love,' she greeted her niece. 'I have only just left my room and you have already taken Nelson for his morning walk.'

'Then we may break our fast together, ma'am,' Grace replied, sitting down at the table.

'And I am very glad to see you up and about,' remarked Aunt Eliza, as Jenner filled their coffee cups. 'You were so quiet at dinner last night I was afraid you might have caught something in that dreadful gaol.'

'No, no, I am quite well,' Grace reassured her. 'I was merely troubled yesterday.'

'And no wonder,' said Aunt Eliza. 'Mr Arrandale's plight is indeed very worrying. I was horrified when you told me he had been locked up for the murder of that poor woman. I am as convinced as you are that he is innocent, but thankfully he has his brother to support him now, to say nothing of the rest of the Arrandale relations, so there can be no need for you to go to that horrid prison again.'

Grace helped herself to a bread roll. 'On the contrary, I intend to visit Mr Arrandale again today.'

'My dear girl, you cannot be serious!'

'Never more so,' she replied, not looking up. 'As Papa's daughter I must help those in need.'

'But you said yourself Mr Arrandale has funds enough to pay for his comforts; surely one visit to him is enough. Heavens, my love, you ransacked my library to find works he might enjoy. I will not say I begrudge him the books—after all they have been sitting on the shelves since Mr Graham died and *I* shall never read them—but surely there can be no need for you to go back again.'

'If Papa were here it is what he would do.' Grace felt the colour heating her cheeks as those disturbing doubts returned. Of course she did not *want* to see Wolf. Indeed, she would be far more comfortable if she could put him right out of her head, but how could she do that, when the shadow of the gallows hung over him?

She said aloud, 'My mind is made up, Aunt Eliza, I shall visit Mr Arrandale every day while he remains in prison. It is my Christian duty.'

'Well, you are of age and I cannot stop you. Although what your fiancé will say I am sure I do not know.'

Grace silently finished her breakfast. She would have to tell Loftus something of her activities in London and he might even decide to withdraw his offer of marriage. But that was for the future. For now, she could not abandon Wolf Arrandale, whatever it cost her.

Richard Arrandale was to see his brother every morning, so Grace timed her visit for later in the day. She took her maid, but Janet was reluctant to enter the prison and Grace left her in the carriage while she went in alone to see Wolf. She arrived to find Kennet with his master, playing backgammon. They both rose at her entry and although Wolf scowled and told her she should not have come, the glow in his eyes gave the lie. There was an awkward moment of silence. The valet coughed and muttered that perhaps he should go.

'Yes—no,' said Wolf. 'What do you say, Miss Duncombe, would you prefer Kennet to stay?' When she shook her head he waved a hand towards his man. 'Come back in an hour. No, make it a little longer.'

Wolf had not taken his eyes off her and Grace struggled to keep still under his scrutiny.

I can do this, she told herself. *It is no different from visiting any of Papa's needy parishioners.*

When they were alone he said again, 'You should not have come.'

'My father always asks after you in his letters.'

It was a poor enough excuse, but Wolf nodded.

'Very well, then, Miss Duncombe. Will you not sit down?'

The days fell into a pattern. Grace was at her aunt's disposal each morning, but every afternoon she made her way to Horsemonger Lane. Kennet was often in attendance, but as soon as Grace arrived he would excuse himself and leave them alone to talk. Grace had no fears for her safety, Wolf kept as much distance as possible between them during her visits. He might walk with the devil, but nothing could have exceeded his civility towards her.

The guards grew accustomed to Grace's visits and soon gave no more than a cursory glance at her basket filled with books and a few little delicacies to augment the meals Kennet brought in from the local tavern. She also included extra pastries for the guards, who fell upon them with relish and it earned her a smile and a cheerful word from the warders as they escorted her to the prisoner.

Grace knew Richard was trying to build a case for his brother's defence, but by tacit agreement she and Wolf never spoke of it. Instead they talked of unexceptional subjects such as books and art and the latest reports from the newspapers that Kennet brought for his master every day.

After an hour, or sometimes a little more, Grace would take her leave, pulling down her veil to hide the despair that choked her every time she left Wolf's cell. Once a rogue tear escaped and splashed on to the page when she was signing out and after that the officer in charge waved her away, saying with gruff kindness that they could not have her spoiling their visitor register and he would sign her out in future.

Grace hoped that the parting would grow easier as the days went by, but at the end of the first week she felt more desolate than ever. She returned to Hans Place, hoping to slip upstairs unnoticed, but her aunt was waiting in the hall and asked her to step into the morning room.

'My love,' she said, as they sat down together on the sofa. 'Another letter has arrived for you, from

Hindlesham Manor. No doubt your fiancé is anxious to hurry your return.'

'Quite possibly.' Grace knew she must leave London very soon, but the hours she spent with Wolf were too precious and she could not give them up. Not yet. Under her aunt's watchful eye she broke the seal on the letter and opened it.

'Loftus sends his regards to you, Aunt,' she said, reading quickly. 'And he writes to tell me that the reception for Mrs Braddenfield's birthday went off very well.'

'You missed his mother's birthday?' Aunt Eliza put a hand on her knee. 'Grace, my love, let me speak plainly. You should have been at Hindlesham for such an event.'

'Loftus quite understands that I have not yet finished my business in London. If we were married it would be different.' Grace glanced again at the letter. 'Besides, he tells me Claire Oswald arranged everything perfectly. Indeed, as his mama's companion she was by far the best person to do so.'

Aunt Eliza gave a little tut of exasperation.

'My love, tell me honestly, do you still mean to marry Sir Loftus? It is not kind of you to keep him waiting, you know, if you mean to jilt him.'

'Jilt him?' The letter slid from Grace's fingers

and she bent to retrieve it. 'Good gracious, Aunt, why should I do such a thing?'

'Because you are showing more interest in visiting a prison than seeing your fiancé.'

'I...I want to help Wolf, that is all.'

Aunt Eliza's brows rose. 'So it is Wolf now. You are mighty friendly with that young man, Grace.'

'The injustice of his situation shocks me. Papa urged me to support him and I have done so.' She added, as much to convince herself as her aunt, 'It is not friendship or anything warmer that draws me to the prison, but duty.'

'Well, I am relieved to hear it,' said Aunt Eliza. 'I was afraid you were in danger of throwing away your chance of lasting happiness for a man who is not free, and who, barring a miracle, is like to hang before the year is out.'

Aunt Eliza's words haunted Grace as she made her way to Horsemonger Lane the following day. She lifted her eyes to the prison roof and a little shiver of foreboding ran through her as she stared at the scaffold. The feeling of disquiet grew even stronger when she found Richard with his brother, and looking grim. She stopped in the doorway, clutching her basket before her, until Wolf invited her to come in.

'Is there news?' she asked, as she took the proffered chair. The men glanced at one another and she said quickly, 'Please tell me.'

Richard pulled up a second chair and sat down.

'Wolf is to be tried at the Sessions House in a se'ennight,' he said.

'So soon!' Grace looked at Wolf, who nodded.

'And Urmston is funding my prosecution for Meesden's murder.'

Grace frowned. 'Is that not unusual?'

'Florence was his cousin,' said Richard. 'And since Meesden was her dresser Urmston says it is his moral duty to see justice done.'

'Justice!' Wolf's lip curled. 'If there were any justice it would be Urmston standing in the dock. As it is he lays my wife's death and the theft of the diamonds at my door, too. A very neat end to his machinations.'

'Sophia has directed her lawyers to handle this case,' put in Richard. 'They approached Urmston to settle this privately, but he will not budge. He is determined to see you hang, Brother.'

'Of course. He wants me to take the blame for his crimes.' Wolf scowled. 'He knows what happened to Florence, I am sure of it. I have had plenty of time to think while I have been locked up here. When we went to see Meesden, Grace, do you remember her words? *"She would have been happier with—"* She did not say with whom, but I believe she meant Charles Urmston. He and my wife were very close, you see. Too close. That was the reason for our argument the night she died. I told her I was damned if I'd be cuckolded in my own house.'

He began to pace about the room, head down, thinking. 'It is all tied up with the diamonds. Urmston would sell his own grandmother for a groat. Perhaps he wanted the necklace and Florence did not want him to take it. I think Meesden, too, knew what happened that night. Urmston may well have paid her to keep quiet and her subsequent disappearance did not matter until I returned to England and began to ask questions. And Urmston now seems quite anxious to find the necklace. He asked me about it again when he came here.'

'Well, it is worth a fortune and his funds are certainly at low ebb again,' said Richard. 'When I ran into him in Bath the summer before last he was once more in need for a fortune and trying to find himself another heiress. Even tried to abduct Ellen. My stepdaughter,' he explained to Grace, adding with a grin, 'She's a minx, but fortunately too clever to fall for his tricks. She even bamboozled me into marrying her stepmama.'

Grace saw his face soften as he thought of his wife and felt a momentary pang of envy. Not that it was *Richard* Arrandale she wanted to think of her with affection. A glance at Wolf showed him lost in thought, his countenance very grim, and she sought around for some glimmer of hope.

'You say your great-aunt has hired lawyers to defend you? They will be the very best, I think.'

Wolf shook his head. 'With the evidence against me there is little hope of an acquittal, even in a fair trial. But here, where Urmston already has the magistrate in his pocket—' He leaned on the table. 'There is no alternative, I must get out.' His stormy eyes fell on Grace. 'You had best leave, my dear. I would not have you compromised by what we are about to discuss.'

'You plan to escape, sir?'

'I am going to try,' he said. 'I have done many foolish things in my time, but I will not be hanged for crimes I did not commit.'

'Then let me help you.'

'No.' He shook his head. 'You have risked enough for me already.'

'But—'

'Go back to Arrandale and marry Sir Loftus. Then I need worry about you no longer.'

Grace winced as his words cut into her, but she would not let him dismiss her so readily. Her determination manifested itself in a steely calm. She gazed at the two men.

'Do either of you have a plan?' When neither of them spoke she said, with no little satisfaction, 'Well, I do.'

Chapter Ten

It took a while for the brothers to accept Grace's idea. Richard finally acknowledged that it might work, but Wolf stubbornly refused to agree.

'What you suggest is madness,' he declared. 'I cannot let you take such a risk for me.'

'The risk is all yours,' she replied. 'I shall be safely away from here before you make your escape.'

'No!' he said explosively. 'I cannot have you involved in this!'

Grace sat back on her chair. 'Can you think of a better plan?'

Wolf glared at her, his look a mixture of frustration and fury.

Richard laughed. 'I have to admit, Miss Duncombe, we cannot.'

'Then we must use mine.' She rose. 'It is time for me to go.'

As she walked to the door she heard Wolf's smothered exclamation behind her.

'No, Grace, I cannot let you do this!'

She looked back. 'I do not think you have any choice, sir, unless you want to hang.'

Grace hurried back to her carriage. The cool resolution she had shown in the prison had been replaced by a nervous energy that made her blood sizzle. How was she ever to explain this to Aunt Eliza, let alone to Loftus? The sad truth was that she had no intention of telling them of her involvement in this daring plan. Indeed, if everything went well there was no need for them to know anything about it. Her part in it was negligible. She would tell Papa and she prayed he would understand, even if he thought her misguided.

A memory stirred. When Henry had been brought back to the vicarage and it had been explained how he had been stabbed protecting a woman from her husband. Papa had given way to emotion then and for once he had railed, saying Henry had been impetuous and misguided to tackle the man alone. Now Grace remembered dear Henry's words as she nursed him through his final hours.

'I had to try, Grace. I could no more leave them to their fate than I could stop breathing.'

'That is it, exactly,' she murmured. 'Oh, Henry, you understand why I must do this, don't you?'

Wolf paced the floor of his cell. It was five days since they had agreed to Grace's idea and throughout each of them he had worried their plan would be discovered and she would be arrested. Richard had called this morning to tell him everything was in place, Kennet had been despatched with his instructions and now Wolf was waiting for Grace to make her final visit. He wished to heaven she need not come, but to all his protests she had calmly pointed out that it was necessary if their plan was to work.

'All your visitors save myself are searched upon entry here,' she had told him. 'The guards trust me and that is our advantage.'

And much as he disliked the idea of putting Grace in danger, for the life of him he could not think of any alternative.

When the door was unlocked and she stepped into the cell he fixed her with a grim stare. She put back her veil, pale but composed.

'Good day to you, Mr Arrandale. I trust you are well?'

Her greeting was the same every time and he replied with his usual scowl, which always made the guard grin as he locked the door upon them.

'I wish you did not have to come,' he muttered, as she put her basket down beside the table.

'I pray this will be the last time.'

Wolf walked to the door and looked out through the grille. The passage was empty, but he was not taking any chances and kept his voice low.

'Everything is ready?'

She nodded. 'A hackney coach will be waiting for you across the road from the gaol at the appointed time.'

'Kennet has found a couple of choice spirits who are even now spending money in the local gin house. Their customers should be roaring drunk and filling the cells within the hour. So you must go as soon as possible, the streets will not be safe.'

'I am aware. I have an extra footman on the carriage today.'

'And I have your word you will go home tomorrow?'

'Yes. That is all arranged.' She cast a shy glance up at him. 'Shall I see you, at Arrandale?'

Wolf had been expecting this and had his answer ready.

'No. I must go to the Hall, but I will not have you or your father involved any further in this business.'

'But if you can prove you are innocent—'

'It would take a miracle to get a confession from Urmston, and I have never believed in miracles.' He shook his head. 'If we can find the diamonds that will throw doubt upon my guilt. Not enough to convince a jury, I have no doubt that in their eyes the fact that I was found kneeling over the bodies of both my wife and her dresser, with their blood on my hands, would be enough to condemn me, but Richard might convince my daughter I am no murderer.'

'But we cannot give up hope.'

She looked at him, confident that justice could prevail. Experience had taught Wolf otherwise, but her faith was endearing. He wanted to kiss her, to lose himself in her soft goodness. She had responded to his kiss before, she would again, all he had to do was reach out and take her. Mentally he drew back, reining in his desire. She was betrothed to another man. He might seduce her, kiss and caress her until she was unable to resist him, but she would never forgive herself for breaking her vows.

She was too good, too honest to bear the deceit. It would destroy her. *He* would destroy her.

'I shall not stay in England. Richard and I will appoint a good steward at Arrandale and I shall provide a dowry for little Florence, but then I shall go abroad.'

'Within the month I shall be married and living at Hindlesham.' Her eyes sparkled with tears. 'If your innocence is proved you need not leave Arrandale for my sake.'

He forced a laugh and said carelessly, 'Grace, m'dear, this isn't about *you*. The truth is I am too restless to stay in any one place or be faithful to any one woman. I have been a vagabond for too long. I shall never settle down.'

He looked away from the pain in her eyes. He was hurting her, he knew it, but it was for the best. He had never been anything but a wastrel and she deserved so much more than that.

He said, 'It is time for you to go. Let us get on with it. If you are ready?'

She nodded silently, looking so unhappy that he crossed the space between them in a single stride and took her hands, carrying them to his lips.

'I am more grateful than I can say for what you have done, Grace, believe me.'

'Thank you,' she whispered. The dark lashes swept down, shielding her eyes. Her fingers trembled in his grasp, he felt her steeling herself for what was to come. Gently she freed herself and gave a little nod. 'Now. Let us finish this.'

Wolf grabbed the chair and sent it crashing behind him, saying in a loud, angry voice, 'Damnation, woman, I am *sick* of your moralising!' He strode across the cell and pounded on the door, exclaiming, once the guard's footsteps rang on the stone flags, 'If all you can do is preach at me, madam, then you had best go now. And good riddance to you!'

As the guard opened the door Grace flicked her veil over her face and hurried out. As expected, the outer office was bustling. The usual officer was not yet on duty and she signed herself out. No one questioned that she was leaving within minutes of her arrival and she hurried away to her carriage, tears of despair welling in her eyes. She had been foolish enough to think she was the reason Wolf would not stay at Arrandale and he had lost no time in correcting her. It should not matter, she was marrying Loftus, if he would have her, so why should she care what Wolf thought of her? But she *did* care. Today in that cheerless little cell she had admitted to herself something she had been so resolutely ignoring for weeks. She was in love with Wolf Arrandale.

Wolf threw himself down on his bed while he waited for the hour to pass. He hated parting from Grace in so rough a fashion, even though they both knew it was contrived. He hated parting from her at all, but it had to be. There was no future for them and he consoled himself with the fact that she would soon forget him, once she was married to her magistrate.

From above came muted shouts and angry voices as drunken rioters were brought in to spend the night in the lock-up. That part of the plan seemed to be working and a few moments later he heard the jovial banter and rough insults that accompanied the changing of the guard. Wolf sat up. That was what he had been waiting for. The officers on duty now would not have seen Grace leaving early and with luck they would not question the veiled figure who would shortly be making her way out of the prison. Quietly, listening intently for any approaching footsteps, he gathered together the clothes Grace had smuggled in for him over the past five days.

* * *

Wolf's escape from the gaol was almost ludicrously easy. The guard was so used to Grace quitting Wolf's cell at this time that he hardly looked at the cloaked and veiled figure waiting to be let out and he barely glanced at the dark shape on the bed. The dim light helped to disguise the fact that there was nothing more than pillows and blankets beneath the covers.

Above stairs was a scene of uproar. Constables argued with their more drunk and belligerent charges and, as Grace had predicted, the beleaguered officer in charge merely waved the veiled figure on her way without even looking at the register. From beneath the veil, Wolf watched several drunken men crowd the desk, berating the guards. It might be hours before they discovered the deception. Wolf kept his large hands hidden inside Grace's swansdown muff and shortened his stride to a more ladylike step as he made his way out of the gaol. No one accosted him, but he did not breathe until he was in the coach and driving away from Horsemonger Lane.

Quickly he discarded the bonnet, cloak and skirts that had masked his identity and replaced them with the hat and riding jacket he found on the seat. Looking out of the carriage, he gave a small grunt of satisfaction. They were travelling south, away from the river. If anyone did remark them they would think he was heading for Dover. So far so good, but he would feel happier once he had reached New Cross, where Kennet should be waiting with the horses.

Darkness was falling by the time the coach pulled up at a busy inn. If the driver thought it odd that a heavily veiled lady had climbed into his carriage and a fashionable gentleman was leaving it, he showed no sign and Wolf tossed him a silver coin to add to the handsome payment he had already received for his services. Glancing back along the road, he caught a flash of movement on the horizon, riders outlined against the last remaining strip of daylight. Wolf's eyes narrowed. They were approaching fast. He had hoped for a little more time before his escape was discovered.

Recalling his brother's instructions, Wolf crossed the inn yard and out through a narrow gate on the far side, into a back lane. Once he was out of sight of any casual observer he began to run. In the dim light of the rising moon he could just make out a stand of trees a short distance ahead of him. As he approached he heard the faint snuffle of a horse.

'Kennet?' He spoke softly. 'Are you there?'

Two horses emerged from the black shadows of the trees but the figure leading them was not Kennet, it was too tall. The pale moonlight fell on a youth, a stripling dressed in riding clothes and a neat jockey cap. Wolf frowned. There was something familiar about the slender shape, the dainty profile.

'Grace! What the devil—!'

She cut him off. 'There is no time to explain. I saw the riding officers approaching the inn. They will be searching here very soon. We must go. There is a horse ferry waiting for us at Woolwich.'

Something blazed through Wolf. He ignored the reins she was holding out to him and dragged her into his arms.

Grace's nerves were at full stretch and she was defenceless against the onslaught of his kiss. It was fierce, ruthless and possessive. It promised everything she had dreamed of. Everything she knew she could not have. With a superhuman effort she kept her hands clenched on the reins and resisted the temptation to respond. It was over in an instant. Without a word he threw her up into the saddle and scrambled on to his own horse, wheeling the restive animal towards her.

'Woolwich, you say?'

She dragged her thoughts back, forcing herself to think. Wolf's life depended upon her now.

'Yes. Follow me.'

She headed into the trees. The path was barely discernible, but they reached the other side without mishap and she set her horse at a gallop across the open fields. The trees at their back screened them from the inn and as they crested a ridge she risked a quick glance behind. There were no signs of pursuit so Grace steadied the pace to a canter, avoiding roads and skirting villages until at length they reached a crossroads.

'You appear to know your way around here very well,' commented Wolf, as she slowed to a walk.

'Your brother supplied Kennet with very good directions, which I have committed to memory.' She looked around, then pointed north. 'That way, I think. You see the church tower over there? We head for that and it will bring us to a small dock, well away from the arsenal.'

'There is an *arsenal* at Woolwich?' Wolf cursed under his breath. 'That means the military. It is madness to consider crossing the river at this point.'

'And thus no one will expect it.'

As she gathered up the reins, ready to ride on, Wolf reached out and caught her arm.

'Go back, Grace. It's not too late. Let me go on alone, do not involve yourself with me.'

She shook her head. 'I *am* involved, Wolf. There is no going back for me now.'

Wolf's head was buzzing with questions as she cantered off along the road, but they must wait. For now all he could do was follow. They took a circuitous route around the town and approached the river through a series of narrow lanes.

'How the devil did my brother find this place?' he murmured as they rode between two derelict warehouses.

'I believe you are not the only Arrandale with dubious connections.' Grace reached into her coat and pulled out a pistol, which she held out to him. 'You should have this. It is loaded, but I am not familiar with firearms.'

'You surprise me,' said Wolf drily. He checked the weapon and carefully put it in his pocket. 'There is a light ahead. Could it be our ferryman?'

'It is certainly the signal,' she said, peering into the darkness.

'It could be a trap,' he muttered. 'Stay here in the shadows.'

She shook her head. 'We stay together.'

There was a stubborn note in her voice and he decided not to waste time arguing.

'Very well, but let me go first.' Wolf touched his heels to the horse's flanks and led the way towards the swinging light. His eyes darted about and he strained his ears for signs of danger, but there was no one save the ferryman, who silently beckoned them towards the waiting barge.

It took time and patience to persuade the horses to embark, but at last they were tethered securely and there was nothing for the passengers to do but to sit down out of the way while the crew plied their oars and rowed them across the wide expanse of the river. The night air was chill and they wrapped themselves in the thick cloaks that had been strapped to the saddles. They were far enough from the crew to talk without being overheard, and Grace braced herself for the questions she knew Wolf was burning to ask.

'So why are you here rather than my valet?'

'He can barely ride.'

'What? Why the devil didn't he say so?'

'He saw it as his duty to follow your brother's instructions.'

'But to let you take his place,' Wolf exclaimed wrathfully. 'Of all the cowardly—'

'Not at all. It was perfectly sensible that I should do so. I learned to ride astride as a child. You must admit I have not held you back.'

'I will admit nothing.'

He sounded so much like a sulky schoolboy that Grace laughed and was immediately shocked at her reaction. There was nothing amusing about their situation. It was perilous. Wolf's life was at stake, to say nothing of her reputation. Her amusement argued a most unfeminine lack of sensibility. Not what gentlemen wanted at all, she thought bleakly. Gentlemen liked weak, decorative females whom they could cherish and protect, not practical women with their own opinions. Years running her father's household had taught Grace to be strong and resourceful, and much as she enjoyed the romances that graced her father's library shelves she knew she was not suited to be one of those heroines who quailed in the face of adversity and turned to a hero to rescue her from danger. She was a practical female and there was nothing she could do about it. Thankfully, Loftus had not shown any romantic inclinations. Theirs would be a practical marriage and the most she expected from it was that her life would be useful.

Useful and dull.

'Where is Kennet now?'

Wolf's voice brought Grace back to the present.
'He is taking your things to Arrandale.'

He leaned closer and said menacingly, 'And just how, madam, did you discover he could not ride?'

Grace folded her hands in her lap.

'From my maid,' she said calmly. 'Kennet was in the habit of talking to her while she waited for me outside the prison each day. She quizzed him today because he was looking so unhappy and he confessed he had not been on a horse more than a dozen times in his life, but he was determined to do his duty. I, however, thought that might wreck everything, so we drove to New Cross and I persuaded him to give up his place to me.'

'No doubt you carry a set of boy's clothes with you, for just such an eventuality.'

His sarcasm made her smile.

'We were fortunate that it is market day. Janet purchased them for me.'

'And then Kennet and your maid left you alone to carry out this hare-brained scheme.'

'They were neither of them happy about it, but they could see it was for the best. I wrote a note for my aunt, telling her to send Janet and all my luggage on to the vicarage tomorrow and I will go there directly. No one will know I did not arrive by coach.'

'Unless we are caught.'

'Then we must make sure that does not happen.'

Her cool response shook a laugh from him. He reached for her hand and raised it to his lips.

'I begin to think you will be wasted as the wife of a magistrate.'

Grace pulled her hand away. His words stung her cruelly. Wolf did not want her so why should he mock her for her choice? And if Loftus discovered what she had done she doubted he would marry her. She would live out her days as her father's house-keeper. The choices were stark and neither of them appealing. The future stretched ahead of her, as dark and depressing as the river flowing silently around them.

Wolf rose. 'We are nearing the bank. Let us get to the horses.'

They disembarked into an eerie, midnight world. Not a light showed in any of the buildings as they cantered through the deserted streets, heading northwards and guided by the stars. Grace had been warned that the land was marshy on this side of the river and they would need to keep to the roads, but eventually they left the flat plains behind and found themselves hedged about by woodland. Grace hesitated, not sure of her direction.

'I had friends in this area as a boy,' said Wolf. 'We can ride cross-country and pick up the Newmarket road at Epping. I know the way.'

'Thank you.' Grace yawned and rubbed a hand across her eyes.

'You are exhausted. We must find somewhere to rest.' She tried to protest, but he cut her short, saying brutally, 'You are no good to me if you are too fatigued to ride hard. If my memory serves we shall soon reach the Colchester road. Let us cross that and we will find somewhere in the forest to sleep.'

Grace nodded, too tired to speak. They set off again. It took all her concentration to follow Wolf and keep her horse from stumbling on the uneven ground. Clouds scudded across the sky, hiding the moon and plunging them into an even darker night. Wolf rode without pause and Grace marvelled at his ability to find his way unerringly along the most twisting lane, heading ever northwards. They crossed a broad highway and plunged again into thick forest. Grace was nearly dropping with fatigue by the time they reached a small clearing and Wolf announced they would stop for the night.

Grace wrapped herself in her cloak and sank down against a convenient tree, apologising that she had not thought to include any food for their journey.

'No matter.' Wolf dropped down beside her. 'We will be in Arrandale in time for breakfast.'

The silence settled comfortably around them. An owl hooted softly in the distance and Grace instinctively moved closer to Wolf, who put his arm about her.

'Do not tell me you are afraid of the dark,' he teased her gently.

She chuckled. 'Not at all. You are softer to lean against than a tree trunk.'

Her head had fallen to his shoulder. It was so comfortable resting against him, breathing in the faint but unmistakable masculine scent. She must sleep now, but perhaps, when she woke, she might turn her face up to his for another kiss. A delicious sense of anticipation filled her at the thought. She put her hand against his chest and snuggled closer.

'Excuse me, I must check the horses.'

He eased himself away and Grace bit back a little mewl of disappointment. Hot tears pressed against the back of her eyes. She felt bereft, in need of comfort. Wolf was talking softly to the horses and she hoped he would come back to her soon. She felt safe when he was near, even though she knew she should not feel safe at all, especially when she was consumed by such a yearning to have him make love to her.

The memory of his kisses made her body hot then cold, as if a huge hand was squeezing her insides and turning them to water. She thought of what could happen here, in this sheltered glade. Helping her father in the parish, she knew the dangers of being too free with a man, but somehow that was of no consequence now. She wanted Wolf to lie with her and satisfy the aching longing that gnawed at her.

She would be ruined, of course. And there could be no question of marrying Loftus, but that seemed unimportant. She had always known she did not love Loftus, to cry off would hurt his pride, but not his heart. But what of her professed love for Henry? She had always believed she could never love anyone else but now she knew she loved Wolf Arrandale, and although nothing could come of it, she wanted to give herself to him, to feel the comfort of his arms, his body. Just once. Was that disloyal to Henry? It was strange that she should face this question now, when her mind and body were so tired, but perhaps that was why she could think of it, while her mind was clear of all the other obstacles.

Henry was dead. She had loved him, part of her would always love him, but Wolf had shown her that she could love again. What would Henry say to that, if he knew? She yawned and felt herself slipping further into sleep even as her imagination discussed it with him.

Wolf stood by his horse, smoothing the velvet nose and breathing deeply to fight down the desire that raged through his body. He had needed to get away from Grace and the almost unbearable temptation of having her in his arms, her body pressed so comfortably against his. She was a parson's daughter, a virgin. She had risked everything to help him and he would not repay her by seducing her.

Why not? whispered the devil on his shoulder. *She wants you, she was almost giving herself to you.*

He closed his eyes. She was a lady. He knew she would not be able to enjoy a brief liaison and then walk away without being hurt.

You could marry her.

No.

Even if by some miracle he could prove his inno-

cence, the stains of his past life could not be erad-
icated. She was too good for him, he could never
make her happy.

You do not know that.

The devil would not be silenced.

*Put it to her. Lay your heart and hand before her
and let her decide. She is a woman and capable of
making her own choices.*

He stilled.

'I could do that,' he murmured as the horse snuf-
fled softly and pushed against his hand. For the first
time he saw a glimmer of hope.

*She believes I am innocent. She has risked every-
thing to help me. Perhaps, after all, she might care
enough to marry me.*

He straightened his shoulders. It would be her
choice. He would move heaven and earth to prove
his innocence and make her mistress of Arrandale,
but if not, if he failed, they could live abroad, content with each other's company.

If she truly loved him.

She certainly did not love her fiancé and Wolf decided if Grace was going to throw herself away on
a man it should be him. He would love her as she
should be loved. He would worship her.

Wolf's spirits rose higher than they had done for a

long time as he walked back to Grace. In the darkness he could just make out her soft shape, wrapped in the cloak. Silently he lay down beside her and rested his hand on the swell of her hip, felt the dip where it fell away to the dainty waist and his blood heated again. He would wait for the parson to marry them, if she wished it, but if she wanted him now... He closed his eyes. It must be her choice.

'Grace, love.'

She stirred. 'You understand, do you not, my dear? Oh, Henry.'

The words were soft as a sigh but there was no mistaking them, or the name she spoke so tenderly.

Wolf rolled away. Disappointment, bitter as gall, flooded through him. Stifling a groan, he turned to look at her. In the darkness her face was no more than a pale blur, but in his mind it was clear. He knew every detail of it, the straight little nose, the determined mouth and those dark lashes that now fanned out over her ivory cheek.

'Oh, Grace.' Wolf dropped a kiss lightly on her sleeping head. 'That puts you out of my reach more surely than an ocean. I cannot compete with a dead man.'

Chapter Eleven

Grace awoke with a delicious sense of wellbeing, but as full wakefulness returned she realised she was lying on the ground, warm enough in her thick cloak, but very much alone. It had all been a dream, then, lying in Wolf's arms, feeling safe and secure and with the promise of delights to come, once they were both rested. She struggled to sit up, rubbing her eyes. It was early, the first grey fingers of dawn were creeping through the trees but everything was still and quiet. Not even the birds were singing yet.

She looked around and saw Wolf standing by the horses, strapping his cloak to the saddle. Somewhere in her foolish, naïve imagination she had expected to wake and find him lying beside her, that he would roll over and make love to her here in this forest glade. What a romantic notion for such a practical person!

A sigh escaped her and Wolf turned. The closed look in his face sent the rest of her happy thoughts crumbling to dust.

'It is time we were moving.'

'Of course.' Grace scrambled to her feet and shook her cloak to shed the twigs and dead leaves that clung to the wool. The man was flying for his life. He had no time for dalliance, least of all with a woman who meant nothing to him. She should be grateful.

'Shall I pack up your cloak?'

'No.' She threw it back around her shoulders. The excitement of the adventure had gone, she felt exposed and rather foolish in her boy's clothes. 'I am cold.'

'The ride will soon warm you up.'

Silently Grace climbed into the saddle. It would take more than exercise to remove the ice in her heart.

Three hours hard riding brought them to the outskirts of Arrandale. They cut into the woods that bounded the park, where there was less likelihood of being seen than if they followed the road.

'You should go straight to the Hall,' Grace suggested. 'I will leave the horse at the stile and you can send someone to collect him.

'No, I will escort you.'

Wolf did not look at her. He did not want to see the pain in those lustrous eyes. Last night they had been so close, so companionable and he had almost succumbed to the temptation to make her his. Thank heaven he had moved away when he did. She still loved her precious curate, and although he might have made her forget the fellow for a time, in the days ahead she would measure Wolf against her saint and find him wanting.

When they reached the gates they were closed but unchained, suggesting Sophia had arrived. The village street was deserted, those who worked in the fields were already departed and the rest had not yet breakfasted. He turned to Grace.

'Give me the reins. I'll take the horse back with me.'

'Yes, of course.' She made no move to dismount.

'Go carefully. Grace.'

'I have only to cross the street. That back lane will take me directly to the vicarage garden.'

Wolf nodded. He had used it many times as a

boy to steal fruit from the parson's orchard. What would Duncombe say, if he knew how close Wolf had come to stealing his daughter?

She sighed. 'So this is goodbye.'

'Yes.' He could not meet her eyes. 'We shall not meet again.'

'Will you not shake hands with me?'

After the long ride the animals stood quietly side by side. How could he refuse, after all she had done for him, risking her life, her reputation, to help him.

He took her hand, forced himself to look into her face.

Ah, Grace, if things had been different. If I had not led such a rakehell life. If we had met before you fell in love with your saintly curate. We might have stood a chance.

The words screamed in his head, but he could not say them.

'Goodbye, Grace Duncombe.'

She clung to his fingers. 'Wolf, last night—'

He shook his head at her. 'One day, my dear, you will thank me for my forbearance.'

She looked as if she might argue so he tore his hand free and caught her reins.

'Go now. Every moment you delay endangers us both.'

She recoiled from his harsh tone and he bit back the impulse to apologise. Without another word she jumped down and scrambled over the stile. Wolf watched her disappear into the lane, then he turned and headed for the Hall. If this was what it felt like, doing the right thing, he wanted none of it. Clearly he was not made to be a saint.

Wolf noticed the changes as soon as he approached the Hall. Two men were scything the lawn and they stopped to watch as he rode down the drive. When he reached the stables they were bustling with activity. An elegant travelling chaise was visible through the open doors of the carriage house and two young men were removing the weeds from between the cobbles in the yard. They were being watched closely by an older man who looked up as Wolf clattered in. He ran across to take the spare horse from him.

'Morning, Mr Arrandale. Welcome home.'

'Who the devil are you and what's going on here?' demanded Wolf.

The man touched his cap.

'I'm Collins, sir, groom to Mr Richard. He sent me here to meet you and to look after the stables. And not a moment too soon, if you'll excuse my saying so, sir, since Lady Hune is determined to set everything here by the ears.'

'So my great-aunt's installed herself at the house, has she?'

A wide grin split the groom's craggy features.

'Aye, sir, the dowager marchioness has brought her whole retinue with her, and then some. All trusted folk and loyal,' he added quickly. 'You needn't fear for your safety, sir.'

'Glad to hear it.' Wolf slid to the ground. 'I'd better go in and see what she has been doing with my property!'

'Just one more thing, Mr Arrandale.' The groom lowered his voice. 'Mr Richard ordered a fast horse to be kept saddled and ready in the stables at all times.'

Suddenly Wolf was twenty-four again, angry, confused and thrust out of the house by a father who was convinced he was guilty. If he had stood his ground ten years ago, this sorry mess might never have happened. And Richard was clearly prepared for the worst.

'Much obliged to him,' he said shortly and strode off towards the house.

He had not gone far before he was intercepted by Robert Jones.

'Her ladyship said she had orders from Mr Richard, there was nothing I could do,' he said, eager to explain himself. 'She just swept in and took over, sir, brought all her own people with her, too. Hundreds of 'em.'

'I doubt if anyone could withstand Lady Hune in full flow,' muttered Wolf.

'But I don't mind saying it's good to have the house staffed again, sir. 'Tis quite a responsibility, looking after a place this size. Why, I couldn't even offer Sir Charles any refreshment when he called.'

'Sir Charles Urmston was here?' Wolf stopped. 'When was this?'

Jones rubbed his nose. 'Oh, weeks back, sir. Just after you left. He came to the house, saying as how he was in the area and wanted to see where he had spent so many happy days.'

'You let him into the house?'

'I didn't see how I could stop him, his having been such a favourite of the old master and cousin to Mrs Wolfgang.'

'But you went with him?'

'Oh, yes, sir. He wandered through the reception rooms, sighing and lamenting.'

'And you were with him the whole time?' When the servant hesitated Wolf put his hand on his shoulder. 'Answer me honestly, man. It is important that I know the truth.'

'Well, sir, when we gets to the hall he looked at the spot where your poor wife died and he covers his face, upset-like. Then he asks for something to drink. I told him there was nothing fit and he says as how he would take a glass of water, if I would fetch it.'

'And where was he when you got back?'

'Sir?'

'Was he still in the hall when you brought the water?'

'No, sir, he was on the landing. Said he had been musing on how his poor cousin could've fallen from that very spot.' Jones shook his head, clearly disapproving. 'Didn't seem proper, sir, to be going over something that happened so long ago.'

'He was standing near the balustrade, was he? Could he have been in any of the bedchambers?'

'He might have done, sir, but I wasn't gone that long.' Jones screwed up his face in an effort to remember. 'And he was wiping his hands on his handkerchief, sir, as if they was dirty.'

'And what did he do then?'

'Well, he comes down and I gives him the water, which he took no more than a sip of before going off.'

'He didn't ask to see over the rest of the house?'

'Now you comes to mention it, Mr Wolfgang, he did say as how he thought his horse was going lame and could he stay the night, but I told him that wouldn't be possible, sir, not at all. I offered him the use of the old gig we keeps in the stables to take him to the Horse Shoe, if he didn't want to walk, but he said his horse would get him that far. I didn't see him again after that, sir. Nor anyone else, until her ladyship arrived. And now I'm not sure what I should be doing.'

Wolf squeezed his shoulder.

'Keep your head down, Robert. This will all be over soon.'

'And then will you be living here again, sir?'

The footman's hopeful look caused Wolf a pang of remorse.

'No, Robert, I won't. But I shall make better provision for you all before I go this time, you have my word on it.'

The house was even busier than the stables, with sounds of activity echoing around the hall, where Croft, his great-aunt's butler, was directing an army of servants. When he saw Wolf, the butler waved away his minions and bowed.

'Her ladyship is in the drawing room, sir. She is expecting you.' He added quietly, as he opened the door, 'May I say that we are all delighted to see you here safe, sir.'

Wolf nodded. He had no doubt of Croft's loyalty and he knew his formidable great-aunt would have brought no one to Arrandale who could not be trusted to keep his presence a secret.

Sophia, Dowager Marchioness of Hune, came away from the window as he entered, her bearing as upright and regal as he remembered, despite the use of a cane, but when he was close enough to press a salute upon her hand he could see how much she had aged, her face more lined and the blue of her eyes a little less intense, although the look she fixed upon him had lost none of its power to intimidate.

'I am delighted to see you here, ma'am,' he said politely.

'So you should be.' The claw-like fingers clung to him. 'Help me to a chair. Once Croft has brought in the refreshments we can talk.'

'You have lost no time in making yourself at home,' he observed.

'You could not expect me to stay in this barrack of a house without a few comforts.'

She fell silent when the butler came and served them both with a glass of wine. Wolf sipped it appreciatively.

'Did you bring this with you, ma'am? It is superior to anything I recall from these cellars.'

'Your father was always a nip-farthing when it came to good wine.'

'So you brought your own. And all your servants, too, by the look of it.'

'Not only *my* servants.' She looked up to make sure they were alone again. 'I had some idea what would be required to put the place in some sort of order, so I asked the family for assistance.'

'The family?'

'Your brother and his wife and Lord and Lady Davenport. The staff were all carefully chosen for their loyalty and discretion, I assure you.'

Wolf frowned.

'I do not doubt it, ma'am, but I would rather you had not dragged Alex and his new wife into this.'

'They are Arrandales and will wish to be involved. Do not worry, your secrets are safe enough, my boy.'

'I do not doubt it, but it comes hard to trust so many people, when I have been accustomed to fending for myself.' He looked up, one brow raised. 'The two fellows scything the lawns as I rode in. They looked useful fellows to have with one in a fight.'

He saw the familiar glint in those faded eyes. 'Your brother sent them, lest Sir Charles Urmston should turn up, although there has been no sign of him as yet.' She paused. 'They might also buy you a little extra time to make your escape, should it be necessary.'

'You have not discovered the Sawston diamonds, then?'

'No. I have had the house turned out of doors, but my people have found nothing.'

'Did Richard tell you to pay special attention to the dresser's room?'

'He and Phyllida are going over it. I presume they have found nothing or they would have come down by now.'

'What?' Wolfgang exploded. 'They are here?'

'They arrived last evening, although they have sent little James off to Brookthorn with his nurse.'

'Thank heaven they have shown some sense!' declared Wolf. 'I do not want the family interfering in my affairs any further.'

'I think you must accustom yourself to it, Wolfgang. These days Arrandales stick together. You should think yourself fortunate that Ellen Tatham,

Phyllida's stepdaughter, is touring the Lakes with her old teacher at present or she would have been here, too, and she would set us all by the ears.'

'Even you, Sophia?'

Lady Hune allowed herself a faint smile. 'Even me. However, I think you should prepare yourself to see the Davenports here tomorrow. And they *are* bringing the children with them.'

Wolf clapped a hand over his mouth, as if to hold back even more explosions, not so much of wrath as consternation.

'Send them an express,' he said at last. 'They should not come.'

'Do you not wish to meet your daughter?'

'Yes, very much, but I want to meet her as a free man. I do not want her to see me arrested and dragged off in chains.'

'Do you think that is likely?'

He nodded. 'If I delay here too long. Urmston will make sure Arrandale is searched, once the trail to Dover goes cold. If the necklace is not found within a day or two, then I must give up my plans to see little Florence and leave the country.'

'If that is the case then naturally you must go, but you may be sure we shall continue the search.'

'Thank you, ma'am, I—'

He broke off as the door opened and a cheerful, musical voice floated across the room.

'Go away, Croft, we will announce ourselves.'

'Cassandra!' The words had hardly left his mouth before a petite dark-haired beauty threw her arms about him. 'What the—the deuce are you doing here?' he demanded, frowning over her head at Raoul Doulevant, who had followed her into the room. Raoul merely lifted his shoulders in a very Gallic shrug.

'My wife, she thought we should support you.'

'You knew I was coming here?'

'I guessed,' said Cassie, twinkling up at him. 'As soon as Grandmama wrote to tell me she was coming to Arrandale I knew something was afoot. We set off as soon as Raoul had made arrangements for leave from his duties.'

'Then you can make yourself useful by helping to search the house for the Sawston necklace,' snapped Lady Sophia.

Wolf glanced at the dowager marchioness. Despite her sharp tone he could see she was delighted to have her granddaughter with her and she even greeted Raoul with more warmth than Wolf expected her to show to a mere surgeon.

'The diamonds?' said Cassie, going to sit on a sofa beside her husband. 'You think they are here?'

The dowager nodded. 'Wolfgang thinks so, although so far we have found nothing.'

Wolf exhaled fiercely. 'Perhaps I am wrong, but Meesden was adamant the diamonds had not been stolen. Grace and I both remember her saying so.'

'Grace?' Lady Hune pounced on the name. 'Your brother mentioned a young woman was helping you.'

'Miss Duncombe is the daughter of the local vicar here in Arrandale,' he said carefully. 'She was visiting her aunt in London.'

'Indeed?' Wolf found himself subjected to another of the dowager's piercing stares. 'I should like to meet her.'

'I think not,' he said quickly. 'She has had too much contact already with the Arrandale family. And she is about to marry the local magistrate.' Wolf stared moodily into the fire. The thought of Grace married to another man tore into him. It was made even more painful by the obvious affection that existed between Cassie and her husband. If only Grace could love him in that way, but her heart was buried in the Arrandale churchyard, along with her first love.

He rubbed a hand over his eyes, the long ride was catching up with him.

'I need to sleep,' he said, rising. 'Then I will help you search the house. The diamonds are here, I know it, and I am determined to find them.'

Grace slipped into the vicarage, thankful that there was no one on the stairs to see her in her boy's clothes. In her room she found the maid, humming tunelessly as she ran a cloth along the mantelshelf. On hearing the door open, Betty turned and immediately dropped the Dresden figurine she had been dusting.

'Ooh, Miss Grace, you did give me a scare!' She looked in dismay at the shattered porcelain pieces lying in the hearth. 'And what the master will say when he knows what I have done I don't know.'

Grace quickly closed the door.

'Leave that for now, Betty. I will make it all right with Papa, but first you must help me to change. I cannot go down to him dressed like this.'

'No, indeed.' The smashed figurine was forgotten as the maid put her hands on her hips and regarded her mistress. 'I thought I'd have time to clean your room before you got home and you turn up, bold as brass and dressed like a, well, like I don't know what.' She wrinkled her nose. 'And if you don't mind my saying, Miss Grace, you looks like you've been pulled through a hedge backwards.'

Grace stooped to look at her reflection in the mirror on her dressing table.

She gave a rueful smile. 'Perhaps it would be as well if you fetched me up some hot water.'

Betty hurried away and the smile faded. Although the pain of the past few hours was lessened a little by being home, she felt so tired and unhappy that she wanted nothing more than to curl up on her bed, but that would have to wait. Papa would want to know why she had arrived in such a precipitous manner and she was not quite sure how much she could tell him.

'Papa?'

Grace peeped into the study. Her father was sitting at his desk, staring out of the window, deep in thought. At the sound of her voice he looked up and smiled.

'My love.' He rose and held out his arms. 'We did not expect you until dinnertime!'

'I rode on ahead,' she said, walking into his embrace and surreptitiously scrubbing away a rogue tear on his shoulder. 'I have such a lot to tell you...'

* * *

An hour later her tale was done. She was sitting on a footstool next to her father's chair. He had kept his hand on her shoulder throughout and shown no signs of censure or approval as she told him everything that had occurred since she had left Arrandale.

Well, not quite everything, she thought now, as she rested her head against his knee. She had not mentioned the way Wolf had held her, kissed her.

'So you helped Wolfgang Arrandale to escape, then rode through the night with him.'

'Yes, Papa. Was it very wrong of me?'

'I am sure you believed you had good reason, my love. How much of this do you intend to tell Sir Loftus?'

She looked up at that. 'Everything I have told you.'

'Oh, my love, he is a magistrate, and in helping Wolfgang to escape you have broken the law.' He sighed. 'I blame myself for this. It was I who insisted you and Mr Arrandale should travel to London together. I do not doubt you thought it your duty to help him, but I had not expected you to go this far.'

'You taught me it was my duty to fight injustice,

322 The Outcast's Redemption

Papa, and Wolfgang would surely hang if he was brought to trial in Southwark.' Her voice shook. 'We both hated the fact that poor Henry's murderer was hanged, imagine how much worse for it to happen to an innocent man, and I sincerely believe Wolf is innocent.' She took his hands. 'I could not in all conscience do other than help him, surely you must see that.'

He smiled sadly. 'I see a young woman who is very much in love.'

Grace quickly looked away.

'Do not say so, Papa.'

'After Henry died you shut yourself off from the world, Grace. I am glad to see that you can love again, I only wish it was your fiancé and not Wolfgang Arrandale.'

'I wish it, too, Papa.' She put her head back on his knee. 'What shall I do?'

'We shall pray, my child. And you must not show yourself until your carriage has arrived. Then I will write a note to Loftus telling him you are home and inviting him to dinner tomorrow. By then who knows what might have occurred at Arrandale?'

Grace went up to her room to rest. As soon as she lay down on her bed exhaustion overcame her and she slept soundly until Betty came in, telling her it was time to change for dinner.

'Have my trunks arrived?' asked Grace, rubbing her eyes.

'Aye, miss, they have, and Mrs Graham and her maid with them. Such a to-do there was, Mrs Graham not knowing whether you was safe, but the master put her mind at rest and now she's in the guest room, changing her gown, and Mrs Truscott's fretting about dinner and worrying that the capon she's got on the spit won't stretch.'

'I will go and talk to her. And I will arrange my own hair, Betty, so that you may be free to help in the kitchen. Now, have my luggage fetched upstairs and we will look out one of my new gowns to wear.'

Grace marvelled at how easily she was slipping back into the role of keeping house for Papa. There was at least some comfort in that.

Dinner was excellent, as Grace had known it would be, and if she had no appetite it was nothing to do with the quality of the chicken, nor the boiled tongue and potato pudding that accompanied it. She did her best to eat the lemon jelly that was served with the second course, knowing Mrs Truscott had prepared it especially for her homecoming, but in truth she tasted nothing. She spent most of the dinner hour in silence while her aunt discussed with Papa the best way forward.

'When Mr Wolfgang was clapped up Grace visited him every day,' said Aunt Eliza, casting a reproachful glance across the table at her niece. 'Perhaps you will say I should have stopped her, Titus, but I confess I do not know how I might have done so.'

'My daughter was merely doing her Christian duty,' murmured Papa and Grace threw him a grateful look.

'But then, when I received her note, saying she was riding home and wanted her things sent on to you today I vow I could not sleep for worrying!'

Grace said softly, 'I am very sorry if I caused you anxiety, Aunt, but as you can see I am here, safe and sound.'

'Yes, yes, but what if it gets out that you have been aiding and abetting a felon?'

Grace sat up very straight. 'Wolfgang Arrandale is an innocent man.'

'I think we may be sure that Mr Arrandale will say nothing of my daughter's involvement in his flight,' said her father. 'We must hold to our story, that she left London with you this morning. But let us hope that no one asks.'

'I vow you are as bad as Grace,' declared his sister with a little huff of exasperation. 'After she lost her first fiancé we were all relieved when Loftus Braddenfield proposed.' She glanced at her niece. 'You will forgive me if I speak plainly, my love, but you are nearly five-and-twenty and unlikely to receive another offer. I very much fear all this has put the match in jeopardy.'

'Let us wait until tomorrow and see what Sir Loftus says,' replied Papa gently. 'After all, he is a reasonable man.'

'Not so reasonable that he will condone his fiancée careering around the country with a man,' muttered Aunt Eliza. 'Especially an Arrandale.'

Grace said nothing, but she very much feared her aunt was right. To the weight of her own unhappiness was added the knowledge that she had disappointed her family. By the time they retired to the drawing room she was feeling very low and she excused herself, saying she was going out.

'There is at least an hour's daylight left and a little fresh air will clear my head. I am only going to the churchyard, Papa, but I think I shall go straight to bed afterwards, so I will say goodnight to you both now.'

Grace went upstairs to fetch her cloak and found the maid turning out the trunks.

'You should have left that for me, Betty, I am sure you have been rushed off your feet today.'

'Nonsense, Miss Grace, it's been a pleasure to put away all the new clothes you bought in London. Well now, I never expected to see this old gown again.' She lifted out the yellow muslin. 'You must have had it for at least four years.'

'I had the hem repaired while I was in town,' said Grace, trying not to sigh at the memory. 'It was done by a lady who used to work up at the hall, you may remember her. Annie Meesden.'

'Oooh, yes,' said Betty, her face lighting up. 'She was brutally done to death, wasn't she? Mr Truscott read it in the master's newspaper. It said Mr Wolfgang Arrandale had been taken up for it.'

Grace did not know how to reply. She felt suddenly stifled by memories and her fears for Wolf. She needed to get out into the fresh air.

'So she was reduced to taking in sewing, was she?' said Betty, inspecting the gown. 'Well, she did a good job on this, I must say.' She frowned and peered closer at the muslin. 'Hmm, she thought a lot of herself, sewing her mark into the hem.'

'Yes, I saw that,' murmured Grace, hunting around for her cloak.

'But it's not her initials, is it?' Betty continued. 'That would be "A.M". And look, miss, she has embroidered "M.K. One-six, one-six". I wonder why?'

Grace barely glanced at the embroidery on the hem of the old gown. She did not want to think any more about the dresser, or murder. Or Wolf. At last she found her cloak and threw it around her shoulders as she hurried away.

Outside the house Grace took a deep, steadying breath. Even with a low blanket of cloud covering the sky it felt so much cleaner and fresher here than Hans Place, where the dust and dirt of the ongoing building work hung in the air. She walked briskly to the churchyard. Tomorrow she must see Loftus and explain everything, but tonight there was something equally important she must do, for the sake of her conscience.

The flowers she had laid by Henry's headstone before going to London looked withered and grey in the fading light.

'I am sorry I have not brought fresh ones,' she

murmured, sinking to her knees. 'And I am sorry for a great deal more.' She gazed sadly at the ground. For five years she had thought her heart was buried here, with Henry. She knew that the innocent, girlish passion she had conceived for Henry Hodges was nothing to the love she now felt for the dark and brooding Wolf Arrandale.

'But he is as lost to me as you are,' she whispered, running her fingers over the rough lettering inscribed on the headstone. 'More so, because he does not want me. And even if he did, I am promised to Loftus. All I can do is to pray that Wolf will prove his innocence. I want him to be happy, that must be enough for me.'

There. She had made her peace with Henry. Grace blinked away the threatening tears, fixing her eyes on the final words engraved on the headstone.

We are the children of God
Rom 8:16

She froze. The air in the graveyard was very still. Nothing moved, there was no sound. In her memory she was seeing again the delicately embroidered numbers and letters on the yellow gown.

'It is not a seamstress's mark at all,' she muttered. 'It is a biblical reference!'

* * *

Wolf was in no mood for family reunions. The sight of Richard and Cassandra, both deeply in love with their partners, only intensified the aching emptiness of his own life. After dinner he remained in the drawing room for barely half an hour before retiring, declaring he was too tired to stay awake.

As he crossed the hall there was an urgent knocking at the door and he stepped into the shadows beneath the stairs. Had his pursuers caught up with him already? Croft opened the door and Wolf heard a familiar voice enquiring urgently for Mr Arrandale.

'Grace?' He strode forward and she ran past the astonished butler.

'Thank heaven I have found you! I must tell you—'

'Hush now, come into the library where we may talk privately.'

He led her across the hall. The library was in a state of disorder, for Sophia had ordered the servants to examine every book in their search for the missing necklace. Two servants were still going through the shelves, but Wolf dismissed them and gently guided Grace to a chair beside the empty fireplace.

'Have you run all the way here?' He asked, kneeling before her and clasping her trembling fingers. 'Let me get you something to drink.'

'No, nothing, thank you.' She was still out of breath, but he noted now that her eyes were gleaming with excitement and not distress. 'I think, I am sure, Meesden left us a clue about the necklace. On the gown she repaired for me. Her landlady said she had been working on it when Urmston came to see her. It was neatly folded and left on the table with her Bible resting upon it. I think that in itself was a message.'

'Go on.' He watched her intently. Just seeing her lightened his heart.

'She had embroidered "M.K. Sixteen, sixteen" on the hem of the gown. I took it for some sort of trademark, but now I am sure it is something quite different.' Her fingers twisted and gripped his own. 'It is a biblical reference,' she explained. 'Mark, *Chapter* Sixteen, *Verse* Sixteen.'

'And do you know what it is?'

She shook her head. 'I am not familiar with that text.'

'And you a parson's daughter.'

Grace heard his teasing tone, saw the glint of amusement in his eyes and for the first time that day she felt like smiling. 'Surely the Arrandales are not so degenerate that they do not own a Bible.'

'Aye, of course we do!' He rose and looked around the room. 'The thing is, where to find it...' He grabbed one of the branched candlesticks from the mantelshelf and strode across to the desk, where several large leather-bound books had been piled up. 'Here it is... What was the reference again?' Quickly he turned to the pages. 'Mark... Mark... Chapter Sixteen, Verse Sixteen: *"He that believeth and is baptised shall be saved; but he that believeth not shall be damned".'*

Grace had jumped up to join him, but as she listened her excitement faded.

'Oh, dear. That is no use at all.'

'Isn't it?' said Wolf, with an intense look that sent her heart skittering. 'Baptism. She's telling us the diamonds are in the font.' He held out his hand. 'Come along.'

Chapter Twelve

They headed for the chapel, Wolf carrying a lantern to light their way through the heavy darkness that had descended. Grace pulled her cloak more tightly about her while he unlocked the chapel door and she followed him inside. The lantern threw grotesque shadows against the pale walls and she kept close to Wolf, resisting the temptation to clutch at the skirts of his coat. She took the lantern so he could use two hands to lift off the ornately carved wooden lid from the font and she peered in eagerly.

It was dry and empty.

Wolf lowered the heavy cover to the ground and ran his fingers around the rough grey stone of the basin as if he did not believe his eyes.

'It has been ten years,' she said gently. 'Perhaps someone took it.'

'Perhaps.'

He would not give up. Not yet. There were candles on nearby pricket stands, dusty with age, but once they were lighted he carried them closer and inspected the old stone font, looking for possible hiding places.

'My great-aunt said the chapel had already been searched, so if the diamonds are here they will not be easily found.'

He bent to inspect the base of the font. There was not so much as a crack where anything might be secreted. The cover itself looked more promising, but there was nothing hidden amongst the intricate carvings of fruit, flowers and cherubs.

'Nothing.' He picked up the cover to put it back on the font, twisting it to give a cursory glance to the base as he did so.

'Wolf!'

He had already seen it. The bottom of the cover had warped badly and split, providing a narrow pocket that stretched across the base. Carefully he reached in with a finger and thumb and tugged at the material tucked inside. It fell into his palm, weighted by something wrapped in its discoloured folds.

'Wolf, is it…?' Grace held up the lantern as he gently unfolded the linen.

'Yes,' he said, his voice not quite steady. 'It's the Sawston necklace.'

Grace reached out. He expected her to touch the diamonds twinkling on his hand, but instead she lifted a corner of the wrapping. It was a handkerchief with initials embroidered on the edge. The same letters and flourishing style he remembered seeing on Urmston's perfume-soaked handkerchief. From the other side of the font Grace was smiling, hope shining in her eyes.

'Do you still not believe in miracles? We can surely prove your innocence now.'

We. It was like a shaft of sunlight on a stormy day and it warmed his soul.

'I will take that.'

The words echoed around the darkened church. Urmston was standing just inside the door, the light glinting from the barrel of a pistol in his hand.

'I think not,' drawled Wolf, ignoring the weapon aimed at his heart. 'The diamonds are wrapped in your handkerchief. What more proof do we need that you stole them?'

'You are not a fool, Arrandale. You know I will not let you leave here alive.'

'Then you must kill us both,' declared Grace. 'I will not let you get away with murder.'

Urmston stepped a little further into the chapel.

'Brave words, my dear, but that is precisely my intention. Only I shall say that Wolfgang killed you, before I shot him. I have already informed the magistrate that the fugitive is here.'

Wolf's brain was racing. The lighted candles made him and Grace easy targets. He needed to catch Urmston off guard if he was to wrestle that pistol from him, so he must keep him talking and look for his chance.

'So you admit you took the diamonds?' he said, playing for time.

'I did, but I put them back.'

'Of course.' Wolf nodded. 'You did not need to sell them, did you, once you had Thriplow's money.'

'The young fool was ripe for the plucking. When I came back from Newmarket I hid the necklace in Florence's room, behind the loose brick where she used to keep the key to her jewel box. Didn't want the diamonds turning up again too soon. I wanted everyone to think you a thief as well as a murderer. Once you were hanged I would make sure they were discovered and returned to the Sawstons. After all I shall inherit them, eventually.'

'Ingenious,' said Wolf. 'Tell me, Charles, were you and Florence lovers?'

Urmston's lip curled. 'Once she was with child she considered she had fulfilled her duty to you. We bribed Meesden to keep quiet, but although she disliked me she positively *hated* you for marrying her beloved mistress, and once she had begun taking money for her silence she was unable to say anything at all.'

Wolf had guessed as much and was surprised how little it mattered to him now.

He said, 'So the night she died, Florence quarrelled with me deliberately, to leave the way clear for you.'

'She did. That temper of yours made it surprisingly easy for us, Arrandale. Florence had given me a key to the servants' door. I went outside to enjoy a cigarillo, then up the backstairs to join her. If anyone missed me I could say I had been wandering in the gardens.'

'And you took the necklace.'

'It is mine by right,' snapped Urmston. 'I was Sawston's heir, not Florence. Why should I not have it? I needed the money. She laughed when I asked her for it, so I had to take it. She fought like a wildcat, followed me to the landing and tried to scratch out my eyes, so I—' He stopped, a look of anguish contorting his florid features. 'I pushed her away. She fell against the balcony rail and overbalanced. It was an accident. An accident. Then you came in, Arrandale. It was too good an opportunity to miss. I left the way I had come. By the time I was back in the drawing room everything was confusion. I rushed into the hall where you were kneeling over Florence. It was easy to suggest that you had killed her and to persuade your father to get you out of the country. He was glad to see the back of you.'

Wolf's jaw tightened. He could not deny it. He had reminded the old man too much of himself. He looked at the pistol pointed at his chest. Perhaps he deserved this ending. For one black moment he could think of nothing to say to prolong the conversation.

'And what of the necklace,' said Grace. 'Where was that?'

'Safe in my pocket. Meesden's shock when she discovered it was missing was quite genuine, but by that time Wolfgang was gone and everyone thought he had taken it.'

'Of course,' snarled Wolf. 'After all, if I would kill my wife I would hardly balk at stealing the diamonds.'

'Quite.'

Wolf's sharp ears had picked up a faint noise. Thunder, or horses galloping through the park. If Braddenfield and his men had arrived they would see the light in the chapel.

He said quickly, 'And having put the blame on me you went off to Newmarket.'

'Well, I did not wish to intrude upon the family's grief.'

'Generous of you,' drawled Wolf. 'So you took young Thriplow's fortune and left him to blow his brains out.'

Urmston shrugged. 'If it had not been me, someone else would have relieved him of his fortune.' He took another step closer. 'Now give me those diamonds.'

Wolf's hand closed over them and he held his fist across his chest. 'Surely you would not kill us before explaining how the diamonds came to be here and not where you left them?'

'Meesden,' said Urmston tersely. 'She caught me hiding the necklace. I paid her to say nothing, gave her enough for her to buy her shop in London. But she must have realised that it was I and not you who was responsible for Florence's death and decided to have her revenge. When I heard you were back in England I posted here immediately, only to find the diamonds were gone.'

'And you had lost track of Meesden, too.' Wolf spoke quickly, trying to cover what was surely the sound of steps outside the chapel. 'And just how did you know I was back in England, Charles?'

'Your lawyer. I paid him to alert me if he should hear from you.'

'And was it Baylis who gave you Meesden's direction?' asked Wolf.

Urmston stepped closer.

'Yes. The fool thought I wanted her as a witness against you and was only too happy to help, no doubt thinking of the money he would make defending you.'

Wolf saw the merest flicker of light in the doorway and spoke his next words clearly, praying whoever was holding the light would hear Urmston's answer.

'So you forced brandy down Annie Meesden's throat and took her to Vauxhall, where you murdered her.'

'What else could I do? Oh, I tried to reason with her, I sat for an hour while she finished her mending, but she would not tell me what she had done with the diamonds. She even threatened to tell you.

So I had no choice but to kill her. I thought the plan was pretty neat, dispose of Meesden and have her murder added to the list of your crimes. And this will be your final victim.' Urmston stared hard at Grace. 'I saw you at Horsemonger Lane. Wolfgang's lady of mercy. Hatcham thinks you helped him escape.'

'She is innocent, Charles. Let her go.'

'Oh, no. I have seen the way you look at her, Wolfgang. I think her death will hurt you more than the others.'

A boot scraped on the doorstep. Urmston's head came up. He swung the pistol towards Grace. He was so close, he could not miss, but even as he squeezed the trigger Wolf pounced.

He saw the flash from the pistol, felt the searing pain in his side but he kept going, landing against his opponent with such force that they both fell to the ground. Even as the blackness closed in on him he heard voices and the heavy tread of boots on the stone floor. Grace was safe.

Grace froze as the pistol turned towards her. In that same instant she saw Wolf drop the necklace and throw himself in the way. A shot reverberated around the little church and the two men fell, but although Sir Charles continued to struggle there was no sign of movement from Wolf, whose dead weight pinned his opponent to the ground.

The urgent shouts of the men running into the church broke the spell. Grace flew towards Wolf, helping the men to roll him away from Sir Charles. A red stain was slowly darkening Wolf's coat and Grace closed her eyes, praying harder than she had ever done in her life that he might be spared.

'Grace! Are you hurt?' Loftus was lifting her from her knees.

'He is innocent,' she said urgently. 'Wolfgang is innocent.'

He nodded, scooping up the necklace and the handkerchief that was wrapped around it and putting them in his pocket.

'I heard enough to know that, my dear. Come out of the way now.'

She sank down on one of the pews as everyone bustled about. Sir Charles was marched away, Wolf was carried to the house, but when Grace went to follow, Loftus stopped her.

'May I ask what you are doing here?' he asked. 'I received your father's note, saying you had but today returned to Arrandale.'

Grace exhaled. 'I have a lot to tell you, Loftus.'

Then, in the soft, flickering light of the church candles, Grace made her confession. She related everything, from the moment Wolf had first arrived at the vicarage to their night-time flight back to Arrandale. The only thing she kept to herself were the savage kisses they had shared. Those memories were too intimate, too precious to be divulged.

'I have been very careless of my reputation, Loftus,' she said at last. 'I helped him escape from prison and spent last night alone in the woods with him.' She raised her chin. 'I cannot regret it, I did it to save an innocent man. But I *do* regret the pain this must cause you. I beg your pardon for that.'

Silence fell in the chapel. Grace hung her head. Loftus really could not be expected to marry a woman who had behaved so badly. She would go home to Papa. If Wolf lived, if he decided to remain in England after all...

She would not think of that, not yet.

'I cannot deny that I am shocked by your confidences, Grace,' Sir Loftus began, with heavy deliberation. 'But I am also proud. You have integrity, the courage to act upon your convictions and I admire that. I am aware that the world would censure you most severely, if your actions should become known, but you shall not hear a word of reproach from *me*. And I shall not break our engagement. I have always considered it my duty as a magistrate to see that justice is administered and I am not such a hypocrite to turn away from you when you have followed your conscience. No, my dear, with your permission we shall instruct your father to call the banns next week and we will be married within the month. You shall have all the protection my name can give you.'

She felt his hand on her shoulder, a gesture of comfort and reassurance. To Grace it felt as heavy and confining as a yoke.

'He's stirring.'

Wolf was aware of the faint smell of lavender and a cool cloth wiping his brow. He opened his eyes.

'Grace.'

The frail whisper must have been his own voice, for she took his hand and squeezed it gently, smiling at him in a way that made him wonder if he was in heaven, being tended by an angel.

'You are safe now, Wolf.' She added softly, 'You saved my life.'

He glanced down at the bandaging around his chest.

'And who saved mine?'

'That was Raoul.' Lady Cassandra came closer, her husband at her side. 'You should be thankful that he brought his surgeon's case with him.'

Raoul grinned. 'I have learned that where there are Arrandales, there is trouble. However, on this occasion your life was not in danger. The bullet skimmed the ribs. A glancing blow merely.'

'Aye,' said Richard, coming up. 'Another inch to the left and it would have killed you. How do you feel, Brother?'

'Damnable,' muttered Wolf. 'Where am I?'

'In the morning room at Arrandale,' Grace answered him. 'The day bed here was more convenient for everyone to look after you than trailing all the way up to your bedchamber.'

As she spoke Wolf glanced past the four persons gathered around him. Of course. The room was familiar, although in the bright light of day it looked much shabbier than he remembered. Neglected. Like the rest of the Arrandale estate. Ten years without a master was taking its toll. He frowned.

'How long have I been here?'

'The constables carried you in here last night,' said Richard, 'after Urmston shot you.'

As memory returned Wolf wanted more answers.

He tried to sit up, but Grace's gentle hands pressed him back.

'No, no, you must stay there, at least for the present. There is no danger now. Loftus knows Urmston is the true villain. He arrested him immediately.'

'Aye.' Richard laughed. 'Braddenfield was as mad as fire when he found the fellow trying to kill his fiancée!'

Wolf's eyes flew to Grace. There was a faint flush on her cheeks, but she made no attempt to contradict Richard. Wolf caught her wrist as she went to move away.

'Grace, I must talk to you, alone. I need to know—'

The blush deepened. Gently she freed herself from his grip and moved out of reach.

'Hush now, sir. There will be time to talk when you are better.'

That was her answer, then. She loved him, wanted him, but she would not break her promise to marry Braddenfield. Wolf closed his eyes. It was best this way. Grace might love him now, but once the first joyful bliss had faded she would compare him to her first love. Let her marry her magistrate, she would go into that marriage with her eyes open, not blinded by starry infatuation. And as for himself, the sooner he was away from here the better. But first he must see his daughter.

He glared at Raoul Doulevant. 'How long must I stay in this cursed bed?'

'I would prefer you did not exert yourself today.' He put his hand on Wolf's brow. 'There is no fever and the wound is not deep, but it might start to bleed again. You have the luck most extraordinary, *mon ami,* but I beg you will stop putting yourself in the way of bullets. This is the second time I have, how do you say, *patched you up* and I may not be on hand if you should be shot again.' Raoul put his arm about Cassie's waist and pulled her close. 'You should settle down. I can recommend it.'

Wolf caught the adoring look that passed between Cassie and her Belgian husband and his spirits plummeted. The man was a hero, worthy of any woman's regard. What had he ever done, save spread mayhem and murder? The opening of the door caught his attention and his sister-in-law came in with Lady Hune.

Wolf's breath hissed out. 'Am I to have no peace?'

'Ungrateful brute,' Richard admonished him cheerfully. 'When the family have gathered here to support you! But we will be relieving you of our presence shortly. Now we know you are in no danger Phyllida is anxious to return home to little James.'

Ah, yes, Richard and Phyllida's son. And they were expecting another child, which might well be another heir. Wolf's black mood deepened. He did not begrudge Richard his happiness, but it served to highlight his own bleak existence. Well, at least a nephew ensured the entail was safe and lessened the need to stay in England. As if to give an extra twist to the knife, Phyllida announced that the Davenports had arrived.

'Alex and Diana?' exclaimed Richard. 'Why the deuce are they here?'

'They have brought Florence,' said Phyllida.

'My daughter.' Wolf's hand clenched at the bedsheet. 'I must see her.'

'Not today, I think,' said Phyllida gently. 'It might frighten her to see you like this.'

He tried to sit up again. 'Then let me be dressed and I can sit in a chair.'

There was an immediate outcry. Phyllida and Cassie pushed him back against the pillows, talking over his protests until Lady Hune rapped her cane on the floor and called for quiet.

'This is a medical matter,' she declared. 'Let us ask the surgeon when Wolfgang may get up.'

All eyes turned to Raoul.

'Tomorrow,' he said. '*If* you rest today.'

'I will,' said Wolf. 'I will rest now and Grace can sit with me.'

'That is not possible.' Again that flush mantled her cheeks and she refused to meet his eyes. 'Kennet is here and he is anxious to attend you.'

Wolf was about to consign his valet to the devil, but Richard squeezed his bare shoulder.

'Miss Duncombe sat by your bed all night, Wolf. It is well past noon now; she must be exhausted.'

'Yes. Yes, of course,' said Wolf. 'Send Kennet to me, then.' He glanced again at Raoul. 'I feel weak as a cat, but you say I should be able to get up tomorrow?'

'If you rest today, yes.'

'We'll leave you now,' said Richard. 'And it is not only little Florence who will visit you tomorrow. Sir Loftus wants to see you. We managed to put him off today, but he represents the law here, Brother, and will not be gainsaid.'

'No,' muttered Wolf, his eyes on Grace. 'Sir Loftus carries all before him.'

Grace went out with the others to the dining room, where a light meal had been laid out, but she had no appetite. Loftus had reluctantly allowed her to stay and nurse Wolf overnight, but only after she promised to leave as soon as he was out of danger. She had prayed so hard and vowed never to sin again if Wolf was spared and now she must keep those vows. She had behaved outrageously in London, but Loftus was willing to stand by her, to give her the protection of his name. His affection for her was deeper than she had realised and although she could not love him she must be a good and faithful wife. He deserved at least that.

Grace had already received an early morning visit from Papa and Aunt Eliza. She had been expecting it, because Loftus had promised he would call at the vicarage and assure them that she was safe. What *had* surprised her was their reluctance to remove her from the Hall. Papa said she could be of more use there than at the vicarage and as Wolf had not by that time regained consciousness, Grace had returned to his bedside. But now she wished Papa had taken her away. Then she would not have seen the warmth in Wolf's eyes when he awoke. It made leaving him so much harder, but it must be done. She was not free. She had pledged herself to Loftus and she could not withdraw. A line from an old poem went through her mind.

*I could not love thee, dear, so much, Lov'd I
not Honour more.*

A knot of unhappiness settled in Grace's stomach
and she picked at her food, something that Cassandra, sitting opposite, was quick to notice.

'Oh, dear, are you too fatigued to eat nuncheon?
Perhaps you would prefer to sleep first and we will
order a tray to be sent up for you.'

'No, no—you are very kind and I *am* tired, but I
was thinking that perhaps I should go home.'

Her suggestion brought a storm of protests, from
Phyllida's insistence that she had had a shock and
was not yet recovered, to a plea from the newly arrived Diana, Lady Davenport, that she stay to meet
the children.

'I shall bring them downstairs later,' she said,
smiling. 'And I am sure you would like to meet
Wolfgang's daughter.'

Grace knew that would be a bittersweet moment,
but in the face of everyone's kindness, she finally
gave in.

'Very well, but only until Sir Loftus calls tomorrow.' She coloured faintly. 'I shall write a note, asking him to bring his carriage so that he can convey
me to the vicarage. I am sure my fiancé will want to

take me away with him, once he has spoken with…
once he has finished his business here.'

Having won their agreement, Grace gave up any
pretence of eating and went off to rest. She fell
asleep almost immediately, waking only when a
maid came in to inform her it was nearly dinnertime. Aunt Eliza had brought over her trunk, filled
with the gowns she had purchased in town. Grace
would have preferred something older and more de-
mure, but in the end she settled for an evening gown
of deep-rose silk with a snowy lace fichu filling
the low neckline. She blinked when she found her
aunt had also put in her jewel box. Heavens, what
was she thinking? This was not some elegant house
party. However, the company did include a dowager marchioness and a countess, so she decided it
would be reasonable to wear her pearl ear drops.

Not that it matters, she thought as she made her
way down to the drawing room. *I am not trying to
impress anyone.*

And Wolf would not be there to see her.

When Grace walked in, the buzz of conversation halted abruptly. She hesitated, wondering if
she was perhaps overdressed for the occasion, but
a quick look around the room showed her that everyone had changed for dinner. Lady Phyllida came

forward to draw her into the company, her manner so warm and welcoming that Grace was reassured. She saw two little girls, the Davenports' wards, and recognised Florence immediately. With her dark hair and serious grey eyes she reminded Grace so strongly of Wolfgang that her heart contracted painfully. She forced herself to smile and talk with the children, all the time telling herself that this unhappiness would pass. As soon as she was away from this house she would be able to forget Wolfgang Arrandale.

Lady Hune's French chef had risen nobly to the challenge of working in an outdated kitchen, and after her refreshing sleep Grace was able to enjoy the lobster and asparagus and even a flavoured rice pudding. Richard Arrandale, sitting beside Grace, kept her glass filled with wine and conversed so pleasantly that the meal was not the ordeal she had been expecting. He excused himself from the table when the dessert course was served and went off to see his brother, but he returned quickly, looking exasperated.

'Wolf has not yet dined,' he declared, going back to his seat.

'I gave instructions that he was not to be disturbed, if he was sleeping,' put in Raoul.

'Well, he is awake now and in the devil of a temper because Kennet has gone off to press his coat for the morning.' He swung round to look at Grace. 'I know it is presumptuous of me, but would *you* accompany Croft when he takes in my brother's dinner tray and remain while he eats it?'

'Me?' Grace recoiled. 'No, that cannot be necessary.'

Richard shook his head at her. 'It is very important that he eats well, to aid his recovery. Ain't that so, Doulevant?'

'Very important,' Raoul agreed solemnly.

Lady Cassandra leaned forward. 'We would take it as a very great favour if you would do this, Miss Duncombe. Wolf is far less likely to throw the dishes at you than at any of us.'

Something close to panic fluttered inside Grace. She had refused the syllabub, so she had no reason to stay. She glanced around the table, but everyone was either intent upon their dessert or looking at her hopefully. There was no escape.

The morning room was washed with the soft glow of candlelight. Wolf was on the daybed, propped up on a bank of pillows and with a white nightshirt covering his upper body. Grace thought how achingly handsome he looked, his lean cheeks freshly shaved and his dark, curling hair falling over his brow. He watched her, unsmiling, as she came in, but the look in his dark eyes was unreadable. Grace straightened her shoulders. She reminded herself that they would be bound to meet occasionally if he decided to stay at Arrandale, so she would have to get used to this. She summoned up her most cheerful manner.

'Croft has brought your dinner and I am here to keep you company while you dine.'

She stood aside while the butler placed the tray across Wolf's lap and a footman put a second, smaller tray with wine and glasses on a table at Wolf's elbow. When the servants withdrew she sat down upon a chair at a safe distance and folded her hands in her lap, watching Wolf pick at the succulent morsels the chef had served up to tempt his appetite. He looked pale, and a little tired, but he was calm enough. A suspicion began to grow that the Arrandales had planned this. They wanted her to be alone with Wolf. But to what end?

They want him to marry you and settle down at Arrandale.

Impossible! Had he not told her he was too restless to marry? That he could never be faithful to any one woman? Even if she was not promised to another man he did not *want* to marry her. He would certainly not want to be coerced into marriage by his well-meaning family.

'Will you join me in a glass of wine?' Wolf asked her politely.

Grace nodded, glad to be doing something, but as she poured the wine into two glasses her hand trembled and she spilled a little on the tray.

'Are you afraid of me, Grace?'

'Do not be ridiculous.'

'You are shaking.'

'I should not be here,' she said in a low voice. 'I should not be alone with you.'

'Then why are you here?'

Her shoulders lifted a fraction. 'Your family…'

'What?' He gave a mirthless laugh. 'Surely they know you are betrothed to Braddenfield?'

'Yes.' She handed him a glass. 'I told Loftus what had happened. I thought he would not wish to marry me once he knew everything.' She did not look at Wolf, knowing he was watching her intently. It was as much as she could do not to sigh. 'He admires my integrity.'

Wolf had finished eating so she moved his tray

to the side table. She said, trying to sound cheerful, 'He is a truly noble man, I think.'

'Aye, damn him.'

'I do not know why you say that—'

'Don't you, Grace? Don't you know that I hate him because he will have you and I won't?

'No,' she whispered, her heart beating frantically. Wolf grabbed her wrist.

'Oh, I know it is fixed. There is no getting out of it now. You are promised to him, but that does not stop me wanting you.'

He was stroking the inside of her wrist with his thumb, setting her whole body on fire. From her toes to the crown of her head, she was aware of him. There was a lightness in her head and in her womb, her breasts tingled, they felt full, swollen and aching for his touch. She wanted to sink to her knees beside the daybed, to close her eyes and delight in the sensual feelings he aroused in her.

I could not love thee, dear, so much...

It took a supreme effort of will to pull away.

'I will not break my promise to Loftus,' she said, her voice catching on a sob. 'Neither will I allow you to behave dishonourably.'

His eyes held her prisoner. She felt the threads

that bound them, strong as steel, tightening and pulling her towards him. One word and she would be lost. She would give herself to a man who would only love her for a short time, then he would move on. He would cease to love her and she would lose him, as she had lost so many other people she had loved. Grace crossed her arms, as if to hold herself back.

'Please, Wolf, help me. We must not do something we would both regret.'

His eyes blazed, but she dare not acknowledge what she read there, lest the final shreds of her control should snap and send her tumbling into his arms. Then, just as she thought she could hold out no longer, he looked away.

Wolf rubbed one hand wearily across his eyes. He had come pretty close to declaring himself, but what good would that do, she would not break her vows. It would only make her suffer even more. He had to keep to his original plan. Better she should think him unworthy.

'Go then.' He added harshly, 'You were never mistress material.'

'Wolf—'

'Go!' he snarled. 'Get out, damn you.'

Blinking away the tears, Grace turned to leave.

'And tell Croft to bring me the brandy,' he called, as she reached the door. 'I intend to get damnably drunk.'

Grace fled. In the empty hall she stopped, irresolute. Voices were coming from the drawing room, but she had no wish to join the family. They would know soon enough that their scheme had failed. If marriage had been their goal. Perhaps they were all as dissolute as one another and had wanted to see her disgraced. She ran to her bedchamber and locked the door, wishing with all her heart that she had never become mixed up with the infamous Arrandales.

Chapter Thirteen

The next morning Grace rose early and packed her trunk, instructing the maid to have it taken downstairs ready to be loaded into Sir Loftus's carriage. Then she sat in her room, determined to remain there until it was time to leave. She had kept her book and her tambour frame with her to while away the time, but both remained untouched as she stared out of the window.

You were never mistress material.

The words had haunted her throughout the night and she had soaked her pillow with hot, bitter tears. How dare he even suggest such a thing! But with the dawn had come resignation and it settled over her heart like ice. She could not change him. Wolf was a rake and a vagabond. He could not settle down with one woman, he had told her so himself. And he was right, she was not cut out to be a mistress.

There was a knock at the door and Phyllida appeared.

'Grace, my dear, Sir Loftus has arrived and asks that you join him in the morning room.'

'The morning room? Oh, no—I would prefer to wait for him here, or in the library, perhaps.'

'He needs to interview you and Wolfgang.' Phyllida put out her hand. 'Come.'

Bowing to the inevitable, Grace accompanied her down the stairs.

The daybed had been removed from the morning room and Wolf was dressed and sitting in a chair. Sir Loftus was standing in the centre of the room and when Grace went in he took her hand and kissed it. He was looking very serious.

'Is all well?' she asked him quickly. 'Sir Charles is safely locked up?'

'Yes, and on his way to Southwark for trial. With my testimony and that of the constables who also heard him confess to everything, there is no possibility of his escaping justice.' He took a turn about the room. 'I have been talking to Arrandale about the circumstances of his escape,' he said at last. 'We are agreed that no purpose would be served by mentioning your part in it.' He fixed his serious gaze upon her. 'We shall admit you visited the prisoner in Horsemonger Lane, but as far as the world is concerned you travelled to Arrandale with your aunt. As for what happened in the chapel, you brought a message for the family and became caught up in events. I think we might even avoid having you called as a witness.'

'Thank you,' she whispered, her eyes lowered. 'I am much obliged to you, Loftus.'

'Aye, well, it would serve no purpose to drag you further into this sordid business.'

'Quite.' Wolf eased himself out of his chair. 'Is that everything?'

'You will need to give evidence at the trial, Arrandale, but with Lady Hune to stand surety for you I do not see any need to lock you up again.'

'Much obliged to you,' drawled Wolf. 'Now if you will excuse me, I shall leave you.' He turned to Grace. 'We shall not need to meet again, Miss Duncombe, so let me thank you now for all you have done for me.'

A brief, polite nod and he was gone. The cold indifference of his parting cut Grace to the quick. She stared at the door, too numb even for tears. Behind her she heard the soft pad as Loftus paced back and forth across the carpet. He cleared his throat.

'Since we are alone, Grace, perhaps…there is something we must discuss.'

She was still looking at the closed door. She wanted to weep, but there was no time for that now. She turned, forcing her lips to smile. 'Yes, Loftus?'

He was frowning at the carpet. 'Sit down, my dear.'

Grace sat on a chair, wondering how much more she could bear. Loftus had been more understanding than she had any right to expect. Was he going to demand some penance from her?

He coughed again. 'I have been thinking, Grace. About us. The other night I promised I would stand by our engagement and give you the protection of my name.' He took another turn about the room and at last came to stand before her. 'I cannot do it, Grace.'

She hung her head. A confusion of emotions flooded her: shame and dismay that she had grieved this good man; relief that she would not be tied to a marriage she did not want. And regret. If she had not thought herself promised to Loftus, she would have given herself to Wolf last night.

And the eventual parting would have been even more painful.

She sighed. 'It was a very noble gesture, Loftus, but I quite understand.'

Impatiently he interrupted her. 'No, no, it is not that. I...my feelings have changed. I love another.'

So it was not her behaviour that had caused his change of heart, thought Grace. That was some small consolation.

'Claire Oswald,' he said. 'My mother's companion. She has always been such a comfort to Mama, but it was only these past weeks, when you were in town buying your bride clothes, that I realised she had become necessary to my comfort, too.' He coughed. 'If it was only my own inclinations then I would have fought against it, but I have reason to believe, to *hope*, that she returns my affections.'

'Of course she does, Loftus, how could she not?' She rose and gave him her hands. 'I am very happy for you.'

'Thank you. But I am aware this leaves you in a very difficult situation. I know better than anyone that your father's finances are very limited. The marriage settlement—he was looking to me to provide for you.'

'I shall explain it all to Papa. I hope...' Something was blocking her throat and she was obliged to swallow hard before continuing. 'I hope he will be pleased that I am not leaving him, after all.'

'And there will be speculation. With everything that has happened people will talk.'

She put up her chin. 'It will die down once it is seen that you still come to the vicarage.' She added, with an attempt at humour, 'I trust you do not intend to cut our acquaintance, Loftus?'

'No, indeed.' Some of the anxiety left his face. He picked up her hand and kissed it. 'Thank you, Grace. I had no reason to expect such understanding from you. I shall go home and speak to Claire immediately!'

Grace was so lost in her own thoughts that his last words did not register until he had quit the room.

'Loftus, wait!' She jumped up, but the soft thud of the front door told her he had left without her. No matter. She would ask Croft to arrange a carriage for her.

She sank down on the sofa. She should find Wolf and tell him she was no longer betrothed, but her heart quailed. It was one thing to succumb to him in the heat of the moment, quite another to offer herself so blatantly. And for what? A few months of happiness, until his restless spirit wanted to move on. Then he would leave her, or worse, he would stay and she would watch his love slowly dying. The unhappiness she had kept in check all morning now welled up and she dropped her head in her hands.

'Why are you weeping?'

The childish voice had Grace hunting for her handkerchief. She had not heard the door open, but now little Florence was standing before her, regarding her with her dark, serious eyes.

'I am being very foolish, I beg your pardon.' Grace wiped her eyes and smiled. 'Were you sent to fetch me?'

'No, I was looking for my father,' said Florence, climbing on to the sofa beside her. 'I wanted to see him. Diana said he was too ill yesterday and she would take Meggie and me to the drawing room this evening before dinner, but that is *such* a long time to wait.'

'It is indeed.'

'And he is *my* papa, not Meggie's, and I want to see him *first*,' declared Florence.

'Of course. I can quite understand that.'

'But I am a little bit frightened,' Florence confided. 'Will you come with me?'

'Me?' asked Grace, startled. 'No, no, I could not.'

'Why not? He likes you. I heard Aunt Diana and Lady Phyllida talking about it when they came upstairs last night. They said…' Florence screwed up her face as she tried to remember. 'They said he should marry you and settle down at Arrandale Hall, and I could come and live with you.'

'Oh.' Blushing, Grace slipped an arm around the little girl's shoulders. She said gently, 'I am not going to marry your father, Florence.'

'Why not? Is it because of me? Perhaps you would rather have babies of your own.'

Grace's blush deepened.

'No, it is not you, sweetheart. Your papa does not want to marry me.'

'But Lady Phyllida said she had never seen two people more in love.' Florence fixed her candid eyes upon Grace. 'Isn't it true?'

Looking into those innocent eyes, Grace was unable to tell a lie.

'Well, I love *him*,' she said sadly. 'With all my heart and soul, but he does not love me in the same way.'

Something made her look round. Wolf was in the doorway and suddenly Grace was on fire with mortification. How long had he been standing there?

She was aware of Florence shrinking closer and she put aside her own concerns. She forced herself to speak cheerfully.

'Ah, so there you are, sir. Florence came here in search of you.'

'And I was looking for *her.*'

'Then I shall leave you alone. If you will excuse me.'

As she rose, Florence jumped off the sofa and took her hand.

'*Please* do not leave me.'

Grace looked down at the little girl, but she addressed Wolf: 'Lady Davenport should be here.'

'She has taken Meggie riding,' offered Florence.

'Oh,' said Grace. 'Perhaps Lady Phyllida could—'

Florence shook her head and clung even harder to Grace's hand. 'She is lying down.'

'Well, we must fetch someone,' said Wolf. 'Miss Duncombe has to leave. Sir Loftus will be waiting for her.'

'Do you mean the man who came to see you earlier?' the little voice piped up again. 'He left a long time ago. That's why I came here, looking for you.'

Grace felt Wolf's eyes boring into her.

'He left *without* you?'

Wolf had entered the room, expecting to see Florence with her aunt and instead he had walked in upon a tête-à-tête between his daughter and the

woman he thought he could not have. But if Braddenfield was gone and Grace was still here…

He must go carefully, she was looking as nervous
as a hind and might bolt at any minute.

'Well then, if Miss Duncombe does not have to
leave immediately, perhaps she would consent to
bear us company while we become acquainted.'

'No!' cried Grace, distracted. 'Sir, we have nothing to say to one another.'

'But I have much to say to my daughter, Miss
Duncombe. And she wants you here while we talk.
Is that not so, Florence?' Wolf dropped to one knee
before the child and smiled. 'There, my dear, I am
far less threatening now I am not towering over
you, am I?' He shot a quick glance up at Grace. 'I
really do not wish to frighten anyone away.'

She was frowning, but he guessed she would not
leave while Florence was still clinging to her hand.
He turned back to his daughter.

'So, Florence, you were looking for me?'

The child nodded silently, apprehension in her
eyes.

'Florence wanted to become acquainted with you
before everyone meets in the drawing room this
evening,' Grace explained.

Wolf marvelled at her kindness in speaking for

his little daughter, even when she would clearly prefer to be anywhere else.

'An excellent idea,' he said. 'I wish I had thought of it.'

Florence looked at him warily. 'Do you?'

'Why, yes. One can never say everything one wants to say in a crowd. For instance, we must decide what we are going to call each other. I would like to call you Florence, if I may?'

'Of course, that is my name.' She looked at him shyly. 'And may I call you Papa?'

Wolf smiled. 'I should like that very much. And there is something else that I need to say. I must apologise for behaving like a brute.'

Florence giggled. 'But that's silly. We have only just met, so there is no need to apologise.'

'Oh, there is.' Wolf risked looking directly at Grace, hoping she would read the message in his eyes. She averted her gaze and he turned again to Florence. 'I am very sorry that we have not been able to meet until now, but you see, I only recently learned I had a daughter, and as soon as I could I came to England to see you.'

'You, you did? Uncle Alex said it was dangerous for you to come here. That you were very brave when the bad man shot you.'

'It was Miss Duncombe who was the brave one. Did you know she nursed me through the night? And I was so ungrateful that I said some very cruel things to her. Things I did not mean and for which I am deeply ashamed. But you see, I thought she was going to marry someone else and I could not bear it.'

'But why should she do that?' asked Florence, puzzled. 'She said she lo—'

'That is quite enough about me,' Grace interrupted her hastily. 'Perhaps your wound is paining you, sir, and you should leave this interview for another time.'

He ignored the hint.

'It does hurt a little,' he admitted, climbing to his feet. 'It would be easier if we could all sit on the sofa.' He held out his hand to Florence. 'You could sit between us, what do you say?'

'Very well,' she said, but she clung even closer to Grace.

He sat down at one end of the sofa with Grace perched nervously at the other. Florence was between them, leaning against Grace and holding her hand. Wolf smiled at Florence, but when he raised his eyes to Grace she put her chin in the air and looked stonily ahead.

'Do you know, Florence,' he remarked, 'since your mama died I have been wandering the world, quite lost.'

'Like a prince in a fairy tale?' said Florence. She was gazing at him much more openly now. 'Did you have lots of adventures?'

'Hundreds,' he replied promptly.

'Tell me!' Florence was no longer leaning against Grace.

'Well, there was the time I helped your cousin Lady Cassandra escape from the French...'

Most of his adventures were not suitable for a little girl, but this one kept Florence transfixed. Her eyes positively shone when he described how he had jumped on his horse and ridden away, chased by the French officers while Cassie and Raoul made their escape.

'They were taken on board a smuggling vessel and carried safely to England,' he ended.

'And did you escape from the soldiers unhurt?' breathed Florence, wide-eyed. He noticed that she had moved a little closer to him.

'Not quite. I was wounded and unfortunately my faithful horse was shot from under me.'

'Was that your black stallion?' asked Grace.

'Yes.'

Wolf was surprised she had remembered that. He was heartened, too, but she was already turning away and looking very stern, as if angry that she had been drawn into speaking to him. He turned back to his daughter. She had released Grace's hand and was now turned towards him.

He said, 'I have been thinking, Florence, that I should settle down and make a home for myself here at Arrandale. Do you think that would be a good idea?'

Florence considered this. 'Would I have to come and live with you?'

'You do not have to do anything,' he said quickly. 'I have discussed it with Alex and Diana, and they are happy for you to live with them for as long as you wish.'

The little girl nodded solemnly. 'I like living with them. And with Meggie. She is my *bestest* friend.'

'Then I would not take you away from her.'

Wolf smiled, but it was an effort. They were strangers still, he could not expect his daughter to throw her arms about him and beg to come and live with him.

'Perhaps you and Meggie could stay at Arrandale sometimes,' Grace suggested. 'It would be a holiday for you.'

Wolf threw her a grateful look, but she was still resolutely ignoring him.

'It would be a holiday for me, too,' he said. 'But I would need to learn how to go on. I have never had such young guests here before.' Wolf paused, then decided to risk all. 'It would help if I had a wife. What do you think, Miss Duncombe, do you know anyone suitable?' Grace was sitting very still. He added softly, 'Someone who loves me with all her heart and soul.'

Grace fought down a gasp of dismay. So he had heard that. It was embarrassing, but it made no difference. She would not give in.

She said icily, 'No, sir, I do not.'

He was not noticeably dashed and addressed his next remarks to Florence.

'It is important she loves me, because I must restore Arrandale. There are years of neglect to put right and I have to repay Richard too, so I cannot offer her a life of idle luxury. But then, the lady I have in mind would not want that.'

Grace maintained a dogged silence and after a moment he continued.

'And of course I must love *her*, too, with all my heart and soul, if we are to live happily ever after.'

'I do not believe in fairy tales, Mr Arrandale,' said Grace, goaded into a reply.

'Not even Beauty and the Beast?' he asked her. 'Where the hero is transformed by the love of a good woman?'

Florence giggled.

'That is what happened to Alex,' she confided to Wolf. 'He says he was *very* bad before he fell in love with Diana.'

Grace was surprised into a laugh which she quickly turned to a cough. It was too ridiculous for words! She tried very hard not to look at Wolf, but it was impossible. One shy, tentative glance showed her that he was smiling and her pulse leapt erratically when she saw the glow in his eyes. She tried to calm it, to keep her heart and her feelings wrapped in an icy numbness.

'There you are then,' he said softly. 'Miracles can happen.'

'No, they do not,' she retorted.

'That is not what you said when we found the necklace,' he reminded her.

She ignored that.

'I stopped believing in miracles five years ago when all my prayers and tears could not save Henry.'

'Who is Henry?' asked Florence.

'He was the best man who ever lived,' said Grace, chin up and eyes fixed firmly on Wolf. '*He* was no restless vagabond to capture a maiden's heart with false promises. His love was steady, constant.'

'And yet he left you,' said Wolf softly.

Grace winced.

'I must go,' she said. 'Pray be good enough to summon your carriage to take me home, Mr Arrandale.'

'Grace—'

He broke off as the door opened and Lady Davenport appeared.

'Oh. I beg your pardon; I was looking for Florence.'

Grace knew that Diana's keen eyes would assess the situation instantly: her own rigid posture, Wolf half-turned in his seat, gazing at her, and little Florence between them, blissfully unaware of the tensions swirling around.

Diana continued with barely a pause. 'I have been looking for you, my love.'

The little girl slipped off the sofa and went over to her.

'I have been talking to my papa.'

Florence said the words proudly, but Grace hardened her heart against feeling anything for Wolf's daughter.

'I am very glad to see it.' Diana smiled and held out her hand. 'But it is time to change your dress. No, no, do not get up, Miss Duncombe. I shall take Florence away and we will meet again at dinner.'

She whipped Florence out of the room and closed the door before Grace could force out one word. Even her limbs refused to move. She remained on the sofa, staring ahead, and all the time Wolf's gaze was on her face.

'I cannot stay,' she managed at last, although she still could not tear herself from her seat.

'Why did you not leave with Sir Loftus? Are you still betrothed to him?'

'He…he was going directly to Hindlesham.'

'Are you still betrothed?'

She bit her lip. 'I am not,' she admitted. 'But that makes no difference. I will not stay. Please order a carriage to take me back to the vicarage.'

'Of course, but hear me out first.' When she put up her hand to stop him he said urgently, 'Let me have my say, then, if you still wish to leave, I will send you home and never trouble you again. You have my word on that.'

No, I must leave. I must go now, before his siren words break my heart.

But she remained on the sofa as he began to speak.

'Heaven knows mine has not been a good life, Grace. I was always in scrapes as a boy and I lived wildly in London, gambling, drinking, wenching. My marriage to Florence was arranged by our fathers, but even when I knew I could never love her I was determined to be faithful. A novel concept for an Arrandale, but I was determined to try.

'Then everything went wrong and I was exiled to France. I believed my family had abandoned me and I wanted nothing more to do with them. I struggled to survive, Grace, I admit that my life there was not blameless, but I *did* survive, I even prospered. I returned to England with a small fortune.' He slipped to his knees and took her hands. 'I want to stay in England, Grace, I want to restore Arrandale and make a home here for little Florence, but I cannot do it without you. I want you beside me. As my wife.'

She tried to free her hands. 'I will not marry you for the sake of your daughter!'

'No, for my sake,' he said, holding her even tighter. 'I love you, Grace, I cannot live here without you, knowing you are at the vicarage and as unhappy as I am.'

'Then *I* will go away!' She wrenched her hands from his grasp and ran to the door.

'So you would run away, even though you love me. I thought you had more courage than that.'

She stopped, her hands pressed against the wooden panels as his words cut deep.

'We love each other, Grace,' he said. 'Why does that frighten you? Is it because you think I might leave you?'

'No! Because you will stop loving me!' She gave a sob. 'I have dealt with loss before. My mother, my aunt, when she married. Henry…but I n-never doubted their love. I am afraid you would stop loving me.'

She felt his hands on her shoulders.

'I might indeed,' he said quietly. 'But not in this lifetime.'

Gently he pulled her around, but still she would not look up.

'I have never met anyone like you, Grace Duncombe. I have never felt a love like this before. It consumes me, but *your* happiness is paramount.' He put his fingers beneath her chin. 'If you cannot be happy with me then so be it, but do not expect me to remain at Arrandale, where there are so many memories of you. That would destroy me.'

She was obliged to look up, but his face swam as tears filled her eyes.

'I do not wish to destroy you, Wolf.'

'Then marry me, Grace. I will do my best to be worthy of you. I hope in time I can prove myself, even if I cannot change the past—'

Grace gave a little sob. 'Oh, Wolf.'

She put her hands up, cupping his face and pulling him closer until their lips met. He did not respond immediately, as if afraid to believe what her kiss was telling him. Then, suddenly, his arms swept around her and he returned her embrace with a passion that left her reeling. She clung to him.

'I do not care about your past, my darling,' she whispered. 'Only the present and the future.'

His arms tightened. 'I shall try not to disappoint you.'

She turned her head to kiss his cheek and when she tasted a salty tear, the final shreds of resistance melted. Her mouth sought his again and this time there was no hesitation. He plundered her and she retaliated, matching him kiss for kiss, allowing her instincts to guide her. She drove her fingers through his hair, pressing herself against him and feeling his body respond. She revelled in her power, threw back her head as his lips moved from her mouth and began to burn a trail down the column of her neck.

'I want to make you mine, here and now,' he muttered against her skin.

She shivered, her insides curling in delight. Wolf raised his head. She was pressed against the door, trapped by his body, and his eyes bored into her, so intensely that she thought they danced with blue-violet flames. 'Stop me now, Grace, or it will be too late for you.'

Impatiently she pulled his head down again.

'It was too late for me a long time ago, Wolf. I know that now.'

He swooped down for another kiss. She heard the click as he turned the key in the lock and the next moment she was being carried back to the sofa.

'Wolf, you are wounded!' she protested, half-laughing as she helped him out of his coat and waistcoat. 'You should not exert yourself.'

'I feel nothing,' he muttered, lowering her down on to the cool silk. 'Nothing but an overwhelming desire to worship you!'

With a rapturous sigh she took him in her arms. At first she tried to avoid his bandaged ribs, but soon they were forgotten. Each kiss heated her blood and set her skin tingling. Every caress carried her away until she was almost fainting with the delight of it. She melted beneath his touch, revelling in the feel of his hands on her shoulders, her breasts, her thighs. She was softening, blossoming like a flower with his caresses, instinctively offering herself up to him. Gentle fingers readied her for the union to come. Gentle words eased her fears. She moved restlessly against him, feeling the pull of unfamiliar muscles deep within, the yearning ache to be one with this man. He enveloped her, her heightened senses breathed in the male scent of his skin, the smell of spices and leather and man.

She tore off his neckcloth and unbuttoned his shirt, desperate to explore him. The bandage around his ribs prevented her from running her hands over his chest, but she gripped his shoulders as her body began to slip out of control. She was kissing the line of his throat when she felt the cords of his neck tense. She cried out as he pushed into her and he grew still.

'Am I hurting you?'

'No.' It was an effort to speak. Something was building inside her, like the pleasurable swell of a giant wave. 'No. Go on, go on.'

Her body welcomed him. She was surprised to

feel completed, not invaded, and bucked against him, forcing him deeper. They were moving together, skin on skin, slick and hot, his rhythm matching the pulsing waves in her core. He was carrying her higher, until she was flying, falling, and she cried out with the sheer joy of it as he gave one final thrust. She heard him calling her name as she tumbled from the heights into near oblivion and then they were lying together, panting and gasping in each other's arms.

A delightful lassitude had stolen over Grace. Wolf's body was pinning her down but she did not mind, she wanted to stay like this for ever. She cradled him until his breathing became more regular and all too soon he stirred, raising himself on one arm so he could look at her, seeing her contentment. His slow, teasing smile appeared.

'It is quite wanton, you know, to make love fully clothed.'

She smiled back. 'Then I must be very wanton, sir, for I found it quite delightful.'

He dropped a kiss on her brow, but when he raised his head again the smile had disappeared.

'Are you sorry we did not wait until we were married?'

'A little,' she admitted. When she saw his troubled look she added quickly, 'A *very* little. I have wanted you and imagined this moment for weeks now. This is the consummation of all my hopes and dreams.'

'It is merely the beginning, my love.' He kissed her again. 'Your father shall marry us, but it must be by special licence. I will not wait a day longer than I must to call you my wife.' His smile was tender, but a little rueful, too. 'I am afraid, my angel, you are no longer a virgin.'

She smiled up at him, tenderly brushing a dark curl from his brow.

'And you, *I hope*, are no longer a vagabond.'

'No.' He kissed her again. 'I have come home.'

* * * * *

If you enjoyed this story,
make sure you don't miss
the other three books in Sarah Mallory's
THE INFAMOUS ARRANDALES
miniseries

THE CHAPERON'S SEDUCTION
TEMPTATION OF A GOVERNESS
RETURN OF THE RUNAWAY